THE NORTH POLE SANTA PATROL

Save the world from Unbelief

ROBERT BOWMAN

Smart and Smarter Publishing

For more information regarding copyright and
permission, write to:
Smart and Smarter Publishing
Post Office Box 1815
Zillah, Washington 98953

ISBN 13: 978-0-9713530-3-9
ISBN 10: 0-9713530-3-4

This is a first edition printing.

Printed in the United States.

DEDICATION
For Dad, who knows what Upstairs is.

CHAPTER ONE
The Candy Cane

Friday, December 10th

"What do you mean you can't come? It's Friday. It's the weekend!" Jason looked at his watch for a moment. "It's almost Christmas Break. It's time to celebrate with a little pre-Christmas party."

"I can't. I already told you. I've gotta get ready," Erik replied, grinning.

Jason put a hand on each of Erik's shoulders, changing to a serious tone. "This is the first Christmas party of the year. You realize this? We're seniors. Our job is to relish every moment, every opportunity for fun available to us, and Lisa's party is one of those opportunities."

Erik laughed. "Jason, I want to go, but I already told Lisa that I couldn't make it."

"And she let you get away with that lame excuse that you have to go to some winter camp?"

"It's not an excuse," Erik said, pushing Jason's hands off his shoulders. "I have a responsibility."

"To what? What's this camp about again?" Jason

asked skeptically.

Erik chose his words carefully. "It's a camp where we help spread Christmas spirit. You know, helping kids."

"Helping kids do what?"

"We help kids . . . with problems."

"What kind of problems?" probed Jason.

Erik sighed. He'd explained this to Jason and his other friends many times over.

A loud honk from an old Ford Bronco took Erik's eyes off Jason to the parking lot of Interlake High School. As usual, it was congested with students in their cars trying to get out of the poorly designed lot that always bottle-necked after school. Erik hoped he'd beat the traffic today but Jason had stopped any possibility of that.

Again, Erik chose his words carefully. "Mostly kids that have problems with belief — belief in themselves and stuff."

Jason looked bewildered. He had never heard of a camp like this, especially in winter.

Erik had to admit his answers were vague, but telling the truth, the whole truth, was something he could not do. Not for Jason, not for his parents, not even for his girlfriend, Jennifer, who walked up behind him.

"Aren't you gone yet?" she said sweetly, brushing her straight brown hair from the sides of her face.

"Was trying to beat the rush," Erik said, pointing to the line of cars, "but Jason . . ."

"Yeah, I grabbed him and told him he's got to come to Lisa's," Jason said, looking at Jennifer as if finally now there was someone to talk some sense into Erik.

"He can't go to Lisa's," Jennifer said seriously. "He's got to pack for camp. He flies out tonight."

"You know about this camp?" Jason asked, as Jennifer stood next to her boyfriend of almost a year.

"I haven't been there, but Erik's told me a little. It's very prestigious. Not very many people get selected to be counselors."

"You're a counselor?" Jason stared at Erik.

"That's part of the job."

"You can't just go to the party for a little while?"

Erik shook his head. "I can't."

Jennifer took Erik's hand and smiled at him. "Always committed."

"With this, always. It's my third year — my last year. It's gonna be special, and I've got to be ready."

"You're not going to do it next year?" Jennifer asked, looking into Erik's very blue eyes.

"I can't," he replied disappointedly, running his hand through his thick red mop. "Nineteen is the oldest you can be, and that's me."

"You old man," Jason said sarcastically. "Held you back a grade, huh?"

"No. My parents put me in kindergarten late, so I'm an old senior."

"Okay, old man. You're gonna miss some real fun," Jason said, finally conceding.

"You have some for me."

Jason smiled, thinking that wouldn't be a problem. "I'll see you then when you get back, I suppose. Merry Christmas."

"Merry Christmas, Jason."

"I'll see you tonight, right Jen?" Jason asked, as he walked backwards slowly, moving to his two-door truck.

"I'll be there."

"Good. See you."

"Bye," Jennifer said with a wave. She turned and faced her boyfriend.

"I'll miss you," Erik said kindly.

"You'd better," Jennifer replied sarcastically, still holding Erik's hand tightly. She pulled him forward and hugged him.

William Wood was nineteen and lived with his parents while going to the nearby technical trade school in his hometown of Leavenworth. Had it not been for his brutal calculus final he had to take at ten that morning, nothing could've stopped him from leaving the house. After all, it was December tenth.

The calculus final, as it turns out, wasn't as bad as he anticipated, and by the time he got home, it was almost noon. He was hopeful that the package hadn't arrived yet, so that maybe, in his final year, he would see how they did it — how they delivered it.

He clambered through the front door, slid his backpack off his shoulder, and was surprised to hear someone in the kitchen. Ah ha! He had finally caught them in the delivery. He rushed down the hall and turned abruptly to his right, his face ripe with anticipation. However, he was quite let down when he saw his mother putting away dishes from the dishwasher.

"Ah, Mom," he said, disappointedly.

"Do you have to say it like that?" his mother turned

to answer him before putting away a bowl.

William slumped into one of the kitchen chairs.

"Were you expecting someone else?" his mother asked, continuing to put away dishes.

William wanted to say, "Yes!" but doing so would raise questions and he knew that questions were something he needed to avoid. "No, I was just . . . why are you home?"

His mother laughed. "William, I'm taking my lunch break and thought I'd come home and fix lunch. Is that okay?"

"Well, yeah, but I . . ."

William caught himself.

"You . . ." his mother said, stopping and looking at her son curiously.

"Nothing. I was hoping to be here when a package arrived."

As soon as he said this, there was a sudden glow around his mother's head. He instantly knew what it was. His heart raced. They *had* delivered it while he was gone. Oh, they were good. No doubt they knew his school schedule.

"Mother," William said slowly, "what kind of a package arrived today?"

His mother blinked innocently. The glow around her head now pulsated with soft white and red in small bursts of what looked like exploding stars.

"Oh, it was such a nice package I found leaning against the door," she said airily.

"Was it a Candy Cane?" William said, not hiding the obvious excitement in his voice.

"Why yes, it was. It was so smooth and radiant."

"Where did you put it?"

"Up in your room," his mother answered, still in a tone of wondrous bewilderment.

William immediately stood up. "You know what this means, right Mother?"

"Of course. You're off to camp. Oh, William. It's so nice they invited you back for another year."

William laughed warmly, looking at his mother with both love and humor. She had no clue what was happening, and even though William had seen this look of hers now for a third straight year, it never got old. "I'm going to go up to my room and start packing. I leave tonight."

"Yes." His mother smiled. "By train?"

"No, Mom, that's for other kids. I leave by air."

"Yes, yes. By air. How silly of me," she giggled innocently.

"The power of the Candy Cane," William whispered under his breath.

"What was that?" his mother asked.

"Nothing, Mother. Go ahead and go back to the dishes."

"Right, right. The dishes," she said, turning her attention back to the open dishwasher.

William hurried up the stairs to his room.

There it sat, glowing softly with a blend of red and white, the same colors that circled his mother's head downstairs and would continue to circle it for the days ahead.

This Candy Cane looked identical to the ones he had received the last three years. It was the epitome of all candy canes — perfectly shaped, four feet from bottom to rounded top. The red and white swirls did not blend together like cheap candy canes. No sir. This Candy

Cane was perfect. Not only did it glow, but an incredible aroma of peppermint filled the room. It was amazing how the pleasant odor relaxed one instantly.

William moved to his bed and sat down, admiring the work of art. How he had wanted to see them place it, and exactly how they would do it. Was it the same way they sent off suitcases? Alas, it wasn't meant to be, and that was all right. It didn't matter. In just a few short hours, he'd be on his way.

He moved his right hand over the Cane and let his fingers dangle down, barely touching the top swirl of red. Immediately, a warmth filled his body as though he'd been dipped in thick hot chocolate. If only he could have a Candy Cane all the time. Heck, if everyone could just have one it would make the world such a better, safer, gentler world. But Candy Canes, the type he was holding, were not at all easy to make, and he understood that.

———————————

It had taken Erik a full hour to say his good-bye to Jennifer, wait patiently through the student traffic, and drive the six miles to his house after school. It was as though he was a kindergartner again, full of curiosity and excitement. Even though he knew what to expect, even though he knew that for a third year he would not see them deliver it, he knew without a doubt that it would be waiting for him.

He pulled into the driveway and took little notice that no other cars were parked there. Both his parents wouldn't be getting home from work until six. He bolted out of his Honda Civic and jumped the three cement stairs that led to the front door. He had always had this fear that someone would take it, that somehow some other person could see it and steal it. But to his relief and immense joy, there it was, leaning against the front door, glowing a soft red and white.

He threw his hands up in the air and shouted with joy, "Yeah! Yeah!" right before he went into a kid-like dance, hopping up and down in a bad attempt at an old Irish jig. He did not care what the neighbors thought. He did not care if one of his friends would have happened to drive by. That didn't matter. The only thing, the most important thing, was that he was going. He had been invited and now it was time for him to get ready for his third and final adventure.

When he finished his jig he breathed deeply and picked up the Candy Cane with both hands, admiring it with every ounce of appreciation he had. A warmth spread across his body — an exhilarating feeling that gave him goose bumps from head to toe, that made the hair on this forearms stand straight up. He fumbled for his keys and opened the front door. Once inside, he did another small jig, laughing all the way to his downstairs bedroom. He tossed the Candy Cane onto his bed that was littered with yesterday's and some of yester-weeks clothes and simply stared, taking a long, slow breath that brought him somewhat back to reality: He needed to pack.

CHAPTER TWO
Preparations

Erik finished packing by seven o'clock that night. He had found the largest suitcase his parents owned, stuffed it with clothes, gloves, ski pants, a stocking cap (totally essential for the snowball fight), along with jacket, boots, and all his necessary bathroom essentials.

He'd just finished zipping the last zipper when his father called him up to dinner. Tonight was pizza, delivered from one of the best pizza parlors in the area, The Pizza Pickler. The name sounded somewhat strange, but there was little doubt their pizza was the best in their area.

Like the last two years, he wondered if the conversation would start the same, if the Candy Cane's aura would produce the same results. To his satisfaction, it did. After sitting down at the round oak table, he took a slice of pizza (which did not have pickles on it by the way), and looked at his mother. Red and white bursts of light emanated around her head.

"So, honey, are you packed for camp?"

Erik grinned widely. "Yeah, Mom, all set."

"That's good, son, keeping on top of things," his father said, chiming in with a mouthful of pizza. He, too, was surrounded with bursts of red and white light.

"Isn't that smell wonderful?" his mother said breezily. "The smell of fresh peppermint. It seems so Christmassy."

Erik took a bite of his pizza and shook his head.

"Now, you're leaving tonight, is that right?" his father asked.

"Right, Dad."

"And they're coming to pick you up like last year?"

"Right."

"Oh, very nice. It must be a wonderful camp. It's such an honor for you to be going, to help kids, kids all across the world," his dad said proudly.

"It *is* an honor, Dad. That's for sure."

"You count your blessings," his mother said, shaking a finger from across the table. "Not very many people get this kind of an opportunity."

"I know how fortunate I am, Mom."

"You'll do a splendid job," added his father.

Erik took another bite of pizza and thought that this part, the waiting part, was the worst of the whole deal. Knowing that you are going but having to wait for your midnight ride was the most difficult. There was no other event in his life that he looked forward to more than this day, this night, and the days and nights to follow.

"You look so much like your father," William's mother said kindly, looking over at her son as if she hadn't seen him for a long time.

"All except that chin," his father teased. "That crack

in the middle . . ."

"All right, Dad," responded William playfully. "It's not a crack, okay? It's a clef."

"It's a crack," replied his father equally as playful.

"At least you got your father's features. That black hair and rugged look," his mother said blissfully.

"There's nothing wrong with your features, Mom," replied William kindly.

"Oh . . ." his mother said, as sparkles of red and white swam around her head.

"Now, now," his father said, patting his lips with his napkin. "You've got everything you need for the trip?"

"Yeah, Dad," William replied, wrapping a heaping forkful of spaghetti and putting it in his mouth.

"Gloves, winter pants . . ."

William nodded.

"I just can't get over that they're asking you for a third time. It's such an honor, son," his mother said proudly.

"Yes, indeed. William, you make us proud. I have no doubt that you will help people in need while you're there," his father added, red and white sparkles encompassing his head as well.

"That's why I go."

"It must be so fun," his mother reflected.

This produced the largest smile of the night. "Mom, you have no idea. Fun really isn't an adequate word for what I'll do, and this year, being my last year, and the new responsibilities . . . it's going to be fantastic!"

"Will they have you doing anything new this time?" his father asked.

"There is one new thing that's going to happen, Dad. I hope."

"What's that, son?"

William wanted so desperately to tell his mother and father. But with the aura of the Candy Cane, it was pointless. They wouldn't really remember in detail if he told them now.

Erik Sweet lived in northern Maine, which by mid-December means you are shoveling snow from sidewalks. This year was no exception. Everything was covered in a glistening white blanket.

Erik stood atop the roof of his house, glancing down at his watch that glowed midnight. Next to him was his thick rolling suitcase stuffed to the brim with his necessities. It'd been a chore getting it up to the top of his two-story home, but with the ladder and his father's help, he had managed.

Part of the Candy Cane's power was that Erik's father didn't question helping his son haul his suitcase up the ladder at near midnight. It didn't bother Erik's dad in the least. And when Mr. Sweet had gone back to bed and his head touched the pillow, he slept more soundly than any other night, as did every neighbor within a five-mile radius. This, of course, was due to the Candy Cane that was now propped conspicuously in the corner of Erik's bedroom, next to his nightstand. It would spread its magic for the duration of camp, never ceasing from its warm pulse of red and white light.

The air was crisp and cold. The moon was full and cast a grayish-white across the row of houses along Fortieth Street. Erik thought it was the quietest night he'd ever seen.

He'd been smiling from the moment he had set foot on the roof in anticipation of his ride. He scanned the clear sky and wondered who was to be his escort. He knew it wouldn't be Rudy, which meant he had a one in eight chance of guessing correctly. Last year it had been the big B. He was banking that it would be him again, and sure enough, as though he had read Erik's thoughts, emerging from the sky, high above as though he had just popped out of a star, was none other that Blitzen.

Erik watched as the magnificent reindeer flew toward him, galloping across the air as if it was a meadow of grass. Now, unless you're one of the chosen Members, you'll have never seen a reindeer fly. Picture an eagle, soaring majestically with the wind currents high above the trees. Combine that image with the gallop of a stallion on a sandy beach and you'll have as close to a description as I can give you as to what Santa's reindeer look like when they take flight. It's glorious!

"Blitzen . . . Blitzen! That's you, buddy!" shouted Erik in elation.

The animal drew closer and circled the rooftop as if to make sure he knew exactly where to land. After all, housetops were not as easy to land on as the Strip in the North Pole. But Blitzen had been Erik's escort last year, and remembered quite well where to approach and land.

The reindeer touched down loudly, slamming its hooves hard against the snow and wooden shingles, finally stopping just a few feet away. The animal was astonishing to look at. His all brown fur was smooth and groomed, and the first thought that entered Erik's mind as he stared in wonder, was that Hailey, the head caretaker of the reindeer, hadn't lost her touch in caring for her reindeer.

"Look at you! Look at you!" Erik said, a grin so wide it hurt his cheeks.

Blitzen quickly nodded his head twice, obviously excited to see Erik as well. He jumped up and down, breaking a few of the cedar shingles, but Erik didn't care. It wasn't as if Blitzen was going to wake the neighbors. That was impossible.

"It's so good to see you," Erik said, grabbing the animal around the neck and squeezing tight.

Erik was close to six foot. Blitzen, one of the bigger reindeer of the Nifty Nine, stood seven-and-a-half-feet tall.

"Yeah, whew!" Erik shouted, pulling away.

Blitzen shifted wildly.

"This year has gone by so slow! It seems like I've been waiting forever, pal! So," Erik rubbed his hands together, "same plan as last year?"

Blitzen nodded vigorously.

"We're meeting William in Kansas at Strother Field, right?"

Blitzen again nodded.

"This Christmas is going to be awesome. This is my last one, you know. I've gotta make it great. Not that last year wasn't, but the thought of it all coming to an end after Christmas this year . . . well, I don't want to think about it. You're here, I'm here. Let's fly, Blitz. Let's fly!"

The reindeer moved his head and motioned toward Erik's large suitcase.

"Yeah, that's my stuff. Don't look at me like that. I packed better than last year."

Blitzen snorted in disbelief.

"Hey!"

Blitzen snorted again, and took two steps toward the luggage. He lowered his head until his nose touched the top handle. There was a burst of red and green light that illuminated the roof for an instant. When the light faded, Erik's suitcase was gone.

"That's so cool," Erik said.

Blitzen stood upright and snorted again, as if to suggest that what he had just done was quite normal.

"May I?"

Blitzen nodded slowly. Erik grabbed what he could of the fur on Blitzen's neck, and hoisted himself up until he was comfortably straddling the animal like a horse. He scooted forward, and grabbed hold of the tall, thick horns of Blitzen's massive rack.

Erik's heart pounded with energy and anticipation. Although he knew what to expect, he was still giddy like a child on Christmas Eve. There was no ride comparable than on the back of a reindeer as you soar toward the NP.

———————————

William Wood stood on the rooftop of his house and stared at the thick fog that hovered a few hundred feet above him. Large snowflakes, the size of pennies, tapped his face, the lampposts providing him with enough light to see that this evening, the Leavenworth valley was in for what looked like a healthy snowstorm.

William was dressed in jeans and wore a thick ski jacket over his sweater. His hands were jammed inside the pockets of his coat and when he breathed, he could see his breath appear momentarily before whisking away into nothingness.

He stared at the lampposts and watched the snow continue to fall peacefully until all at once there was a loud crash to his left. He turned quickly, knowing that it could only be one of the Nifty Nine, and sure enough, there he stood, all seven feet of him.

"Dancer!" William said enthusiastically.

The large reindeer pranced forward.

"It's great to see you again!"

There was no mistaking Dancer, simply because the animal danced whenever he could, and this celebration called for a circle dance, in which the reindeer jumped up and down in a circle, kicking his legs out each time he lifted into the air. More shingles crushed and broke apart nosily, but it didn't bother William. No one would hear.

Dancer's appearance was very much like the other reindeer. He was completely brown and very manicured. His black eyes were narrower than the other reindeer, which helped to identify him.

William stared at the animal, his heart racing. "I just have one bag," he said, pointing to his suitcase.

Dancer stepped forward, bent down, and in an instant the suitcase disappeared among a wild flurry of red and green light. The animal then turned and threw his head back; an invitation for William to jump on. William didn't wait. He pulled himself up and took hold of Dancer's horns and found himself giggling like a tickled child.

Riding bareback on a reindeer might seem uncomfortable. After all, you don't have a saddle to cushion the many bumps you encounter while traveling. But with the Nifty Nine and Juveniles, you needn't worry. It was going to be the most comfortable and enjoyable trip William had ever taken, and he knew it.

"A third time?" William said, patting Dancer's neck. "Are we meeting in Strother Field again?"

Dancer nodded excitedly.

"All right then. Let's go!"

The reindeer took a quick two steps forward and jumped. Immediately, he rocketed upward, galloping as though he were on the ground. The reindeer flew into the thick fog, making it impossible for William to see, but it didn't last as Dancer continued upward until reaching the clear night sky.

The moon shown brightly in all its glory, illuminating the fog below in a brilliant silver hue. It was a sight that many people will never see and as William looked below him, he couldn't help but think he was the luckiest person on earth.

Like most things in the NP, these reindeer were special in many ways. Not only did the Nifty Nine fly, but their passengers didn't feel the effects of the flight. William could not feel the air whipping against his face or that the temperature was lingering around ten degrees. To him, he felt only warmth and comfort while staring around in awe at the magnificence of the night.

William figured he had a few minutes before he was in Kansas to meet with Erik. Though the two of them had spoken half a dozen times over the phone this year, it was nothing compared to what they were going to do in the days to come. They would be the best days of his life. He knew that. No matter what life had in store for him and his future, William Wood believed that whatever it was couldn't compare to the joy and happiness he was going to feel. Just riding on Dancer's back, gliding through the air with steady ease, would've been reward enough.

The exhilarating feeling filled his body with mental images of the NP and what he expected it to look like, to smell like, even to taste like. He hardly noticed the snowstorm Dancer navigated through once they crossed into Kansas. Large quarter-sized snowflakes descended in every direction, canceling out all light and surrounding the reindeer in complete darkness.

Not that this bothered William . . . it didn't. He knew perfectly well that Dancer was capable of finding the large rooftop of the printing factory. Within a minute, he could make out the lights below that lit up the building within the shroud of snow.

As Dancer made his approach to the flat roof of the four-story, square factory building, William could make out the silhouettes of two people standing in the snow, and a larger silhouette that was unmistakably a reindeer. Dancer steadied himself before touching down gently and trotting to a halt in the fresh, powdery snow.

"Well, well . . ." Erik said enthusiastically, walking toward Dancer as the reindeer came to a stop.

William disembarked and greeted Erik with a strong hug. "Good to see you."

"You too," Erik said, pulling away and examining his friend. "You've grown."

"Yeah, two and a half inches since the last time I saw you. I'm a size fourteen shoe now."

"Fourteen?" Erik laughed, trying to get a look at William's boots, but it was no use. They were buried in snow. "That's like . . . not right."

"Tell me about it. You wouldn't believe how hard it is to find shoes."

"Ah, to be young again," came Gustavo's voice. The portly man gently pet Blitzen's neck.

"Hey, Goose," said William pleasantly, "how are you?"

"Fine. However, I'd appreciate it if you used my real name."

"Don't give me attitude. The nickname fits."

"But I prefer . . ."

"I know, you prefer Gustavo, but to me, you'll always be the Goose," Erik said.

The old man, who stood a hunched-over-five-foot ten, smiled gently. "Youth today."

"Gotta love 'em," Erik countered playfully.

"How'd everything go this year with the printing?" William asked.

The seventy-year-old ran his hand through his thinning gray hair, drenched from the snow. Erik and William were perfectly dry. "Busy but good."

"How many did you print?" William wondered.

"This year, the big S wanted almost fifty thousand."

"A little more this year, ay?"

"Right," Goose said proudly. "The boxes are in the main terminal on the bottom floor. I just need one of the reindeer . . ."

Dancer stepped forward and bowed his head slowly. Goose was immediately excited. He stepped forward and mounted the reindeer with surprising ease. It was obvious he had mounted a horse or two in his lifetime.

"This is my twentieth year doing this and it still is amazing," Goose said delightedly. "Fly me around the place a couple of times, will you, Dance? Then you can take me to the side door and we'll go in through there."

The reindeer raised and lowered its head in a nod, and in an instant was carrying Goose into the air, the old man laughing the entire time.

"So, what's new? How's Jen?" William asked, watching as Dancer took Goose on his first circle.

"Good." Erik smiled. "She's really helped a lot this year. What about you and Holly?"

William stared a long time at Erik. "You ready to be my best man?" he finally said.

"You're serious? You guys decided?"

"More or less. Holly's already got things lined up," said William.

"What about your parents?" asked Erik.

William sighed. "I didn't tell them. It wouldn't do much good anyway with the Candy Cane's aura working."

Erik understood. "This year is going to be weird. Picking our replacement just doesn't feel right, you know?"

William nodded while Goose and Dancer descended toward the ground and out of sight.

"I wish there wasn't the Twenty Rule," said Erik in a dejected voice. "It's too bad we can't change it."

"I think that's impossible. It's been in place for so long," said William, watching the snowflakes fall, none of which he or Erik felt, due to magical protection.

Erik looked at Blitzen, who stood quietly. "In just a couple of minutes, we're going to be back again. We're going back to the NP, baby! The NP!"

CHAPTER THREE
Meet Hannah Green

Hannah Green was a ninth grader at Fisher Heights High School in Gresham, Oregon. She had bright red hair that touched her shoulders. She was about five-foot-five and twenty pounds heavier than most girls her age. The weight thing didn't bother her much. Hannah was a confident, independent, and most importantly, compassionate person. She was, by far, the most liked freshman at Fisher.

The day in which she found the letter was on Friday, December seventeenth. She had fifteen minutes before first period started and was just about to open her locker, but had to wait for a group of upper classmen to get by. A frequent occurrence. Hallways at Fisher were worse than Portland traffic jams, as impossible as that is to believe. Fisher was the oldest school in three counties and was designed and built to hold a maximum capacity of eight hundred students, not the current student body of over twelve hundred.

When the bulge of adolescence finally passed, Hannah put in her combination and opened her beleaguered locker. She was an organized marvel.

One look inside and you knew you were dealing with someone with purpose. She had bought shelves that fit the locker perfectly, giving her a way to store her books so that it was quick and easy to get what she needed and move on. After all, with so many students, getting from class to class in the five short minutes allowed.

She reached in to grab her science book for first period when she noticed *it* resting on the first shelf. It was a red and white striped envelope. It reminded her of a Christmas card, but how did it get into her locker in the first place? No way someone, somehow slid it in. The locker was impenetrable. The only way someone could've gotten in was to actually open the locker, but who could do that? No one knew her combination, not even her best friend, Emily. And Hannah was one of the lucky ones that didn't have to share her locker. Bethany, her old locker partner, had moved two months ago, leaving her with the luxury of the entire space.

She glanced to her left and right, searching to see if someone suspicious might be looking to see how she would react, but there were so many people it was a blur of walking hormones.

She returned her attention to the picture-laden inside of the locker and to the letter. She picked it up. She could have sworn, for a fraction of a second, that the card glowed softly white, like Christmas lights you decorate the tree with.

Her name was engraved in green calligraphy on the front of the envelope. It was obvious whoever wrote it was a talented calligrapher. It wasn't a stamped name or some cheap trace-out you buy at a store. This name was a work of art. Her name never looked better.

She carefully peeled the envelope open and

withdrew a hard piece of old parchment paper, yellowed and faded. In the same wonderful letters as her name was the message: *We're watching you.*

What did this mean? Who was watching her? Was this some sort of sick threat or something? She scanned the hall again, trying to find anyone that looked as though they were focusing on her. She couldn't find anyone. The noise and movement made it impossible to spot anyone suspicious.

She looked at the old parchment again and stared unbelievably. Her heart thumped noticeably harder. The message now read: *Yes, we're watching you.*

"Who are you?" she blurted. The ambient noise around her drowned out her outburst.

Another scan of the hallway — this time much longer and deliberate.

Nothing.

She steered her eyes to the card again and gasped: *You can't see us yet . . . but remember, we're watching you.*

"Who?" she said.

The words on the card disappeared in a flash of green light and another message appeared: *The NPSP.*

Hannah's heart pounded like a possessed timpanist. She grabbed Angelina Brewster, a couple of lockers to her left, by the arm.

"Hannah, what are you doing?" Angelina said, as she rummaged through her locker hurriedly.

"Look at this card! Look at what it says!" Hannah said, somewhat hysterically.

She shoved the card in front of Angelina's face and waited. Angelina stared blankly.

"Well?" Hannah said. "What's it mean? 'The NPSP?'"

Angelina continued staring at the card, then looked

at Hannah. "It doesn't say anything. It's blank."

Hannah stared down at the card incredulously: *They won't be able to see the words.*

"There, there," Hannah pointed, again shoving the card up to Angelina. "It says, 'they won't be able to see the words.'"

"No, it doesn't. It doesn't say anything."

"What?" Hannah said, staring at the card again. The words were still there. "Yes it does. It says it right here in fancy calligraphy."

"Hannah, it's not funny," Angelina said, somewhat miffed, turning her attention back to her locker search.

Hannah stood, dumbstruck. The words were on the card. She wasn't hallucinating. They were there!

The next few minutes as she walked to class, she did so in a sort of trance, holding the card and mumbling, "The words are there. The words are there."

As she took her seat in class, she shoved the card into her backpack and took out a couple pieces of paper, along with a pen, in anticipation of Mr. Lampert's genetics lecture. She had to put the card out of her mind. She tried to dismiss it as a prank, but she had to admit, if it was a prank, it was the best prank she'd ever had played on her. The changing of the letters like that . . . now *that* was a trick.

Into his lecture about ten minutes, Hannah was busy writing notes as fast she could. She was a thorough student and prided herself on her work ethic and effort. She moved her eyes up to the white board to write the next set of important notes when she froze as though she had been petrified.

The board.

The white board.

On it, in the same green calligraphic words as her letter was a message, covering Mr. Lampert's important notes he wanted the students to copy down.

Keep believing.

Her palms were suddenly sweating and her heart was again resuming a brisk, nervous pace. Right before her eyes the message changed again in a flash of green.

You have been chosen.

"All right, all right," she suddenly blurted loudly. "This isn't funny!"

There was an odd silence in the room of thirty kids. Hannah sat at the back table and every eye turned and fixed on her.

Mr. Lampert, a fiftyish man with a low voice, stared inquisitively for a moment, then said, "It's not meant to be funny."

"The words! It's you, Mr. Lampert. You're the one who placed the card and now your board. . . ."

Mr. Lampert looked stunned. "Hannah, I don't know what you're talking about."

Hannah pointed at the board, her hand now shaking. "You see the message in green. There, right there. It just changed. You see, it says 'They won't be able to see it,'" Hannah said, progressively slower as she neared the end of the sentence.

Mr. Lampert stared at the board, then back at Hannah. "Are you done?"

Hannah looked as though she might faint as the color drained from her freckled cheeks. "The board," she mumbled. "The board."

Mr. Lampert took pity of the poor girl. She was, after all, one of the top students in his class. It was obvious she was stressed out. "Why don't you go to the office and have Mrs. Garney take a look at you."

Mrs. Garney, one of the three counselors at Fisher, happened to be in when Hannah came knocking on the door to her small office ten minutes later.

"Come in, come in," said the counselor, welcoming Hannah into the small office. "Take a chair."

"I'm Hannah Green," Hannah said meekly.

"Hello, Hannah. You're a ninth grader, right?"

Hannah nodded, sliding her hand over her face and moving her bangs out of the way.

"What seems to be the problem?" Mrs. Garney asked from behind her rectangular glasses.

"I think I'm hallucinating. I'm seeing things."

Mrs. Garney's brow furrowed a bit. "What kind of things?"

"Letters . . . messages. I was just in Mr. Lampert's class and this message in green appeared on the board and the same type of letters . . . came on this card I got in my locker and like, it was there before I opened it, and then when I looked at it, it made these different messages, and then the messages changed, and I looked around the hall and I couldn't see anyone staring at me, and the messages kept changing and . . ."

"Hannah, Hannah, slow down. Slow down. Tell me what the messages say."

Hannah perked up in the chair. She reached for her backpack and found the old parchment. Sure enough, there was a message in the green calligraphy: *Never stop believing*.

"You see, you see," Hannah said, pointing to the paper. "You see it?"

"You mean, the message?" Mrs. Garney said skeptically.

"Yes, yes! The message. Right there. It says . . ."

"Nothing," finished Mrs. Garney. "There aren't any words on that paper."

"But I see them. They're right there!" Hannah said, closing her eyes and shaking her head. "I see them. There's a message!"

Mrs. Garney showed great concern. She figured Hannah was under some serious stress. "Hannah, Hannah . . . look at me. There's not . . . look at me! There's not any writing on that card. There aren't any words there," Mrs. Garney said slowly from her burgundy office chair.

Hannah was about to lose it. She felt the tears coming. She was going to burst. Whoever was playing this trick had won because she was losing her mind. Before the first tear fell, though, she looked at the card again.

Stop worrying. You have been chosen. You are special. Therefore, you're able to read this card, but that woman sitting in front of you, can't.

Hannah sucked in a large breath.

In a small flash of green, the message changed: *You must trust us. We mean you no harm.*

Hannah kept staring, totally engrossed.

We have one question for you.

What could this card possibly want to know, Hannah thought.

Do you believe in Santa Claus?

Hannah blinked hard. Perhaps it was all her imagination, perhaps this was a dream. Maybe if she just closed her eyes and thought of something else. It was no use. The question remained. Do you believe in Santa Claus?

Hannah waited for a long time and then whispered, "Yes."

We thought so. Welcome!

Hannah looked up at Mrs. Garney and stared unbelievingly. The counselor sat there, a wide grin across her face, small red and white bursts of light encircling her head. "Are you getting the messages, sweetheart?" she asked sweetly.

Hannah closed her mouth and swallowed hard. "Yes."

"Good, very good. You know, I can't read that piece of paper."

"What?" Hannah said, still apprehensive. Mrs. Garney looked like she was in a drug-induced stupor.

"The card, dear. You can read its messages?"

Hannah nodded slowly.

"Then you are chosen. You are a very special person to be invited."

"Invited?" Hannah said, inquisitively.

"Look at the card, dear."

Hannah looked down at it.

Welcome to the NPSP.

"What's the NPSP?" Hannah asked.

A small explosion of red and green light replaced NPSP with the words: *NORTH POLE SANTA PATROL.*

"The North Pole Santa Patrol?" Hannah whispered.

"Yes, Hannah. A very exclusive group."

"Who are they?"

"You'll find out soon enough, but first, your instructions for the evening."

"Instructions?" Hannah was completely flabbergasted. At any time she was expecting to awaken from the bizarre dream she was having.

"Yes, dear. First, you may not tell anyone about the card you're holding or about any of the messages. Second, you need to pack a large suitcase. You are going to the North Pole, so pack accordingly," Mrs. Garney said matter-of-factly.

Hannah's hand shot up in the air as if she were in class ready to ask a question. "Wait, wait. I'm going . . . to the North Pole?"

"Yes, you leave tonight."

"Tonight?"

"Yes."

Everything was spinning. First the magical card and now Mrs. Garney, who was not acting at all like Mrs. Garney, and who had bursts of white and red stars all around her head.

"Hannah, you are to be a part of the North Pole Santa Patrol, dear."

"What's that?"

"Your questions will be answered soon enough. Please note, it is preferred that you only take one suitcase, however big, to the NP. It's rough on the reindeer when they have to send off more than one in a short period of time."

"What?" Hannah whispered uncomprehendingly.

Mrs. Garney ignored Hannah's confusion and went on. "Be at the top of your roof at exactly midnight, tonight. That's where you'll be picked up."

"What?"

"A reindeer escort will arrive to take you to the NP."

"A reindeer escort . . ." Hannah fumbled.

"Yes, of course — might very well be Donder or perhaps Vixen. I doubt they'll use Rudy."

"Rudy?" Hannah could barely whisper.

"Yes, Rudy."

"You mean, Rudolph?"

"The red-nosed reindeer." Mrs. Garney smiled even more broadly. "You know of him? Splendid. Yes, but I don't think he does pick ups much. You know the song? Let's sing: *Rudolph, the red-nosed reindeer, had a very shiny nose . . ."*

"Mrs. Garney! What's happening to me?" Hannah managed to raise her voice.

Mrs. Garney's pleasant demeanor vanished and was replaced with total seriousness. "Hannah, among the millions of kids on earth, you are one of only a handful that was chosen to help in the greatest cause in this world. You cannot turn it down. You have something to offer Santa and everyone else in the NP. You are needed."

Hannah stared in shock and bewilderment. What Mrs. Garney had just said made absolutely no sense, and yet as crazy as it was, she believed the counselor. But how was she going to help Santa? How was she going to help the North Pole?

"Do not worry," Mrs. Garney said reassuringly. "They're watching you. You're in good hands."

"Who's watching me?"

Mrs. Garney motioned to the card.

Hannah looked down and stared at its message, still continuing to be written in green calligraphy: *We're watching you, Hannah! From Erik and William.*

"Who are Erik and William?"

"I'm afraid I've run out of answers for you, dear. I believe it's time for you to head back to class. I'm going to write you a note . . ."

"Class? How can I go to class with all this

happening?"

Mrs. Garney waited until she had finished writing her note on the small school message pad. "Those who are chosen have the burden of knowing. They have seen the truth, but must carry it inside. You must do the same, Hannah. Tell no one and make sure you're ready tonight."

Mrs. Garney handed Hannah the note and smiled. "Now, off you go."

Hannah slowly stood up, staring at gray-headed Mrs. Garney. Explosions of light emanated from each side of her head.

"Quit staring, child, and get out of my office," Mrs. Garney said playfully, motioning for Hannah to leave.

"But . . . but," Hannah fumbled.

"On your roof by midnight, young lady. Don't be late, and remember, tell no one."

Telling no one, as it turns out, was nearly impossible. She so desperately wanted to tell Angelina in fourth period technology class that she resorted to actually biting her tongue. She wanted to tell Nathan Hawkins in sixth period PE when he asked her what had happened after she left the room during first period. Since they shared both first and sixth periods, he had seen her outburst in class. Hannah played it down as best she could and blamed the whole incident on exhaustion, telling Nathan that Mrs. Garney recommended going home and getting lots of rest.

Lots of rest . . . what a joke. Every time she looked at the card she felt restless. It had a different message every time she read it. When she finally got home and read it, *Midnight on the roof,* she had had enough. She stuffed the card in her backpack and vowed not to look at it again.

She didn't have any intention of going up on her roof at midnight.

She was relieved when she heard her parents drive into the driveway. They commuted to work and arrived home at their customary six o'clock. Hannah greeted them at the door like a puppy that's been locked up all day. She wanted to tell them about the card, but the moment she tried, the moment she opened her mouth to describe the events of the day, something inside her couldn't go through with it.

She decided that she would wait until after dinner. Perhaps a full stomach would provide her with the extra she needed, but the nervousness of the day stopped her from taking a bite and prompted her mother to notice.

"You're not hungry? Are you feeling all right?"

No, she wasn't feeling all right. She was feeling scared and mystified. She needed to tell her parents but, again, she was stymied by something deep within her. A feeling that was so strong, she couldn't go against it.

Eight o'clock rolled around and she tried doing homework at her small desk in the corner of her second-story room, but that was a waste of time. She couldn't concentrate. She was about to search her small bookshelf for a good novel when her mother called from the bottom of the stairs. She opened her bedroom door and stared down at her mother in amazement. She was holding a large Candy Cane, the smoothest, most breathtaking Candy Cane Hannah had ever seen. It pulsated with red and white light, and the smell of peppermint was inviting.

Hannah gazed at it and then noticed the sparkles around her mother's head. Red and white sparkles, just like the ones she had seen popping up all around Mrs.

Garney earlier in the day, had now infected her mom.

"I believe this is for you," Hannah's mother said in a droll.

"What is it? Where did you get it?" Hannah asked perplexedly, staring at her mother in wonder and apprehension.

"I found it on the front porch when I went to get the mail this evening, dear. I'm glad I did, too. I wouldn't want you to miss your ride tonight."

Hannah's pulse quickened.

"What ride?"

"Your ride to the NP," her mother answered matter-of-factly.

"Yes, yes," her father suddenly said, joining his wife at the bottom of the stairs. Around his head were bursts of red and white stars.

"Dad, what's happening?"

"Not a thing — nothing to worry about, sweetheart. I just wanted to make sure you were ready for tonight."

"What do you mean?" Hannah asked, bolting down the stairs so that she stood in front of her parents. "What's tonight?"

Her father smiled compassionately. "Tonight is the beginning of an incredible journey that you've been invited to attend."

"I have?"

"Oh, yes," Hannah's mother added. "Hannah, you're going to the most important place on Earth. You've got a job to do."

"I do?" Hannah said, almost in tears.

"You are to be a part of the NPSP."

CHAPTER FOUR
Pick Up

Hannah could not sleep. She had probed her parents the rest of the evening until they went to bed at ten, and yet they gave her little more information about what she was about to embark on.

So far, she knew that she was chosen to be part of something very unique and special that was called the North Pole Santa Patrol. What that was exactly she didn't know, and when she asked her parents, they simply smiled and said that she would find out soon enough. There was no denying that whoever these people were, they had power. That was evident with her parents and Mrs. Garney. Bursts of red and white stars around people's heads wasn't normal and the change of behavior was remarkable, especially Mrs. Garney's transformation from a stressed out, over-worked counselor to a relaxed, if not ditsy, demeanor. And what about the miraculous card messages?

Hannah also knew that she was to be on top of her roof at midnight, but why? And what kind of ride was going to be coming for her? Were these people working for Santa Claus himself? Were they elves of some kind? The questions kept coming like relentless rain for which her parents had, unfortunately, failed to provide an umbrella.

Time wasn't helping either. The closer it crawled to midnight, the more nervous she became. She tried drinking a glass of milk to calm her tight stomach, but could only get two swallows down.

She wrapped a coat around her shoulders and went out to the backyard. She wasn't sure why, but maybe she'd be able to see something that would calm her. The evening was crisp and cold as her breath left in irregular puffs. She stared at the blinking stars, searching for a sign.

Hannah wondered what would happen if she just didn't go to the roof. Could she go hide in the garage and wait until midnight passed? Would they still come for her or would they go away, never to bother her again? She doubted that. Something in her heart told her that whoever the North Pole Santa Patrol were, they did not mean her or her family any harm, and that somehow she was obligated to meet them.

She decided that she would not wait any longer. She went to her room, grabbed a large suitcase that she had packed as if she was going to be visiting Greenland, and shoved it out her window and onto the roof. She followed, taking the suitcase and sliding it nosily across the shingles to her left. She would need to get to the very top of the roof, but that wasn't hard. Her house was designed in three levels and the six-foot ladder her father had set up for her just before going to bed was all she needed.

Carefully walking up the ladder, dragging her suitcase, she made it to the top. It didn't get much stranger than this. What parent in their right mind would let their daughter climb to the very top of the roof at midnight? What kind of father sets up a ladder so his child can get to the top more easily? The reality of what she was doing, and how ludicrous it all sounded, was bearing down on her now more than ever.

Hannah looked at her watch.

Five minutes to midnight. She stared around at the surrounding houses and was surprised at how dark and lifeless they all were. Not even Mrs. Doggett's house was alive with activity, and she had three teenagers who never slept. Loud music was always blaring, but not tonight. Everywhere Hannah looked, houses were sedate.

Her first cue was the sound: rushing wind over her head, like a train had come roaring past. She drew in a frightened breath and stared above, but only stars and a large moon stared back. Then she heard it again, as if it was behind her now. She quickly turned.

Nothing.

The third time she heard it, she knew where it had come from. Descending toward her was something she could not at first believe. She figured she would never see one her entire life. She had stayed up nights trying to see them on Christmas Eve, but without any luck. Yet here two of them were, coming at her majestically, galloping across the air smoothly and naturally.

They were magnificent looking reindeer. Huge racks adorned their heads. Their brown, smooth fur glistened in the ambient light. She was so captivated by them that she barely noticed that each had riders. As the two animals clambered onto the roof loudly, two boys dismounted and stood, smiling.

"Hannah, Hannah," said Erik happily.

The boy that spoke was red headed, and wore a green ski jacket with long red sleeves. In the center of the coat were four letters, each about the size of a tennis ball. Each glowed with a soft, white light.

"NPSP," Hannah whispered in awe.

"Right. That's us," Erik said, stepping forward.

Blitzen snorted as puffs of breath jetted out his nostrils.

"Welcome to the NPSP," William said, moving next to Erik to face Hannah. Dancer inspected the roof and walked in small circles, the shingles cracking beneath his hooves.

"The North Pole Santa Patrol," said Hannah, barely audible.

"That's us and actually now, that's you," said William.

Hannah stared at the two boys unbelievably and then at the reindeer. "Those are reindeer?"

"Not just *any* reindeer," said Erik proudly. "These are Santa's finest. These two are the ones you read about at Christmastime. These two are part of the Nifty Nine. That's Dancer. Notice how he finds it hard to control himself. Okay, Dancer, calm down. And then we have Blitzen, who is much more subdued."

"I never thought I would see one," Hannah said admiringly.

"Not too many do, believe me. Consider yourself extremely lucky. Out of the entire world of teenagers, *the entire world*, you are the one we chose to carry the torch for us."

"What do you mean?"

"Hannah, I don't even know where to begin," Erik said, looking at William. "Remember our first time?

Remember what it was like?"

William laughed. "I was so nervous."

"So was I," admitted Erik.

"Hannah, are you nervous?" William asked kindly. Hannah nodded.

"Don't be. There's absolutely nothing to fear. But we have a lot we need to share with you, so before we actually mount up and go to the NP, we need to answer your questions and get you somewhat prepared for what you're about to see and do."

"What is the NPSP?" Hannah asked quickly.

"Sit down and we'll tell you."

Erik looked around like he was suddenly aware. "Kinda depressing not having any snow here."

"We're lucky it's dry tonight. It usually rains during the winter," said Hannah.

William stood opposite her. "This is going to take a few minutes."

Hannah was captivated, forgetting time and place.

"Dancer, will you calm down! Just sit still!" said William with a slight hint of exasperation. "Honestly, the animal is wound so tight . . ."

"Hannah, the NPSP, short for North Pole Santa Patrol, is a special group of human teenagers. There are only four of us. We have the most important job in the North Pole. We continue to propagate the Christmas Spirit," Erik began.

"Propagate?" Hannah asked.

"We continue the Christmas Spirit. If all of the NPSP were to be killed, Christmas, as you know it, would cease. Part of our job is to continue the Spirit of belief in the NP. We're able to do that because we believe just as you do. We believe in Santa and what he stands for. We believe in the magic and sanctity of Christmas."

"Dancer!" rebuked William again. "Sorry, but this animal . . ."

Blitz was obviously getting annoyed at his skittish partner and snorted loudly twice, finally calming Dancer down enough for the reindeer to stand somewhat still.

"About time," William sighed.

Erik grinned. "What do you think you know about the North Pole?"

Hannah took her eyes off the reindeer and looked at Erik's shadowy face. "The North Pole is cold."

"It won't be any colder than what you're used to in wintertime," William stated.

"But it's the North Pole. It's like the top of the earth. It's freezing up there."

"Like I said, it won't be any colder than you're used to," said William.

"It's part of the aura of the Christmas Spirit that makes it livable," Erik added.

"What else do you know?" William probed.

Hannah thought for a moment. "There's elves."

"Right," Erik said, smiling broadly.

"There's a toy shop for all the kids' toys," Hannah continued.

"Right. Go on."

"I don't know. That's all I can think of."

"Hmmm," said Erik. "You're in for a real treat."

"Oh, yeah," William echoed.

"But why was I chosen? What makes *me* so special?"

"Now that's a good question," Erik admitted, turning to William.

"The interview process that we had to go through to

pick the right person was intense and very challenging. The elves are the most honest beings on the planet. In fact, they do not lie. To do so is against everything they stand for. Each elf has a gift of remembering information far more than normal humans. Each elf in the NP is in charge of monitoring thousands of human beings from all across the world. They monitor them through what they call the Windows of Observation."

Hannah looked befuddled. William caught it right away.

"You'll understand the Windows once you see them. The elves keep track of your good deeds that they observe. Now, granted, they don't see all your good deeds, but you'd be surprised how many they do catch. They then record your deeds into their computers, which are linked to the central computer in the Operations Center."

"Elves have computers?" Hannah asked skeptically.

"Elves may be old-fashioned, but they keep up with technology. Before computers, everything was done by hand. Took ages — had to work deals with Father Time. Now things are much more streamlined," Erik explained.

"So the central computer keeps tallies on all the people's good deeds. In December, when we arrive, we print out a list of the top five teenagers on the planet. And guess what? You were on it. Then we take about a week to observe the candidates, all four of us."

"All four?" Hannah asked.

"Me and William, along with Noemi and Natalya," said Erik.

"During that week, we watch all five candidates at different times of the day," continued William.

"Basically, we spy on them and see which ones we feel will best make the new Patrol members. Now Noemi and Natalya are both sixteen, so they will be members until they turn nineteen, which will mark their final year.

"That's where Erik and I are now. We're both nineteen and this is our last year being on the Patrol. This year, two new members had to be chosen, and you're our pick. A committee of four elves picked the other human."

"How did you spy on me? I never saw you," said Hannah.

"We had a special Candy Cane made last year so that we could see people in person. Took the better part of a year. It allowed us to go invisible and follow you."

"That's amazing," whispered Hannah.

"That's only the beginning," continued William. "We get to greet the person we chose, so we're here. Natalya and Noemi are greeting the other human that the elves chose. His name is Marcel. He's from France."

"I was your pick?"

"All of us picked you. Noemi, Natalya, William, and myself. You were far and away the best one."

"No." Hannah shook her head. "That can't be. I can't believe I'm one of the best in . . ."

"The world," Erik finished. "Out of all the candidates, Hannah, no one had done as many good deeds as you. Four days ago you helped Edith get her groceries without being told to help her, without expecting any reward. I don't know many teenagers that would help a ninety-year-old woman the way you did."

"And what about Nicole?" William chimed in. "She was having a terrible day yesterday and needed a friend, and you took the time to really listen to her problem."

"Anyone would have done that," offered Hannah.

"Not true," came William's quick response. "Nicole isn't very well liked at school, is she? And to be honest, she really doesn't have many friends, but what did you do? You befriended her. That's because you have the type of qualities needed to continue the Christmas Spirit. You have compassion for other people. You have honesty and integrity, and most important of all, you have love — something we need more of in the world today. We read your deeds list and it's amazing. Just watching during that week proved what we thought once we read it: You are the one."

Hannah felt warmth spread through her like she'd just drank a large mug of hot cocoa.

"It is an honor, Hannah. You should feel very proud. Don't be ashamed that we are honoring you. I know it kinda feels weird because you don't want to sound self-serving, but relish the feeling."

"Thanks," Hannah offered quietly. "This is so . . . cool."

"It's going to get a lot cooler," said Erik. "Look above you."

Hannah stared above and immediately saw what Erik was referring to. A streak of white rocketed past, a hundred feet above them. It was a white blur and impossible for Hannah to make out exactly what it was. She turned to Erik.

"You don't know what that was, do you?" he asked with a smile.

"No."

Erik looked at William and winked, then gazed back at Hannah. "Think, Hannah. What do you know about the North Pole that could explain what you just saw?"

Hannah stared at the sky again. She asked herself what could possibly explain what she saw as it related to the North Pole, but nothing came to mind.

"I don't know."

"No, not that easily. Come on, now. Think."

Hannah concentrated and just about the time she was ready to give up once again, a thought echoed through her mind and she realized what the streak was.

She smiled.

"You got it?" asked William.

Hannah nodded. "Is it Comet?"

Before William could answer, the streaky white blur appeared once again, heading straight for them.

"Oh boy," lamented Erik. "He's out of control again!"

"No, he's got it this time," argued William, both boys staring up with anticipation at the approaching blur.

As the mass of white neared, Blitzen and Dancer snorted indifferently.

"Slow down, slow down," whispered Erik. "Come on, Comet, slow down."

Comet could not hear Erik, not that it would have mattered. Comet couldn't do anything slow, including flying. He had been given his name for a reason, and even as a young reindeer, he had control problems, which were about to manifest themselves.

With the loudest crash of the night, Comet slammed onto the roof. Pieces of shingles flew off in every direction, one shard rocketing inches past Hannah's cheek. Both Blitzen and Dancer showed disdain by backing up and huffing loudly while Comet tried to gain control of his landing.

"You're insane, Comet!" shouted Erik, a hint of laughter in his voice. "You've got to slow down!"

Comet steadied and presented himself in front of Hannah, as if for her approval. She looked at Erik and William for guidance.

"He wants you to pet him. It's kinda like you giving your approval."

Hannah moved closer and put her hand out. Before touching him, Blitzen and Dancer gave another snort of disapproval.

"Oh, it's all right," William said, chastising the two reindeer. "He's a good flyer, just a little out of control."

Hannah stroked Comet's neck as the reindeer lowered his head and allowed her access to his mane.

"He never changes," laughed Erik. "The only time that animal doesn't make crazy landings is when he's with the others."

He might have crazy landings, thought Hannah, but she liked him nonetheless. He had character, and his personality appealed to her. "So they call him Comet because he's so fast, right?"

"Yep. He's by far the fastest of any of the Nine. He comes from a long line of speedy reindeer. He can travel at speeds that make him look like a comet, so that's where his name comes from," said Erik.

Comet raised his head and stared at Hannah with his dark, sparkling eyes. She knew that she was incredibly lucky to be standing on her roof, learning things she never knew existed. Whatever apprehension and nervousness she felt earlier were gone, now replaced by curiosity and excitement.

"When do we go?" Hannah asked, admiring Comet's massive rack.

"Are you sure you're ready?" asked Erik.

"No, but I suppose I'm as ready as I'm ever going to be. I know I'm going to have questions, but you'll be there to help me, right?" Hannah asked, looking from William to Erik.

"Of course," William replied earnestly. "All we have left is to send your suitcase, and then we're outta here."

"My suitcase?"

Comet went to the suitcase and touched it with his nose. Immediately, it disappeared in a sea of red and green light.

"How? What?" Hannah said, pointing to the empty spot on the roof where her suitcase had been.

"Reindeer can transport objects with their magical properties. Now," said William eagerly, "climb aboard Comet."

"Climb aboard?"

"Yeah, grab some fur and hoist yourself on."

Hannah swallowed, looking at Comet apprehensively. The animal turned its head and lowered its neck so that Hannah could climb on more easily. She stepped forward and managed to mount the animal quickly, using Comet's horns to help.

"You've gotten on a horse before," said Erik admiringly.

"Yes," Hannah said

"Well, then, let's go."

Hannah found that riding Comet was surprisingly easier than riding a horse, something she had years of practice with since her aunt entered any rodeo within a three-hundred-mile radius and was bent on making Hannah her clone. But riding a reindeer was a smooth and comfortable affair, not a jumpy, sometimes painful experience riding in the saddle often produced.

Hannah had fully expected the crisp night air to brush against her face like icy shards, but she was pleasantly surprised and somewhat bewildered that she felt no air resistance at all. Comet galloped through the air smoothly, following Dancer and Blitzen.

Hannah smiled with joy as she watched the city lights below fade into the distance — her reindeer climbing higher into the cloudless night sky. It was exhilarating to be flying. She gripped Comet's horns tightly and wondered how long it was going to actually take to get to the North Pole. Suddenly, Comet picked up his pace, as did Blitzen and Dancer. They were now ascending at a much steeper incline, and Hannah squeezed her hands tighter on Comet's rack. The reindeer gained momentum and just about the time Hannah was feeling uneasy, white and golden circles of light surrounded her. The brightness blocked out everything. Blitzen and Dancer, along with William and Erik, were nowhere to be seen. It was as if she was passing through a great tunnel of luminescence.

Comet maintained his pace as the white and gold colors surrounded Hannah for nearly ten minutes. During this time, Hannah wasn't frightened, but was filled with wonderment that spawned questions without answers. When the surrounding light finally disappeared, William and Erik were directly in front of her, mounted on their reindeer. Both animals were quiet and still as if they were standing on an invisible bridge overlooking a grand scene from high above.

Comet slowed to a gentle walk until he was adjacent to Dancer and Blitzen. Hannah stared below and could hardly believe what she was seeing. So many people had told her it didn't exist . . . yet there it was.

Erik turned and smiled broadly. "Welcome to the North Pole."

"Yeah," Hannah whispered.

They were high above tall mountain peaks that surrounded a snow-covered valley. At the base of the mountains was a vast forest of what looked like pine trees, their limbs sagging from the heavy snow build up. The land was gorgeous, but it was nothing compared to the valley itself, which was alive with green, red, and white hues and plumes of steam rising into the air.

"Before we go down," Erik said, "William and I thought we ought to give you an aerial tour first."

"Okay," Hannah said, her eyes going from building to building in wonder.

"Directly below us . . ."

"Wait," Hannah cut him off. "The card at school? How did you do that? How did it change messages like it did?"

Erik smiled. "That was a slick trick. We used some magical peppermint, which you'll find out about later once you've been in the NP awhile."

"Magical peppermint?"

"Yes. Now, I want you to look directly below us . . . see all those houses? Those are the elves' houses. It's the Elven Neighborhood."

"It's huge. It's like a city," Hannah observed, staring below at rows and rows of houses that all looked the same, and most of which had small puffs of smoke coming from the chimneys.

"Right. There are a lot of elves in the NP."

"Only elves live there?" Hannah asked.

"Correct," answered William. "Now, move your eyes forward north and what's the first thing you see?"

"It looks like an airstrip. . . ."

"It's the runway for Santa and the sleigh," Erik said, pointing at the flashing red and green lights. Hannah figured it was about as big and long as a commercial airstrip, and it was obvious it had been plowed of snow recently because she could easily see the cement underneath.

"To the left of the Strip . . ."

"The Tree," Hannah gasped, cutting Erik off. "And what's that flowing . . . is that a river?"

"Yeah, well . . . just let me finish," Erik said.

Hannah was mesmerized.

"Uh, Hannah . . ."

"Yes," she said airily.

"Over here. Look over to the left here . . ."

William laughed. "Just like us when we got here."

Erik looked at his partner. "Yeah, huh? We just stared for the longest time."

Staring was exactly what Hannah was doing, especially at the giant Christmas Tree reaching toward the sky, much taller than even the highest building. There looked to be a river that meandered its way lazily through the valley, dividing the land essentially in half.

Erik tried to get back on track. "Hannah, look over to the left. Just stay with me now. I promise this isn't going to take long, okay?"

"Okay," she said, smiling. "Wait! We got here so fast! We're at the very northernmost point of the earth?"

"Fairly close," said Erik.

"Incredible," Hannah whispered.

"It's easy to get here if you're on a reindeer, and you can only see the NP if you're an elf or one of the chosen. For anyone else, they wouldn't be able to see any of this valley, including the trees that surround it. All they would see would be a barren wasteland of permafrost and snow."

"Why?"

"As a protective measure. You'd be surprised how many secret expeditions have been carried out to try and find the actual North Pole. None have succeeded because the search crews could not see what we see."

"Search crews have been sent up here?"

"Many times," answered William, shifting slightly. "Let's continue with your introduction. So, directly below us you have the Elven Neighborhood. Just above there you have the Airstrip."

"Right," affirmed Hannah.

"Okay, see the building to the left of the Airstrip?" Erik asked.

"Yes."

"That's the kitchens. That's where all the food is prepared when we are eating in the Banquet Hall. Now to the right of the Airstrip and a little south is the Blackhole Research Center."

"The what?" Hannah looked at Erik curiously.

"It's where all the secret work is done on new technologies. You have to be a high security elf to get in there or be a part of the NPSP. Right next to the Blackhole are the Mistletoe Gardens."

"Mistletoe?" asked Hannah.

"Yeah, you know the plant that if you stand under it, means you have to kiss the person you're with? That's a whole hanging garden of it. To the right of that is the big Ice Skating Pond."

"It's huge," Hannah observed.

"It's got to be," said William. "You know how many elves ice skate at the NP?"

"You see the square building north of the Mistletoe Gardens? That's the Operations Center. That's one of the most important buildings on the campus. That's where everything is run," Erik said.

"Will I get to go there?"

"Absolutely," said William.

"To the right of the Operations Center is a large hill, you see that?" asked Erik.

"Yes," answered Hannah.

"That's where we go to sled and ski, and right in front is that long, rectangular open space . . . that's the field. Notice it looks like an arena with bleachers surrounding it? It's where we go for our annual snowball tourney. And if you notice, you've got the river cutting through. All the buildings south of the Cocoa River are called the South Campus. Everything north is the North Campus," added William.

"The Cocoa River?" Hannah was lost.

"You can't tell from here, but the water you see down there really isn't water at all. It's hot cocoa."

"The whole thing?" marveled Hannah.

"Yes. It's a flowing river of hot cocoa that you can drink."

"Amazing!"

"Let's continue with the tour. Everything you're looking at now is north of the River. Way over to the left, next to the tree line, you have the building for sled repair and renovation. It's a cool place and run by an elf named Tosh. Good guy. Knows his stuff," said Erik.

"So he does sled repairs?"

"Well, not just sled repairs. He repairs most anything that gets broken in the NP."

"And that building right across the street? What building is that?" Hannah asked.

"Right across from the sled repair? That's the Wrapping Center. Notice how the roof is multicolored green and red, like wrapping paper? That's where all the physical presents are wrapped."

Hannah was enjoying herself as her eyes went to the right of the Wrapping Center, landing on the magnificent Christmas Tree. The star at the top alone was the size of a large truck, and it shone brighter than the strongest of car headlights. The tree was decorated in a myriad of ribbons, tinsels, ornaments, and stars that combined with white, green, and red lights. It had to have taken weeks to decorate with such intricate detail. Even from far above, the tree was a marvel to behold.

"Looking at the tree?" asked William.

"Yes," Hannah said.

"Every time I come up here, I'm astonished. Everything about it says Christmas."

Hannah nodded.

"Okay, to the right of the Tree and just a bit north is the Banquet Hall. That's where we eat. The food is awesome. Directly left of it is the Gift Troubleshooting Shop. Notice it's quite a bit smaller than the other buildings? We don't have too many gifts that need fixing, but once in a while one of them goes a little nuts, and we have to take it in. Ruby is the head elf there. She's great," William explained.

Erik cut in. "Now look way over to the left . . . that

long building there is the Gift Manufacturing Plant. Within that building is the Naughty Department."

"What's the Naughty Department?" asked Hannah.

"It's where all the people on the Naughty List are investigated and verified. That department makes sure people that are on the Naughty List should really be there. Every year it seems there's some poor soul that landed on the list when they shouldn't have been there."

"Wow," Hannah said, leaning forward, looking through the tangle of horns that christened Comet's head.

"To the right and north of the Plant is the Auditorium. This is where we all gather for meetings," Erik explained.

"It's so big," observed Hannah.

"Well, when we call everyone together, there are a lot of bodies. If you look over to the far right, you'll see that barn-like building. That's the Stables where the reindeer are housed."

"Cool."

"And then we have that other rectangular building to the left and a little north. It's all lit up in green. See it? That's the Guest Quarters. That's where we get to stay."

"And what about that small cabin way up north by the tree line? What's that?"

"That," Erik said reverently, "is Santa's cabin. It's where Santa and Mrs. Claus live."

"NO!" said Hannah incredulously.

"Yep. That's it. That's where the big guy spends a lot of his time. It's a cool little cabin."

"You've been in it, Erik?" asked Hannah excitedly.

"Yes. You'll go in too."

"This whole place looks better than I ever imagined," admitted Hannah.

"Let's head on down and we'll get settled in. We won't give you the walking tour until morning."

It was becoming clear to Hannah that the reindeer could understand language because Comet took off just as Erik finished his sentence. Hannah quickly gripped his rack and hung on as Comet rocketed toward the Guest Quarters. As she drew closer, she noticed all the buildings were linked by cobblestone streets that had been plowed of snow. Large snowbanks were in corners, piled high.

Wherever Hannah looked there were elves walking along the streets, some of them with large packages in their arms, others with tools and other items. The whole place was abuzz with life.

Hannah observed that some of the elves were short, much shorter than her five-foot-five frame, and others were just as tall as her. She'd imagined that all elves fit the mold of small, but that obviously was not the case. It also struck her as interesting that all the elves were wearing the same clothing: Tight, red pants, like sweats, a long-sleeved shirt, just as tight and just as red, along with long white gloves that stretched up to their elbows. Each one of them wore a red stocking cap with a white tip at the end, and shiny black high tops adorned their feet.

Comet approached the magnificent Christmas Tree. Up close, it was even more spectacular as Hannah tried to take in every detail of tinsel and bulb hanging from the branches of the gargantuan pine.

Comet passed by it, with Blitzen and Dancer right behind. Seconds later, he touched down in front of the arched entrance of the Guest Quarters. The front of the building was almost entirely windows, each rectangular frame outlined in red lights. The structure itself glowed pleasantly green, although Hannah couldn't tell where the source of the light was actually coming from.

Before she could climb off Comet, an elf about her height rushed out from behind the windowed doors. He reminded Hannah of a butler. He was the first elf she had seen not wearing red and the first she had seen up close. Contrary to what she had believed, the elf's face looked smooth and radiant, without blemish. He looked human, except for his overly-pointy nose and ears. His hair was neatly cut and combed intricately over to the side.

"Good evening, ma'am," he said regally. "May I help you off your ride?"

"Sure," Hannah said without hesitation.

Before she could move, she was lifted off Comet magically and moved to the animal's side, descending to the ground gently until she was standing on the cobblestone. The butler elf smiled.

"Sure, do that for her and not for us, eh, Willis?" said Erik sarcastically.

"By all means, sir," Willis said with great dignity.

Both Erik and William were lifted from their reindeer and placed on the ground just as gently as Hannah had been.

Out the doors came another elf, dressed much differently than Willis, with suspenders wrapped over her green and red body suit. She was a plain-looking woman, with a wonderful glow about her.

"Good evening, Hannah. I'm Hailey. It's a pleasure to meet you. I'll be taking Comet and the others to the stables. Come on, Blitzen. You too, Dancer. Quit that, animal! How many times do you have to do that ridiculous dance? That twirl, kick thing you've got going!"

Dancer ignored the elf's comments and continued his jig. Hailey was having none of it as she ignored him and walked away. It took Dancer a minute before he realized he was being left behind and he hurried to catch up.

Hannah looked down the cobblestone street and was amazed at the level of detail in every object. Every stone in the cobblestones were neatly arranged. The lampposts every couple hundred feet rose ten feet high and gave off soft white light that illuminated the street with a warmth she did not know light could give. In the distance, she could see Santa's cabin, light from a fire flickering in the two windows that flanked the wooden door.

"You'll get to meet him soon enough," said Erik, noticing Hannah's stare.

"Yes, indeed," echoed Willis. "Mr. Claus has been awaiting your arrival. The other guests have as well. Please, if you'll follow me."

"I'm going to catch up with you later," said William quickly. "I've got something I have to do."

Erik looked at his friend mischievously. "You want to elaborate on that a little more?"

William smiled. "Not really."

"You wouldn't be heading to the Mistletoe . . ."

"I shouldn't be gone long," William injected swiftly before turning and heading down the street at a brisk pace.

"Where's he going?" asked Hannah.

"He's in search of something," Erik laughed.

"What?"

"Love."

"I'll say," commented Willis as he opened the windowed door and motioned his two guests through and into the foyer. "Everyone in the NP knows of it."

"What are you talking about?" wondered Hannah.

"You'll find out," Erik said.

The foyer was decorated in maroons and deep greens, with lamps on each table that glowed a gentle yellow. There were framed drawings on the wall of different buildings within the NP. There were cushioned chairs dispersed in different areas in the room . . . a room Hannah figured could easily hold thirty people.

On the back wall was a fireplace. ablaze and casting dancing shadows onto the carpeted floor. To the left and right of the fireplace were hallways. Hannah guessed they led to the rooms and, sure enough, Willis confirmed what she thought.

"Your room is down the left hallway. You're in room three."

"Great," said Hannah. "Am I by myself?"

"Yes. Oh, wait . . . excuse me," the butler elf said suddenly, turning around and quickly walking to the front door. He opened it and escorted the two girls and boy in.

"Thanks, Willis," said the first girl through. She was the shortest of them. Her ebony skin matched the color of her hair, which hung down to her shoulders elegantly.

"Hi, Noemi," said Erik pleasantly.

"Hey, you're here. Great!"

The second girl, who was the tallest, had hair almost

the exact same length as Noemi but looked distinctively different. Noemi had somewhat puffy cheeks and very noticeable dimples. Natalya, on the other hand, had high cheek bones and a narrower face and fair skin. Just as Noemi's brown eyes complimented her hair, Natalya's green eyes highlighted her dirty blond curls.

The boy standing next to them was Marcel — a young man with skinny arms and a narrow waist. As Hannah observed him, she immediately noticed that his gentle smile and warm hazel eyes somehow went well with his short, uncombed brown hair.

"About time you showed up," Natalya said sarcastically.

"How long have you been here?" asked Erik.

"Almost two hours," replied Natalya.

"Two hours?" Erik was shocked. "You made good time."

"Indeed."

"You must be Marcel?" Erik said, changing the subject and sticking out a hand in a gesture of friendship. Marcel stuck out his hand and the two boys shook firmly for a moment.

Marcel spoke, but when he did, Hannah was confused. He'd spoken French. Hannah couldn't speak any foreign language, but she had a fairly good idea of what French sounded like, and this definitely sounded like French.

Willis was on top of things and right away stuck his hand into his inside coat sleeve and withdrew a small piece of what looked like white foam. "You're going to need this," he said, handing it to Hannah.

Hannah took it from the elf. "What is it?"

"It will help you understand. Go on now, put it in."

"Put it in where?" Hannah quizzed.

"Either ear," Willis said patiently.

"What will happen?"

"You'll be able to understand languages."

Hannah took the spongy material and moved it toward her earlobe.

"Now, push it in firmly," the butler elf ordered.

Hannah looked at Erik inquisitively.

"It's all right. Go ahead."

Hannah pushed the soft material down into her ear and instantly, a warm liquid-like feeling filled her canal. Just about the time she was going to say that it felt disgusting, the sensation dissipated and it was impossible to tell she had put anything in her ear in the first place.

"Now you know every language of the world," informed Willis plainly.

"Hi, how are you?" Marcel addressed her in French and incredibly, Hannah understood.

"I'm . . . fine," she answered but was surprised to find that she'd replied in French.

"You speak very well," the boy complimented her.

"Thank you," Hannah responded. "Do you understand English, too?"

"Yes," the boy replied, now in English. "I got one of those things in my ear, too."

Hannah giggled. "Cool."

Erik smiled. "The NP . . . there's no other place in the world like it."

"Shall I show Hannah to her room?" Willis addressed Erik.

"We can do that," said Noemi, reaching over Hannah's shoulder. "It will give us some girl time."

"Don't stay up too late, we have a big day

tomorrow," warned Erik.

"Okay . . . Dad," said Natalya sarcastically, sliding up next to Noemi. "We'll make sure we're in bed by two a.m."

Erik rolled his eyes. "Come on, Marcel. Let's hit the hay."

"Hit the what?"

CHAPTER FIVE
Welcome to the NP

The Mistletoe Gardens were a vast labyrinth of wild growth that hung everywhere. Red berries were always being picked and used to obtain a kiss, and the place was never short of young teenage elves. William was hoping there wouldn't be a lot of people there.

He rounded the corner and his heart raced, just as it did whenever he saw her. Holly was the most beautiful girl he knew. Her long hair dangled past her shoulders and glistened in the silvery shadows. She sat on a bench, surrounded by hanging mistletoe . . . a bench built for two people. William was quickly at her side and looking into her radiant brown eyes. Her face was smooth and her small nose and curved lips were perfect compliments to each other.

He leaned forward and kissed her gently on the cheek.

"I was hoping you'd be here," he said.

"How did it go with Hannah?" she asked.

"Great. She's getting settled in now. We made a good choice, I can tell already."

"I knew you would," Holly said kindly in her honey-like voice.

William moved his gaze to his black boots. He was suddenly second-guessing himself.

"I'm sorry," Holly whispered, knowing what was going through his mind.

"It's not your fault," William said quietly.

"I would change it if I could," she offered.

"I know. You're bound by the laws of the NP. I'm not," he said, turning to look at her. "You're absolutely positive about how you feel about me?"

Holly stared at him with passion. "I'm absolutely positive. I'm in love with you," she said convincingly. "I've loved you for two years now, William Wood.

"It's just my family. They're going to be so surprised. I don't know how they'll take it."

There was a long pause as the two simply stared at one another.

"You know," Holly cracked a smile, "this could have been avoided."

"Oh, yeah? How?" asked William.

"We shouldn't have fallen in love with each other."

"Like I could have stopped that." William smiled. "You're the most beautiful girl . . ."

"Oh?" Holly raised an eyebrow. "What about Elisa?"

"Elisa? Holly, that was a year ago, and I told you, I only went to a dance with her," said William in an exhausted voice.

"Uh huh."

"What about you?" William shot back.

"What about me?" Holly said defensively.

"You and Garn last year?"

"Garn! He . . . he," Holly stammered.

"He tried to kiss you!"

"Yes, and I stress the word tried because that's all it

was."

William grinned. "Speaking of kissing . . ."

———————————————————

The room Hannah stood in was simple and elegant.
The floor was hardwood and glistened as though it
had just been polished. There was a bathroom to her
immediate right with a pearly white sink, a shower,
and a toilet, all of which were impeccably clean. In the
far corner was a queen-sized bed covered with a thick
forest-green comforter. Two lamps illuminated the
cream-colored room. Opposite the bed were a round
table with two chairs, both hand-carved and intricate.
A large window provided a breathtaking view of the
surrounding forest and the cobblestone streets below.

"Like the room?" asked Noemi.

"It's great," said Hannah, walking to the window and
gazing out.

"All of the quarters are decorated differently. I like
this color scheme," said Natalya.

"I've got a question," said Hannah, turning to the
girls. "The tunnel of light I went through to get here,
while I was on Comet . . ."

"The Tunnel of Belief," said Noemi with a nod.
"What about it?"

"Is that the only way to get to the NP?"

"The one and only," Natalya said. "It didn't take
too long, did it? You'd think getting to the North Pole,
I mean *the North Pole*, would take longer, but not with
the reindeer. They're the only creatures that can pass
between Earth and the NP."

"What do you mean?"

"None of the elves can ever go anywhere but here. They can't travel to any other part of the Earth. The only one that can, besides NPSP Members, is Santa and his immediate family."

"Santa has immediate family?" Hannah was curious. "Like kids?"

Natalya laughed and looked at Noemi. "Yes. There's Mrs. Claus and they have a son, Junior."

"Santa has a son?" Hannah sounded astounded.

"Right. He turns fifty this coming January."

"How old is Santa, then?"

"Oh, we figure close to eighty, but he's in good shape. I don't think he'll retire anytime soon."

"Santa will retire?" Hannah said, running a hand through her hair.

"Right. The Santa, the very first Santa, is, of course, dead," Natalya continued.

"Long dead," added Noemi.

"The family continues to live on through their children. When this Santa eventually retires or dies, his son, Junior, will take his place. A son can only take the place of Santa if he is at least fifty years old, unless there's some catastrophe, in which case the son is allowed to take the place of Santa at an earlier age."

"This is crazy! How do you know all this?"

"From being here at the NP and studying in the University Library," Noemi said. "I doubt you'll see Junior around much this week, since he's doing practice flights with the Juveniles."

"Flying what?"

"Sleighs. He'll be out in the Earth flying around, mainly at night, practicing with Juvenile reindeer to get his skills up to snuff. Controlling a sleigh is not easy, and when a son gets to forty-nine years of age, he's allowed to begin practice flights."

"So you're telling me that there have been many Santas?"

"Many," answered Natalya simply.

"But what if Mrs. Claus didn't have a son? Then what would happen?"

"It's never happened. There's always at least one son."

"Junior has a sister five years younger than him. Her name's Alisha. She loves to work at making Gifts. You'll meet her tomorrow."

"So the current Santa has two children, Alisha and Junior?" Hannah asked.

"Yes."

"Fascinating," Hannah whispered.

"The more you learn, the more fascinating it becomes," said Noemi.

"We should let you go to sleep," Natalya offered. "We're going to have plenty to do in the morning starting with the tour. That's after breakfast."

"We'll come get you and head up to the Banquet Hall together," Noemi said, smiling.

When the door shut, announcing her solitude, Hannah flopped down on the bed with a sigh. The comforter seemed to envelope her, like the cushions were alive and knew right where to expand and contract to make it the most perfect comfort imaginable.

The day's events seemed unreal. Everything from the messages at school to her parents' behavior, to the sight of an actual reindeer and sailing through the night sky, to the sight of the real North Pole . . . all of it was unfathomable. Yet, here she was . . . on a bed in a beautiful room within the Guest Quarters at the North Pole.

She thought about changing into her pajamas but wasn't exactly sure where her suitcase was, plus, she was exhausted and mentally drained. She didn't even attempt to find the light switch. She closed her eyes, a smile beaming across her face.

It was only a moment before Hannah Green was fast asleep.

Hannah awoke the next morning to a hard pounding coming from the other side of the door. She got up slowly, rubbing her face with her hands and stretching toward the ceiling. Everything yesterday seemed like a fantasy, yet here she was in the Guest Quarters at the North Pole.

She walked over and opened the door, and was greeted by a smiling Natalya. "How'd you sleep?"

Hannah smiled. "Great. I was tired."

"I bet."

Hannah invited Natalya in.

"You didn't sleep in the pajamas they provide?" Natalya said as Hannah flopped back down on the bed.

"I didn't even know they provided pajamas."

"Oh, yeah. They provide you with everything, even underwear, though it's a bit strange wearing panties with little elves and Christmas trees on them."

Hannah laughed. "Panties?"

"Yep. But most of the time you'll be in this." Natalya gestured to the uniform she was wearing. It looked very similar to the ones Hannah saw the elves wearing last night. The only difference was the embroidered NPSP insignia on the right side of Natalya's chest, just under her shoulder.

"You were wearing that yesterday, too. Where do you get those?"

"The elves took the liberty of stocking your closet for you. You have about a dozen suits, all the same, hanging in there," Natalya said, pointing to the closet.

"My suitcase . . . I packed . . ."

"It's in the closet, but you won't need most of the clothes you brought."

"I won't?"

"No," Natalya said, walking to the window and staring out at the falling snow. "The NP has a regulated temperature of fifty degrees. Your suit will keep you plenty warm. It'll be weird at first that it can be that warm and still, it snows and icicles hang everywhere. It's one of the magical things about this place."

Natalya reached into one of the pockets of her suit and pulled out a large, folded piece of paper. She turned back to Hannah.

"This is your schedule for the day."

Hannah looked at the paper oddly. "My schedule?"

"You have a lot to do today in the NP. The days that follow are going to be the best of your life, but believe me when I say you're going to be busy!"

Hannah stared silently and read.

SCHEDULE
    9:00 –12:00 Gift Manufacturing
    12:00 - Lunch
    1:00-2:00 Window of Observation
    2:00-4:00 Sled Repair
    4:00-5:00 Dinner
    5:00-7:00 General Meeting in Auditorium
    7:00- Free Time

"I'm so excited," Hannah finally said, jumping up from the bed.

"I remember last year," Natalya said reflectively. "It was the absolute best. Everything is so new and incredible. Some things you'll learn will seem impossible but it's all true. It's amazing."

"Like what?"

"Oh, no. I'm not telling you that. You'll have a much better time if you discover things yourself and don't have any information about it beforehand."

"Come on, please!" Hannah pleaded.

Natalya smiled. "Good try, girl. Why don't you get dressed and we can go up to the Banquet Hall."

———————————————

She had never been to this part of the forest before. The trees were immensely tall and thick brush made it difficult to manage her way along the thin trail. She was thankful there wasn't snow on the ground, and the mere sight of green was refreshing, instead of the depressive white she was used to.

Just as scheduled, the man was waiting for her.

Standing between two fifty-foot pines was the human named Dewey. "Did you have problems getting away?" he asked. "I wasn't sure you'd be able to do it."

"Don't underestimate me," the woman whispered in a rough tone. "Why didn't we meet on the island?"

"*He* didn't want that. *He* chose here instead. You have the plans and the times?"

The Elven woman smiled. "Do you have what I asked for?"

Dewey withdrew a black bottle from his jacket pocket and tossed it to her. The woman caught it, raised it up above her head to examine it, and then smiled.

"That should be all the material to finish your little science project."

"Indeed," the woman replied, sliding the bottle into the front pocket of her green coat. Reaching into the opposite pocket, she withdrew an envelope and handed it to Dewey. The man looked skeptical as he took the package and opened it up.

"These are all the plans?" he said, unfolding the paper and examining it carefully.

"Exact plans and times," she answered.

"And you're sure he's not going to change his plans?"

"Quite sure." The woman's voice was confident.

"Excellent," Dewey whispered wickedly.

Hannah stared in the mirror at herself with disbelief. She was clothed in a type of body suit that felt very comfortable and looked like a derivative of Santa Claus's actual suit. Her feet were covered in black boots that went up almost to her knees. Her pants were brick red and felt like cotton. A small, black belt fit around her waist snugly. Her long-sleeved shirt was pin-striped with red and black.

"Wild," she whispered, pulling her hair back into a ponytail and making her way to the door where Natalya was waiting.

"How's it feel?" she asked.

"This suit . . . it feels so . . . cool."

Natalya led Hannah down the hallway and into the foyer. She was surprised that no one, besides Willis, the butler elf, was there. It was such a pleasant room, decorated so serenely, with the fireplace crackling.

"Good morning, Natalya . . . Miss Hannah," Willis said with a courtesy nod.

"Morning, Willis," Natalya said pleasantly.

"Hi," Hannah said, smiling and following Natalya out the windowed doors that Willis held open.

Standing on the cobblestone streets, a sudden gush of joy and happiness spread through Hannah. There was just something about seeing the buildings lit up with white lights, the packs of fresh snow lining the sidewalks, and large snowflakes the size of marbles falling that made her appreciate the holiday season all the more.

"Hello, Hannah," an elf she had never seen before said, walking past her.

"Hi," Hannah replied.

Another elf passed by and smiled. "Good to see you, Hannah. Have a great day. You, too, Natalya."

"Thanks," Hannah said.

"Hope to see you both in the Wrapping Center

sometime today," came another voice from behind.

"Here comes your escort. I'll see you around, Hannah," Natalya said, walking away to the west.

"Hannah, Bobanna," came Erik's enthusiastic voice. "Well, well, you're up."

"Yeah," Hannah said.

"Hey, Talya!" said Erik with a wave.

Natalya turned and looked over her shoulder, waving back at him.

"Time to eat," said Erik. "I'm a starvin' dude."

"I thought Natalya was going to take me."

"Nope. Change of plans. She has to help Jessica in the Gift Manufacturing Plant, so I'm your escort for now."

"Where is the Banquet Hall again?" asked Hannah, now side by side with Erik and trying to keep up with his brisk pace.

"Down this street. You'll get the feel for the place quickly."

"I don't know what it is, but this, all of this, makes me feel so warm inside . . ."

"That's part of the NP. It's the Spirit of Christmas you feel. It's wonderful, isn't it?"

Hannah nodded.

As they walked toward their destination, dozens of elves passed by, greeting them pleasantly, always with a bright smile, and each wearing the exact same looking outfits.

"Everyone's so nice here," Hannah observed as she and Erik veered right and headed toward the large Banquet Hall.

"Too bad the world can't be more like this all the time. Imagine how nice it would be if everyone treated everyone like you're being treated right now," Erik said.

"The world would be a much better place," Hannah agreed.

"Exactly. That's why it's so tough when you have to leave here and go back to the real world. It's somewhat depressing when you first get back."

"And this is your last year here?"

"Right. For me, this is it. I'll never be able to come back."

"Why not?" Hannah asked as they approached the tall, glass doors of the Hall.

"It's part of the Code."

"The Code?"

"Everything revolves around the Code. It's like the rules that everyone lives by. The particular rule that gets me is the Twenty Rule. Once a human is twenty years old, he or she can no longer serve on the NPSP."

"Why not?"

"I'm not sure why the rule exists. Haven't quite figured out where it all started, but I *can* tell you — it sucks."

The glass doors they approached swung open and they were greeted by another elf dressed like Willis, though this particular man was much older and more wrinkled.

"Good morning, Erik. Hello, Hannah," he greeted pleasantly.

"Morning, Wiley," said Erik, guiding Hannah into the extravagant Hall.

"His name is Wiley?"

"Yep. Nice guy."

The Banquet Hall was the fanciest room Hannah had ever been in. It was a grand, rectangular room, filled with hand-carved cedar tables and chairs. It was lavishly decorated with different Christmas Trees — some taller, some shorter, some traditionally green while others were sprayed white. Each was adorned with massive decorations and lights. Poinsettias in large red pots were placed throughout the room, and each table had a magnificent glowing centerpiece of winter flowers.

Everywhere Hannah looked there were elves, eating and visiting pleasantly at tables, most of which sat six. In the far right corner of the room was a small orchestra playing *I'm Dreaming of a White Christmas*.

"What do you think?" Erik asked with a smile. "Pretty awesome, huh?"

"This is great!"

"Over there . . . see William, Noemi, and Marcel?"

Hannah followed Erik through the Hall and was surprised how many times she was greeted and looked at kindly. She took a seat next to William.

"Hi, Hannah," they all greeted her warmly.

"Hi," she replied.

"It's nice that we're all here. Well, all of us except for Talya, but hopefully she'll get here soon," said Erik. "Since this is the first time eating in the Hall for Marcel and Hannah, it's tradition that we have our first-time ceremony!"

"If I could have everyone's attention!" William took over, shouting from his chair and addressing the elves. "Thank you. Since this is our newbies' first time in the Hall, it's tradition that they go through . . ."

"INITIATION!" shouted the elves excitedly.

"INITIATION!" shouted William back.

"INITIATION!" shouted the elves again.

And then it started. The small orchestra played and

the elves launched into song:

You're here in the NP, We see you're on empty
It's good you're in your seat, Because it's time to eat

Welcome to this match, Where you'll need to catch
The food as it flies, The bread as it rises
The waffles that catch air, The syrup under your chair
The eggs in your hair, You'll eat like a bear

Welcome to the Hall, Welcome to the Hall
You're here to have a ball

Chugga-Wugga Chugga-Wugga, Hey, hey ,hey
Chugga-Wugga Chugga-Wugga , Hey, hey, hey

It's the Hall, Not a mall
Where you'll fall, Don't you call

It's time to start, Get your cart
Don't you fart, Have some heart

You're at the Hall
You're at the Hall

YOU'RE … AT… THE … HALL, YEAH!

Marcel and Hannah looked at each other in utter
astonishment. Both felt like they needed to applaud.
Everyone sang with such vigor and intonation that

it sounded like some sort of rendition of a Broadway musical. But before either of them could put their hands together, they were tagged in the side of the head by soggy, syrup-drenched waffles.

"INITIATION!" the crowd of elves shouted.

Noemi, Erik, and William ducked away from the table and what followed next was an entourage of breakfasts being hurled from every direction at the newbies. There were pancakes and sausage links, half-cooked eggs with runny yokes, and quiche being flung. It was all Marcel and Hannah could do to defend themselves. They used the plates in front of them to shield the direct shots but couldn't stop all the food from finding its target.

Some might imagine that being hit by a barrage of food wouldn't be the most enjoyable aspect of life; however, for Marcel and Hannah, they couldn't stop laughing. This food fight or INITIATION, as the elves called it, wasn't malice or mean-spirited. It was all in fun and when Hannah reached to the table and fired back a pancake, there was a cheer from the group and then the *real* frenzy began.

Suddenly, the attacks shifted, being replaced by other attacks on other elves. Instead of concentrating on just Hannah and Marcel, it was all out war. Elf versus elf. About the only thing not flying through the air were utensils and plates but anything that was edible had taken flight in one form or another.

Hannah and Marcel were deep into it now, firing off anything their hands could grab. Marcel tossed an over-easy egg mass and hit one elf with black hair on the side of his cheek. The elf bust open laughing as did Marcel.

INITIATION only lasted about five minutes and

was called to a stop when the butler elf, Wiley whistled so loud it froze everyone long enough for him to say, "ENOUGH!"

The beautiful and plush Hall that had been so immaculately decorated was now drenched in breakfast food. Every table, nearly every chair, the hardwood floor, the circular lamps . . . everything looked nasty.

Hannah couldn't help but giggle. The thought did hit her however, that this was going to take a massive effort to clean up.

"Good INITIATION!" shouted Wiley.

The group of elves cheered and clapped.

"And now, the hard part," Wiley continued. "Clean up."

Hannah wondered how on earth they were going to clean the place up, let alone themselves, when a white flash of light exploded in the center of the room. When it disappeared, the room was miraculously back to the way it had been. There wasn't any sign that a massive food fight had taken place. There wasn't a spot anywhere — not on a table or a chair or clothing or in the hair.

"Don't you love the NP?" said Erik, taking his seat once again.

Marcel stared incredulously.

"It only happens once in a while, but you have to love INITIATION," William commented, sitting down. "But now, it's time to eat for real."

"I don't know if I can," Hannah admitted.

"Oh, don't worry. They have the best chefs in the NP. Believe me, you'll never eat better," said Erik.

———————————————

"It's tonight," Dewey's voice sounded scratchy over the phone.

"You're sure," came a deep voice's reply.

"Positive. The information is very reliable," Dewey said confidently.

"And you know the precise location?"

"Yes."

"I want all of the bots in place and ready. I don't know if we'll have another chance at this."

"I have three other runs he'll be on in case we fail this time," Dewey said.

"Those dates will be useless if we fail our first time. He will undoubtedly know we are after him once we make our attempt. He will know that someone gave us the information. He will not stick with his planned schedule. No, he'll go into hiding and protection at the NP," the deep voice said evenly. "We cannot fail this first time, Dewey."

Dewey swallowed hard. "Right. I'll make sure everything is in place from my end."

"And I will make the necessary preparations. I will be in touch when I have everything ready here."

CHAPTER SIX
Gift Manufacturing

It was true what Erik said about the chefs in the NP. Hannah had never had a better breakfast than the one she had just finished. As she walked side by side with Erik, she felt that if she would've had one more bite of anything (cinnamon roll, Belgian waffle, egg) she would've exploded.

Making her way along the cobblestone street toward the Gift Manufacturing Plant, she was greeted multiple times by elves she did not know. Nearly all of them wore similar attire, the central theme being red and white, with green occasionally mixed in.

"So, did you like the food?"

Hannah looked at Erik, keeping his pace. "It was the best food I've ever had."

"It spoils you, believe me."

"I bet," Hannah said. "What am I going to do at Gift Manufacturing? Am I going to actually make something?"

"Possibly. It all depends what Alisha wants you to do. She's in charge of Gift Manufacturing."

"How long has she been in charge there?"

"I don't know exactly how many years, but it's been a long time."

"Does she help her father deliver the Gifts on Christmas Eve?" Hannah asked as they passed two elves sitting on a bench next to a lamppost, discussing the benefits of stocking caps.

"No, she doesn't. No one helps Santa."

"Why not?"

"The sleigh is actually only built for one person. There's no room for any others."

"But couldn't they make a bigger sleigh so that others could help Santa?"

"Are you kidding?" Erik laughed. "Hannah, that sleigh has been in use for thousands of years. It's *the* sleigh. It will never be expanded. Every year they make minor repairs on it, but that's all. Claus would never allow it to be expanded."

Hannah smiled. She had the feeling that the more she learned about the NP, the more it would amaze and thrill her. Ahead of them was the enormous Christmas Tree that she couldn't take her eyes off. There had to be at least three dozen elves suspended from wires at various spots along the Tree, adding tinsel and a host of other overly-large decorations.

"The Tree is amazing," Hannah observed, staring at the sixty-story behemoth.

Erik stopped and looked to the sky. "Look up," he said.

Hannah cranked her neck back and stared. She'd been so caught up in the other buildings, she'd fail to notice the sky. Above the surrounding mountain peaks was an enormous cloud, illuminated by the sunshine. No direct rays came through, but the cloud was so lit up, it cast a wonderful hue of yellow across the valley.

"The cloud is always there — part of the protection

of the NP. If we relied on the actual sun for our light and heat . . . well, it's the northernmost point. Of course, that's not the case here," Erik explained.

Hannah turned her attention to the Tree. "What are the wires attached to?" she asked, watching as an elf swung over high above to help another.

"The highest branches. You'd be surprised how strong those elves are. I helped decorate a couple of years ago. It was a rush. Spent three days at it."

"I'd never make it," Hannah confessed.

Erik looked at her with a grin. "Yeah, we know. You hate heights."

Hannah blushed. "What are all the tiny stars on the Tree? There's got to be millions of 'em?"

"The stars are Gifts."

"They are? For who?"

"So, what'd you think?" asked the tall elf, staring at William seriously.

"Perfect temperature," William replied, admiring the flask and the brown liquid inside.

"I've been working on regulating a more moderate temperature and I think I've finally mastered it," the elf said proudly.

"These are much better results than last year," complemented William. "You've been doing some serious work here, Jorgen."

Jorgen smiled, his large prominent front teeth beaming. "Thank you, but what about the taste?"

Jorgen motioned with his hands. William looked at

the flask for a moment then brought it to his mouth and drank.

"Well?" Jorgen asked with anticipation. "Everyone that's taken a drink has liked the change. What do you think?"

"I think," William said slowly, "that this is the best flippin' cocoa I've ever had!"

"Yes!" exclaimed Jorgen enthusiastically.

"Well done," William said, slapping the elf on his shoulder. "How long has it taken you to perfect it like this?"

"I started on it about six months ago."

"Bravo, Jorgen. Bravo!"

"So I take it you like Jorgen's new recipe?" came Holly's sweet voice from behind them.

William turned, and there she stood, radiant as always, in her red and white uniform, her hair pulled back into her favorite pigtails.

"Hello, Holly," Jorgen said. "William and I were just discussing the new formula for the River and . . ."

". . . and I'd say he likes it." Holly smiled.

"Yeah, I do," William agreed.

"I have to head back to the Hole. You coming?" Jorgen motioned behind him, toward the Blackhole Research Center.

"I'll meet up with you later," William said, staring at Holly.

Jorgen grinned. "Right. I'll see you when I see you."

"Okay," said William.

"Good to see you, Jorgen," Holly said as the tall elf nodded and went away via the cobblestone path that led back to the facility.

"What are you doing here?" William asked, walking

forward and giving Holly a tight hug.

"I was going to the Stables and saw you and Jorgen. Just thought I'd stop by and see what you were doing."

"I want you to know that I decided on something last night after I left the Gardens," William said seriously. "I know that you wanted to really surprise your parents, but I think we should tell them tonight. Let's not keep them in the dark."

Holly smiled. "You're sure?"

"I know. I just think it's time. It's only a few days away, anyhow. We might as well tell them. I just hope they'll be excited about it."

"Me too," Holly said.

"They still expect me for dinner, right?"

"Yes, they're planning on it."

"Okay then . . . tonight after dinner," said William firmly. "We tell them."

Hannah stood inside one of the most elaborate, fascinating rooms she'd ever been in: the Gift Manufacturing Plant.

"How about this place?" Erik said in an astonished voice. "I've been in here so many times, and still I get goose bumps."

"What . . . this . . . how . . ." fumbled Hannah.

Erik laughed. "Yeah, that's what I did when I saw all this for the first time."

"Now, now," came a woman's voice.

Hannah turned and stared at the woman walking toward them. She had flowing black hair and narrow brown eyes, and was dressed in an all-red uniform.

"You must be Hannah," the woman said, shaking Hannah's hand. "I'm Alisha."

Hannah swallowed hard. "You're Santa's daughter?"

"The one and only," Alisha said proudly. "This is probably your first stop today, isn't it?"

Hannah nodded.

"You're in for a real treat," Alisha said.

Erik backed away. "I'll be working in a different department, but I'll be back in time to take you to lunch," he said, looking at Hannah with enthusiasm. "Have fun. You're going to be blown away."

"Uh huh," Hannah said, staring around in wonder.

"I'll see you later," Erik said to Alisha, and with a wave of his hand, was gone.

Hannah was in awe. The building was a rectangular, completely open warehouse, ten times the size of the biggest grocery store she'd ever been in. Everywhere she looked there were elves sitting, as incredibly as it seemed, on nothing but air. There were some close to the ground, others halfway between, and some up near the ceiling. All were sitting but what they were actually doing, Hannah couldn't tell.

"What you see all around you are the elves making Gifts for kids all around the world," Alisha began.

"What do you mean? I don't see anything. It looks like they're just sitting there, most of them with their eyes closed."

"Right. But believe me, they're busy."

Hannah looked confused.

Alisha smiled understandingly. "We stopped making all physical gifts long ago when the population boom hit. We simply couldn't keep up, even with Father

Time's help. That's when Claus decided for the elves to begin making Gifts that people really needed, not so much what they wanted."

"So you don't make real toys anymore?"

"Oh, yeah. We still make toys. . . . millions of them, but not for every child. It's impossible. Below us is a whole other section this size where elves are making real, tangible toys. You'll get a chance to see that on a different day, I'm sure. For now, you're going to make your first Gift."

Before Hannah could ask how, she and Alisha lifted into the air and soared higher and higher. The building was a painted a vivid green and red. The lights hanging from the ceiling cast a soft glow over everything and created a warm, inviting feeling.

As the two ascended, they were greeted with kind looks and nods from the elves, who glanced over momentarily. Everywhere Hannah looked, elves were busy and all of them, every single one of them, had genuine smiles on their faces.

Alisha stopped abruptly, like she'd been on an elevator. Hannah stopped as well. They were hovering many feet off the floor and Hannah immediately felt queasy.

"I don't like heights," she admitted.

"I know," Alisha said kindly. "That will pass. For now, just try and put it out of your mind and sit down."

"Sit down?"

"Yes. Sit."

"Where?" Hannah asked confusedly.

"Just right there."

"But there's nothing to sit on!"

"Yes, there is. You simply believe that there is

something to sit on. It is that belief that will be made reality for you."

Hannah reluctantly bent down awkwardly and then decided to just let her body go, believing that she wouldn't go plummeting to the floor.

She didn't.

Instead, it was like she was sitting on the most comfortable chair ever.

"You see, there *is* something to sit on. It's called belief. Without it, you cannot accomplish the greatest things in life."

Hannah nodded and watched Alisha sit down next to her. "We begin by first learning who we are going to make the Gift for."

"How do we do that?" wondered Hannah, now completely in suspense. There was something very thrilling and exciting about what was happening.

"You must concentrate, Hannah. Concentrate on it."

"On what?"

"On mankind, on people."

"All of mankind? Everyone on Earth?"

"I know that sounds crazy and impossible, but I assure you it *is* possible. Now, shut your eyes and concentrate on people."

'Concentrate on people,' Hannah thought. How does one concentrate on people? On all people on the Earth? There are billions of people on the planet and Alisha expected her to just think of all of them?

"Keep your eyes closed," Alisha said. "Concentrate."

Minutes passed slowly and as much as Hannah concentrated on people, as Alisha had ordered, nothing was happening. She wasn't getting any feelings or images.

As if Alisha sensed her frustration, she said to Hannah, "Think of a young child somewhere . . . anywhere."

Hannah kept her eyes closed and focused everything she had on a child, any child. Maybe a kindergartner or a first-grader or . . . and then it happened. As if her mind suddenly split open, an image filled it with such force it took her breath away. She could see the girl's face clearly. She was black-skinned with short hair and deep hazel eyes. Her name was Serena. She was six years old. She was in kindergarten.

Emotions flooded Hannah's conscience. It seemed like every emotion the child had ever experienced, Hannah could now feel. Hannah was learning about Serena's most precious memories and feelings, which was precisely what Alisha wanted. It wasn't long before a giant smile crept across Hannah's face and she knew exactly what Serena needed. But how could she give it to her?

In her conscience, she could hear Alisha's faint voice, telling her to 'will the Gift' to Serena. What did that mean to will the gift? But Hannah's question was answered by her own mind. In order for Serena to receive the Gift she needed, Hannah had to give the Gift to her.

Hannah wanted nothing more than for this kindergartner, this little six-year-old, to receive her needed Gift of patience. Serena was an impulsive girl, and did things like most six-year-olds, quickly and without much thought. But Serena was an exception, and more than anything, needed patience with people and situations.

Hannah concentrated and willed Serena to have more patience, to be able to wait on things and people. A great feeling of joy leapt out of Hannah's mind and abruptly, her connection with the little girl ended and she no longer could sense Serena's presence. Hannah opened her eyes and looked at Alisha.

"Well?"

"That was incredible. I felt so happy and then the connection just kinda left me."

"Your Gift . . ."

"It was patience. She needed patience," Hannah said.

"Right . . . well, her Gift has now been sent to delivery, and Serena will receive her Gift of patience on Christmas."

"Delivery?"

"Did you walk by the Christmas Tree today when you came here?" Alisha asked.

"Yes."

"Did you notice the small stars that covered the tree? Millions of them it seemed, didn't it? Most of them silver."

"Yes."

"All of those are Gifts for kids all around the world. The stars will stay on the tree until Christmas Eve when Santa will gather and deliver them."

"So that's what everyone's doing in this room?"

"That's right," Alisha answered, looking around. "Those that are chosen, the ones in this building, work tirelessly to give all children a Christmas Gift. You just gave Serena hers."

"But there are so many kids on earth . . ."

"That's why there are so many of us working. We can go through thousands upon thousands of kids a day, each one of us."

"Is that what I'm going to be doing the next few hours?"

"Yes, Hannah. I want to see how many Gifts you can give with your time here."

CHAPTER SEVEN
The Window of Observation

Erik looked at his watch, which read a quarter past noon. He had spent the last few hours in this department, and although it was necessary, it wasn't the most enjoyable job in the NP.

He was in the small building adjacent to the Gift Manufacturing Plant, where Hannah was completing her first Gift creations with Alisha. Erik was in the Naughty Department. And just as you can imagine, the Naughty Department is for kids that have been, you know . . . naughty.

The building itself was divided into three parts. The first section dealt with those kids on the Level One Naughty Scale. These were kids who hadn't been naughty very much and actually still had a good chance of receiving a Gift from Santa. The second part of the building was reserved for children on the Level Two Naughty Scale. If you're on Level Two, you're really in danger of not being on Santa's list for a Christmas Gift. And the last section of the building, located in the far back corner, was for kids on the Level Three Naughty Scale. These kids were so naughty there wasn't a chance they'd be receiving a Gift at all.

Erik was working with the thirty-five other elves in the Level One department. The room he and his Elven friends were in was rectangular with circular desks randomly placed. Each desk had an enhanced Elven computer (no, you can't buy these in stores on Earth) along with a desk lamp that illuminated the working area enough for them to scribble notes on paper that they might need for each candidate.

Erik looked to his right where Jamille, a thirty-year-old female elf, sat listening as the computer showed images of her candidate and the attributes that led to her being placed on the Naughty List.

"Frustrated?" Erik asked as he waited on his computer.

"My shift is almost over," Jamille said, rubbing her forehead.

Shifts in the Naughty Department were only three hours. Elves are the happiest, most content people on Earth, and working in the "Naughties" (what the elves call the department) could be effective if they only worked a maximum of three hours a day. Any longer and there were issues to deal with that over the centuries Santa found to be not worth fighting against, so he instituted the three-hour rule. Erik understood why. After a couple of hours of viewing and analyzing, his brain felt like a pummeled piñata.

"Norman Dodger, twelve years old," Erik's computer said in a very human, uncomputer-like male voice.

Erik turned his attention to the screen.

The monitor had been red and green. Now he was staring at a white-skinned boy with a freckled nose and large front teeth.

The computer continued its narration. "Norman Dodger, Level One classification. His most recent occurrence was on December fifteenth . . ."

As the computer talked, different pictures of Norman appeared: Norman at school, at his house, talking with his friends on a street corner . . . .

"While riding home from school on his bicycle, Norman stopped to tease Melanie Griffin about the way she played basketball in PE."

There was now an aerial picture of Norman standing in front of Melanie, as if a camera was suspended thirty feet above them.

"Norman was quoted as saying, 'You played like . . .'"

BEEP.

"'and if I . . .'"

BEEP

"'played like that, I'd . . .'"

BEEP

"'just stay home because . . .'"

BEEP

"'who can . . .'"

BEEP

"'play with you!"

BEEP

"Norman has a swearing problem," Erik whispered to himself somewhat sarcastically, continuing to watch the boy on the screen.

For the next twenty minutes, Erik watched scene after scene of Norman's naughtiness. The computer always played the most recent naughty scene and then worked backwards chronologically.

Norman was indeed naughty. Erik had seen worse, no doubt, but, at times, this boy was a tyrant. He hit his younger sister of seven years repeatedly. Keep in mind that the Naughty Department generously allows for sibling violence, but some of the stuff Norman was doing was completely inappropriate.

Norman was also throwing rocks at cars that drove by his house. Not the smartest thing to be doing but then Erik figured that Norman wasn't the brightest star in the world, although deep down, the boy seemed like a good kid. Erik couldn't pinpoint how he knew this nor did he have any evidence that Norman was deserving of a Gift, but he'd analyzed enough Naughty cases to know when there was still some good left in a kid.

"Display last good deed," Erik said to the computer after it had finished chronicling Norman's naughtiness for the past three months.

The twenty-five inch screen blinked white, and now it was Norman helping his little sister (yes, the one that he liked to pick on) as they put a Lego set together she'd gotten for her birthday in November. There wasn't any malice or self-serving motive that Erik could see coming from Norman at that point. He was genuinely helping his sister and enjoying it.

Erik sighed. "Display next good deed."

———————————

"Are you sure it's safe?" the deep voice asked cautiously, his voice distant over the phone line.

"Of course," the female voice answered. She too sounded distant and muffled.

"Where are you now?"

"Doesn't matter. It's almost lunchtime and most everyone is headed to the Banquet Hall or back to their homes."

The deep voice growled. "We went over the schedule."

"And you're prepared?" the female voice asked.

"Most definitely."

"You need to be," affirmed the female's voice. "You have one shot at getting him."

"I know," the deep voice answered.

"And if you don't, I will be exposed!"

"I know. You don't have to worry about that. I have the bots in place where they need to be."

"Don't forget, you are not to harm him until . . ."

"Don't worry," chuckled the deep voice. "I know that you want your chance."

"I've waited too long. I deserve a chance. I'll be in contact again soon."

There was a click on the other end of the line.

Conversation terminated.

When Hannah walked outside the Gift Manufacturing Plant, snow was falling gently. The gravel-size flakes swayed on their descent from a gentle breeze blowing from the east. She was surprised at how well her suit kept her warm. The regulated fifty-degree temperature was not something she relished, but she knew it was much better than the alternative.

Hannah's head was swimming with thoughts. The last few hours of her life were amazing. She'd never dreamed she'd be in the actual North Pole, let alone giving Gifts to children that needed them. She had been through at least a hundred kids, learned all about them, and felt somehow connected to them.

Whether it was Joshua, with his need for more humor in his life, or Tim's need of compassion for others, Hannah had created invisible, intangible Gifts that would help them throughout their lives — Gifts that were invisible, yet essential. Most of the children Hannah saw today were not even aware they needed their Gifts, but nonetheless, Hannah had provided them all with something special and unique to be delivered Christmas Eve.

"You going to eat in the Hall?" an elf asked, walking past her.

This brought Hannah out of her reflective thoughts. "Yeah. I'll be there in a second."

"Oh, I'm not eating in the Hall," the black-haired elf said. "I go home and eat lunch."

"I thought everyone ate in the Hall."

"No, no. The Hall is not nearly big enough to accommodate all the elves," answered the elf kindly. "You did well today with the Gifts."

Hannah smiled. "Thank you."

"How many did you finish?"

"I think about a hundred."

"Not bad for your first time."

"Will I get to come back and make more?" Hannah asked.

The elf thought a moment. "Probably. It just depends on your schedule."

"Right, my schedule."

"See you later, Hannah."

"Bye," Hannah said. "Wait . . . what's your name?"

"Zander," the elf replied, walking south along the

cobblestone street that led to the Elven Neighborhood.

"Hannah, Bobanna!" shouted Erik, walking toward her.

"Hi, Erik."

"Who was that?" he asked.

"His name was Zander," replied Hannah, looking down the street where the elf was walking. "You know him?"

"No. But that's not uncommon. It would be impossible to know everyone in the NP. Was he working with you in Gift Manufacturing?"

"Yeah. He told me I did well for my first day."

"How many Gifts did you make?" Erik asked, pushing his red hair to the side with his hand.

"I think about a hundred."

"Hey, that's good."

"Well, I tried my best."

"That's all that matters in the NP, Hannah. Your best effort. So, you ready to eat?"

"Yeah, I'm surprisingly hungry. Time went by so fast."

Erik led her along the street, walking east toward the Banquet Hall. The cobblestone street was filled with elves, chatting and walking here and there. Everyone was pleasant and greeted Erik and Hannah politely. This impressed Hannah. Never had she seen people so nice and genuinely kind.

"So, did you enjoy making the Gifts?"

"It was incredible. I have to admit my mind is a little, I don't know how to describe it, I guess . . . tired. You learn so much about all these kids and you see what they need and you wonder how the Gift you made is going to turn out."

Erik nodded.

"And there are so many kids in the world. I only did a hundred today. How can the elves get to all the kids?"

"Remember, you weren't the only one working in the Plant. Also, you don't know how many of the other Gifts the elves made. Did you ask Zander how many he made?"

"No."

"I wouldn't be surprised if he made over a thousand," said Erik.

"A thousand in that little of time? That's impossible."

Erik stopped her and stared seriously. "Never say that, ever, especially here! This is proof of the possible. Everything you see here many people do not think is possible. But you're standing in the possible, Hannah."

"All right. Sorry," Hannah apologized, feeling rebuked.

"I'm not mad at you, but impossibility and unbelief don't belong here. Neither do ifs."

"Ifs?"

"Many people live their lives with ifs. *If* it is possible or *if* I can get this, I might be able to get that. There are no ifs in the NP. Anything can happen."

"It's easy, though, to not believe," Hannah offered.

"Things that don't lead anywhere significant are easy. Belief is hard because you're dealing with the unseen, the invisible. One of the reasons you were the best candidate when William and I looked at you was because of your strong belief. No other candidate had your kind of belief. No one. Don't ever lose that, Hannah."

Hannah found Erik to be like a big brother, and she enjoyed his quiet wisdom.

When they arrived at the Hall, it was bustling with elves, laughter, and chatter. The chamber orchestra was engaged in a lively rendition of *Frosty the Snowman*. Even though Hannah had been there in the morning, the elaborate, decorated room still took her breath away. The most impressive thing to her was the marvelously decorated Christmas Trees. Erik led Hannah to a table near a window where Marcel, Natalya, and William sat.

"Hey, guys," Natalya greeted them. "How was Gifts?"

"Great," Hannah said, taking a seat.

"Amazing place, isn't it?"

"Amazing," Hannah echoed.

"Man, I'm so ready to eat," William said, grabbing his stomach.

"I hear that," Erik added, looking around the table. "Where's Noemi?"

"I don't know. She was with us, and then said she needed to go and do something, but she wouldn't give us any details. Seemed a little secretive to me," said William.

"Good afternoon." The table was greeted by a short elf, dressed in a tuxedo and very well combed. "May I start you with an appetizer?"

"You bet," Erik said enthusiastically. "How 'bout some quesadillas, amigo!"

"A favorite. Very good," the elf said regally. "Anything to drink?"

"A pitcher of Liquid Breeze would be great," William said.

"Very good, sir."

The elf did a sort of mini-bow and went away.

"Liquid Breeze?" Marcel asked, looking to Natalya

for help.

"It is a wonderful concoction. I don't know how to describe it to you, Marcel, except that it's a vanilla drink that's served cold and makes you feel . . ."

"Harmonious," William finished.

"Harmonious?" Erik said sarcastically. "How can a drink make you feel harmonious?"

"It does," William defended playfully.

"Harmonious. Don't listen to that noise, Marcel. Liquid Breeze is like a bit of heaven in a drink."

"A bit of heaven?" William countered. Now it was his turn to be sarcastic. "Like something could taste like heaven? What kind of a description is that?"

"A good one," Erik replied, smiling.

"You wish," William retorted.

Marcel changed the subject. "I have a question about the Gift Manufacturing Plant. Natalya was telling me about it. I'm excited to go there and learn about the Gifts, but why do only some kids get them? Why don't all kids get Gifts?"

"Most do," replied Erik. "Those that are on the Naughty scale risk the chance of not getting one."

"But don't those kids need Gifts just as badly as the others?"

"Yeah, every kid needs a Gift, but not from the NP. I can't explain the mentality or why it is. It just always has been. Kids that are the most mean, the most naughty, don't get Gifts from the NP."

"But that's not fair," said Marcel.

"I agree," added Hannah, looking at Marcel. "He's right. Those kids should get a Gift."

"Unfortunately, that's not the way it works here. You are rewarded for your acts, not just belief," Erik said.

"Yes, but if those naughty kids knew that there was a North Pole. . ." Marcel started.

"But they *do* know," said Erik. "Most of them choose not to believe in Claus or the NP. In fact, out of all the cases I've studied of kids who don't get Gifts, I can't think of one of them that actually believed in Santa. Trust me, I've studied a lot of kids. Like today, there was this kid . . . Norman. Good kid deep down, but making unwise choices."

"What Level was he on?" William asked.

"He was a Level One."

"Does he get a Gift?" asked Hannah hopefully.

"Yes, if he doesn't do anything in the next few days before Christmas to screw it up," Erik answered.

"I still don't like the system," Marcel said, folding his arms.

"There's nothing wrong with that, Marcel. Everything isn't fair, not even in the NP," Natalya said.

"But do you like the NP?" Hannah asked Marcel.

"Oh, I love it. It's the greatest place and I'm so grateful to be here. It's just that I want everyone to be a part of it."

"Nothin' wrong with wanting good for others, Marcel. It's one of the reasons the Elven Council picked you," Erik said with a respectful nod.

"Here comes our quesadillas and Breeze. Ooh, yeah!" William said, excitedly.

———————————

Lunch was even better than breakfast. The

quesadillas were the best Hannah ever had and the Liquid Breeze was the richest-tasting, smoothest drink she'd ever sampled. Her table of friends so loved the appetizers that they skipped lunch and kept the quesadillas coming.

She was now staring at a massive door of shimmering silver, like the stars on a clear night. The door was nearly ten feet tall and four feet wide. It looked heavy and reinforced. Hannah got the feeling she was standing in front of a door to a very important building in the NP. Erik had walked her over from the Banquet Hall and waited with her for the door to open.

"What am I going to be doing here?" she asked.

"I could tell you all the things you may or may not see today in the Operations Center, but it really wouldn't help you. You need to experience it without me giving away any of the surprises."

Hannah smiled. "I just thought . . ."

"Thought what?" came another voice just as the door hinged open and an elf with shoulder-length silver hair appeared.

Hannah stared blankly. "Ah, nothing."

"It's never nothing," said the old elf. He walked up to Hannah and surveyed her with his wrinkled eyes. He was a bit taller than her and much older. How old exactly Hannah wasn't sure, but he appeared well over seventy.

"So, Ms. Hannah — coming to the Operations Center for the tour?"

"I didn't tell her anything, Alkin."

"Uh huh," the old elf said playfully.

Erik looked at Hannah. "I'll be back in an hour."

"I have only an hour with this young one?" the old

elf asked.

"That's it, Didmeister. An hour only."

"Do you have to continue to call me that?" Alkin obviously didn't approve of Erik's rendition of his last name.

"Hey, we're family, big guy," Erik said, slapping the elf on the shoulder and turning back down the cobblestone street.

"Big guy?"

"Big guy!" Erik shouted over his shoulder.

Alkin focused his attention back to Hannah and smiled pleasantly. "My name is Alkin Didier. Please come in," he said, gesturing.

Hannah walked in and was amazed at what she saw. It was an enormous building, teeming with elves busily working at their computers on small, circular tables. The lighting in the room was a forest green and cast everything in a greenish hue. Hannah wasn't sure if she liked it at first, but within a couple of minutes, she grew accustomed to it and found the lighting quite pleasant.

Alkin led her up a small flight of stairs to his open office, which had no walls and looked somewhat like a floating island.

"Take a chair," Alkin offered, slipping behind his oblong desk and sitting down.

Hannah sat.

"An hour? That's all we get for today. Well, then, let me tell you what the Operations Center is. Basically, we manage all the buildings and technology in the NP, both Elven and human. Everyone that works here has been to the University and studied advanced crossover technology."

"Is it hard to work here?"

"Yes and no. We encounter problems all the time. Like today, for instance. We've been having strange power fluctuations in some of the buildings. I'm not sure why. Neither is everyone else, and it somewhat worries me. Without power . . . well, we'd have to stop production. But enough about that. You're here to get a tour, and I suspect that most of our time will be spent in the Window of Observation."

A teenage-looking elf walked up the stairs and waited at the top for Alkin to acknowledge him.

"Yes?" Alkin said.

"We've isolated some of the power fluctuations and Thomas believes he may have a lead."

Alkin looked concerned. He eyed Hannah and then the young elf standing at the top of the stairs.

"Gallest, I want you to take Hannah to the Window. Tell her how things work. Give her the full scoop. She has an hour."

Gallest, the teenage elf, looked a little bewildered. "Ah, you want me to show her the Window?"

"Right, Gallest. The Window."

Alkin stood up and came out from behind his desk. Hannah stood up as well.

"Hannah, I leave you in the very capable hands of Gallest. I would give you the tour myself, but I must find out more about these power problems. I will hopefully be able to come and join you soon. For now, Gallest is your tour guide."

Alkin walked briskly past the teenager and moved down the stairs. Hannah felt a bit awkward. Gallest was a handsome elf, with deep brown eyes and dark brown skin. His hair was cut short and his pointed ears stood out noticeably.

"Hi, Hannah," Gallest said in a bumbled attempt. He seemed a bit nervous.

"Hi. Your name is Gallest?"

"Right."

"How long have you worked here?" wondered Hannah.

"It's been about two years now," the elf answered pleasantly. "I started right after I got out of the University."

They looked at each other in silence. Hannah could feel her face burning red. She hated that she had such fair skin that even the slightest embarrassment showed. Gallest quickly broke the silence.

"Let's go ahead and go on down," he said, gesturing Hannah to the stairs.

Hannah followed him. Everywhere she looked, there was a computer station with an elf or two busily hacking away at a keyboard.

"Over there to the left — that hallway there. That's where we're headed," Gallest said, guiding Hannah toward it.

"How many elves work here?"

"I don't know the official count exactly, but every year we have more and more. The test just to work here is brutal. Only the top students get in."

"That must mean you're a top student?" Hannah looked at the boy and smiled.

He didn't blush, but the compliment took him by surprise. "I was fortunate to get in. Frankly, I didn't think I passed the test with a high enough score."

"But you must've because you're here."

"Yeah," agreed Gallest.

They walked in a hallway decorated with small

Christmas trees littered with tinsel and small, green lights. Pictures sketched in charcoal, of elves walking along the cobblestone streets adorned the hall.

At the end of the hallway was a silver door, much like the one in the front of the building. Gallest led Hannah through it and into the circular room. Just like the hallway, the room was decorated with pictures drawn in charcoal of various buildings and scenes in the NP. Unlike the rest of the building, though, the room was lit with soft white light from the high, lofty ceiling.

Besides the pictures, there was nothing else in the room except for a seventy-five-inch screen embedded in the wall. It was the biggest television screen Hannah had ever seen. It was white and without image.

"Welcome to the Window of Observation."

Hannah looked around the room and then to the television screen. "Gallest, there aren't any windows in this room."

"Unless you count the screen in front of you."

"It looks like a television screen."

"Yeah, a big one," Gallest concurred.

"How does it work?"

"The Window is a way to get into another person's life. It is the ultimate spy machine. With it, we can see anyone, anywhere, and at any time. Have you been to Gift Manufacturing yet?"

"Yes, this morning," replied Hannah.

"Then you know that you can get into a person's life when you're in there. Problem with it is that you can't always get who you need to get, and once you've given them their needed Gift, you can't go back and see how they're doing. That's not the case with the Window."

Hannah looked astonished.

"Every elf has certain people they are responsible for watching. Every household in the NP has a Window, albeit a smaller one, but still a Window to be used to monitor their designated people. What you're looking at now is the first Window developed thousands of years ago. It hasn't changed. The only thing that has are the pictures in the room. This room is one of the oldest in the NP.

"Originally, elves came here to monitor their people, but with the population exploding, it was necessary to have Windows in every household."

"Every household has a screen this big in it?"

"No, no. Most of them are about thirty inches," Gallest answered.

"But every elf has one in their house?" Hannah was astonished.

"Yes. And each adult within that family is responsible for monitoring their lists of people on Earth."

"How old are you when you're an adult?"

"In the NP, you're an adult when you're twenty years old."

Hannah studied the screen harder. "How does it work?" She looked for some sort of button, but there was nothing.

"You begin with thought. Since you don't have a list of people to track, you can focus on anyone that you know or have met."

"What do you mean?"

"Think of someone," Gallest said.

"Anyone?"

"Anyone."

Hannah frowned a moment, then nodded. "Okay."

"Look at the screen," Gallest ordered, pointing.

Hannah turned her eyes to the large screen. Almost instantly the white was replaced by an aerial image of a yellow house. Walking out the front door was a girl with long, black hair. Hannah knew immediately that she was seeing who she had thought of.

"Is that the person you are focusing on?" Gallest asked.

"Yes," said Hannah faintly. "Her name is Joanna."

It was like there was a camera above Joanna's head as she walked along the sidewalk. Hannah was amazed at the sounds that she could hear. They were somehow amplified and crystal clear.

"Why did you think of her?"

"I . . . I haven't seen her for years. She moved out of the state and I haven't spoken to her in about a year."

"You were friends?"

"Best friends, but after she moved, things just weren't the same."

Joanna was now knocking on the front door of a neighbor's house. The door opened, and as it did, the view of the camera shifted, as though it was now above Joanna's right shoulder. Looking into the screen directly was a face Hannah hadn't seen before.

"Hi, Joanna," said the girl.

"Hey," Joanna replied pleasantly.

"Come in," the girl said.

Joanna walked in and the camera followed. Now it was inside the house. Hannah turned to Gallest in amazement.

"Don't lose your focus," Gallest said, pointing back to the screen.

Hannah returned her gaze but the image was white

again. "What happened?"

"When you lose your focus, you lose the person you're focusing on."

"Did I just see her in real time, like right this moment?"

"Yes," Gallest said. "You could watch her as much as you like whenever you'd like, if she was on your list."

"So someone watched me?"

Gallest laughed. "Yeah, a lot of people watched you."

"All the time?" Hannah was now feeling a bit strange.

"Most of the time."

"What about our privacy?"

"Well, for those elves that have you on their list, you don't get any privacy. They can watch you whenever."

Hannah thought about this for a moment. "That's not right."

"It's the only way we can verify the Naughty List."

"But, it could be . . ."

"Weird," Gallest finished quickly. "And the elves could see private things? All of this is true. But elves aren't out to get you. They aren't out to hurt you or use what they find against you. We are loving people and we want the best for all humans."

"But you have a Naughty List," protested Hannah.

"Yes."

"You say you love people and you want the best. How can a Naughty List be the best for people?"

"It's always been that way, Hannah," said Gallest earnestly. "We've never questioned it."

"I suggest there shouldn't be a Naughty List at all. Just think, everyone could get a Gift."

Gallest sighed. "You are not the first person to suggest that. The more you see and learn, the more you might come to understand why we have a Naughty List."

"But the worst people are the ones that need help the most!" Hannah raised her voice.

"That's not our department. Those that need the most help do get help, but not from us."

"Then from who?"

Gallest paused as if deciding whether or not to tell her. "They haven't told you about Upstairs?"

"Upstairs?" Hannah didn't know what the elf was talking about.

"The ones Upstairs help those people that need it the most. In fact, they help all of us."

"What are you talking about?" Hannah didn't have a clue where the conversation was going.

"I'm not going to tell you any more. You'll learn as you spend more time here."

"What kind of an answer is that?" Hannah said, stepping forward, closer to Gallest.

"I know it's not the best answer, but it's the only one I can give you. Christmas isn't just about the NP, Hannah."

"Yeah, I know. It's about the entire human race!"

"And more," added Gallest quickly.

"How can there be more?"

Gallest's eyes moved from Hannah to the screen again. He took a deep breath and then said, "You need to practice with the Window. Focus on another person."

"No," said Hannah defiantly. "Not until you give me

a better explanation than what you just gave me about this Upstairs thing."

"I can't, Hannah. I probably shouldn't have said anything in the first place."

CHAPTER EIGHT
Sled Repair

"I want to know about these times here," the man asked in his deep voice, staring at the map folded open on the table.

"Those are the correct times. As you know, NP time is basically the same as Pacific Standard, except on Christmas Eve, of course."

The large man stared at Dewey for a long moment, then returned his gaze to the map. "And the cables are in place?"

"Most of them. They should be completed within an hour or two. Plenty of time before he is to ride."

"She'd better have been right about this position," the large man said gruffly.

"I wouldn't worry, sir. I believe in her."

"But I do worry, Dewey. I don't believe in anyone, not in Santa nor in her. I don't put my trust in people. I put my trust in technology."

"But you trust in me, right?" Dewey asked.

The large man looked amused. "Are you serious? I don't trust you, Dewey. I pay you well to do what you do."

Dewey looked nonplussed. "Sir?"

"You checked to make sure the cables are reinforced?"

Dewey wanted to talk about the trust issue but knew his boss wanted to drop it, and Dewey decided it wasn't worth pursuing. "Yes, sir. They're ready."

Despite Hannah's frustration with Gallest's answers and her ongoing confusion about Upstairs, she found the Window of Observation to be fascinating. Within the short hour she was with him, she watched the lives of some of her closest friends and a couple of distant cousins who lived in Florida.

"Your hour's up," Gallest said, interrupting Hannah's final session with a former friend.

"Ah, just a little more time," Hannah pleaded, not taking her eyes off the screen.

"Sorry, but this is your first day and you're on a tight schedule. I don't want to make you late."

"All right," Hannah said, when her eyes met Gallest's and the screen in front of her went white immediately.

"I know you might be feeling a little frustrated because I didn't tell you about . . ."

"Hey, it's okay," Hannah cut him off. "I get that I have to find out stuff for myself."

Gallest was obviously relieved. He paused a moment and swallowed hard before asking. "Tonight we have a general assembly meeting in the auditorium. Afterwards, maybe we could take a walk or go out for ice cream?"

Hannah felt her cheeks beginning to burn. This was sounding like a date. "Ice cream? There's an ice cream shop in the North Pole?"

"Not on the campus, but within the Elven Neighborhood there are lots of shops and restaurants."

"So you have a University and shops? It's like there's a city within the neighborhood."

"Yeah, a small one. You think you might be interested?"

Hannah felt warm all over. She smiled and nodded. "I'd like that."

"Great!" Gallest said enthusiastically.

There was a long, strange pause as they stared at each other then at the ground.

"I should walk you out," Gallest finally managed.

"Right . . . okay," Hannah answered back quickly.

Gallest escorted her back to the main wing of the building and to the entrance door. Erik was there, talking with a black-skinned elf named Midias.

"Gallest . . . how are you?" Erik asked pleasantly, shaking hands with the elf.

"Fine. It's good to see you, Erik."

"You too. So where's Alkin?"

"He's been trying to troubleshoot some power outages that have been plaguing us the last couple of days."

Erik nodded. "Midias was just telling me about that. Looks like Alkin has most of the department looking into it."

"It's a problem," Gallest said.

"I'm not worried," Midias said, broadening his shoulders. "We'll have it under control soon."

Erik looked at Hannah and grinned. "How was the Window?"

"Fascinating," answered Hannah, deciding not to go

into her frustrations. She looked at Gallest and hoped he wasn't going to say anything.

"I think Hannah would enjoy more time here," Gallest said pleasantly.

"She'll have plenty of time to come back if she wants," said Erik. "Come on, Hannah, we've got to get you to Sled Repair. See you, guys."

"See you," Midias and Gallest said in unison.

Erik led Hannah outside and into a heavy snowfall. The cobblestone streets now had a thin glaze of fresh powder.

"Isn't the Window weird? Kinda makes you feel like you never have a private moment, huh?" Erik said as they made their way to the Sled Repair building.

"Yes. Makes me feel a little violated."

"You get over it. It's not like the elves are going to blackmail you because of what they see. The elves are the nicest people on the planet. I never met one that's been mean."

"Not ever?"

"Not ever," replied Erik earnestly.

The streets were filled with elves coming and going, many of whom greeted Erik and Hannah with smiles and "hellos" as they passed. Hannah got the impression the NP was always busy, especially during the Christmas season. As they rounded the corner and continued west, the splendor of the Tree encapsulated Hannah once again.

"Are there always elves decorating the Tree from those wires?"

"Right up until Christmas Eve."

"It's just so magnificent to look at . . ." Hannah paused.

"Keep moving, Hannah. We're already a couple of minutes late."

A couple of minutes late wasn't the way Tosh, the head elf of Sled Repair, saw it. He took Erik and Hannah's tardiness gruffly. "What's going on, Erik? Tic-toc, man. Let's be on time."

Erik nodded understandably. "Wouldn't have been late if it wasn't for Gallest holding things up."

"Gallest? Did Gallest give you a tour?" Tosh asked from behind a full, white beard.

"Yes," Hannah answered quietly.

"I wonder why Alkin had Gallest do that."

"Alkin had to go examine some power problems," Hannah said.

Tosh looked slightly concerned. "Where are the problems happening?"

"I don't know," Hannah said.

"Hmmm . . . so my son kept you a little late, did he?" the green-eyed elf asked.

"Gallest is your son?" asked Hannah, surprised.

"My one and only. Proud of that boy. I wanted him to come work for me here in Sled Repair but he didn't want anything to do with it. Okay," Tosh rubbed his hands together eagerly, "I have two hours with this young miss, do I?"

"Right. I'll come back and take her to the Banquet Hall," said Erik.

"No need to do that. I'm eating in the Hall tonight. She can walk over with me."

"Great," Erik said. "Have fun, Hannah. See you at dinner."

"Okay," Hannah said, watching as Erik left the building.

The room Hannah and Tosh stood in was no bigger than a bedroom. It had two chairs and one drawn picture of the grand Christmas Tree lit up brilliantly. Tosh turned and made his way to the elevator doors against the far wall.

"Where are we going?" Hannah asked, following him.

"Up," replied the old elf. "This building is divided into three floors. We're headed to the top, the third floor."

"What's there?" Hannah asked as Tosh faced the doors and pushed the up arrow button on the wall.

"You're in for a treat, young Hannah. Today, we're working on the sleigh."

"The sleigh? Like, *the* sleigh?"

"Right. The big guy's. Santa's himself."

Hannah stared incredulously. Santa's sleigh. The actual sleigh Santa uses the night of Christmas Eve.

The doors opened and Hannah followed Tosh into the small elevator, illuminated in soft white and red light. He pushed the third button and the doors shut, the elevator moving upward slowly.

"Is Santa's sleigh broke or something?"

The old elf looked at his wrinkled hands as if he hadn't heard her. Hannah wondered if she should repeat herself, but then he said, "We always tweak the main man's sleigh. Wax the blades, shine the brass . . ."

The elevator stopped. There was a moment's pause and then the doors opened. Hannah followed her guide out and stood in wonderment. In the center of the mammoth open room was Santa's sleigh. Steaming white light from the ceiling illuminated the craft with an angelic, heavenly look.

"Quite amazing, isn't it?" Tosh said, putting a hand on Hannah's shoulder.

"Yes," Hannah managed to whisper.

"You are the only ones working on her today."

"On who?" Hannah was suddenly confused.

"Her . . . the sleigh."

"The sleigh is a her?"

"I'd like to think so," the old elf chuckled. "I sent everyone else out so that you and I can have quality time together and you can get to learn all the intricacies. Come on. Let's climb up."

The sleigh was similar to other sleighs you see at Christmas time. It was contoured and painted red and forest green. A twelve-foot ladder led from the cockpit to the ground. Tosh gestured Hannah to go ahead and go up.

She looked apprehensive.

"Go on. There's nothing to worry about."

Hannah grasped the golden ladder and climbed. This was the *actual* sleigh that has been used for thousands of years. You'd think it would show its years of use, yet it was polished and sparkled like new. When she climbed into the cockpit, Hannah felt powerful. The large seat was embroidered in gold lace and as Hannah put her hand on the red cushion, she could feel that it was a smooth velvet.

"What do you think?" Tosh asked from below.

"It's great!"

Hannah was astonished at how large it was. The cockpit was the very front of the sleigh and everything behind it was like an enormous chasm of space. She looked over the side in wonder. "This is so deep. I can't see the bottom. Shouldn't I be able to see the bottom?"

Hannah asked.

"No," quipped Tosh. "The sleigh has been blessed with many attributes that you can't possibly imagine. One of them is the space issue. Even though we only deliver a fraction of physical gifts to kids around the world, it's still a lot of toys. There's no way we could fit all the toys inside the sleigh if it didn't have some serious storage.

"I wanted you to get an idea of what it's like to sit in it. Just by sitting in the sleigh you feel the power and a certain majesty. To be working on the sleigh is a great privilege, and one that I have taken pride in the majority of my life. It is an amazing craft. Come on down and we'll start on the sleigh blades."

Hannah looked down at the cushioned cockpit. She plopped into the seat, the cushions wrapping around her, instantly providing her with extra comfort. She imagined the reindeer in front of the sleigh. She imagined announcing their names and rising into the night sky.

"Hannah . . . you all right up there?" Tosh asked.

This awoke Hannah from her daydream. "I was just imagining. I'll be right down."

When she climbed off the ladder, Tosh was all teeth. "They picked a good replacement. I can already tell you have a lot of Christmas Spirit."

Hannah blushed.

"Come back here. Take a look at the blades."

They were two feet thick, made of glistening gold.

"The sleigh blades are an important part of the craft. We're going to wax them today. The underside of the blades are the most important since they get the most use. We'll wax the blades over two thousand times this month. You won't find a slicker piece of gold anywhere."

Hannah stared at the blades and then asked, "How are we going to wax the bottom? Are you going to jack up the sleigh or something?"

"No, no," Tosh answered without a second thought. "We'll just flip her over and suspend her right above the floor."

"Suspend her above the floor?"

"Right."

"How?" Hannah asked.

Tosh took in a breath. "Back up a little."

He and Hannah stepped back.

"Sleigh," Tosh said, talking directly at the craft, "flip over and suspend."

Without hesitation, the sleigh obeyed and turned over slowly until at last it was hovering inches above the floor.

"Whoa," Hannah grunted.

"Platform," Tosh said.

Hannah looked at him strangely. "Excuse me?"

Tosh pointed above them.

From high above, the ceiling split open and descending on two cables, one on each end, was a ten-foot-long, five-foot-wide platform. Hannah watched as it slowly made its way and touched down on the floor in front of them.

"We'll use the platform to get us to the blades. Get on," Tosh said.

Hannah walked on cautiously. At each end of the platform was a white ten gallon bucket, filled almost to the top with a thick, red liquid. There were handles sticking out of the goo that Hannah assumed were the brushes.

"Up," Tosh said and the platform slowly ascended. "The wax is a special formula developed thousands of years ago. We'll apply twenty coats on each blade to begin with . . . ."

As he and Gallest stared over Thomas's shoulder, Alkin rubbed his forehead in confusion.

"There," Thomas said, pointing to the flashing red dot. They were staring at a digitized map of the NP, the flashing red dot near the reindeer stables.

"Why are we having fluctuations near the stables?" wondered Alkin.

"Have no clue," Thomas answered honestly. "The stables don't use anywhere near the power of the other buildings. It's as if something is siphoning off power in that area."

"I can't recall ever seeing anything like this," Gallest said.

"Me either," replied Thomas.

"I want you to take a team up there and check it out," said Alkin.

Thomas stood up, brushing his long black hair behind his pointed ears. "Sol and Lyre?"

"That's fine. Take Gallest as well."

"You're not coming with us?"

"No. I've got something else I need to check out."

"Two hours! Two hours of cleaning and waxing the sleigh," Hannah complained before taking a bite of lasagna.

Marcel shook his head in disbelief. "Aren't your arms tired?"

Hannah swallowed. "I can barely move them."

"Tosh makes you earn it," Erik said as he took a bite of his Caesar salad.

The Banquet Hall was packed with elves, enjoying the evening's menu of lasagna, fresh bread, and salad. Hannah found the meal scrumptious. She was famished.

"Repair and maintenance work isn't easy; neither is upkeep. He takes pride in the sleigh. It's his baby," said William, finishing off his bread.

A butler elf came by their table with a pitcher of Liquid Breeze and refilled their glasses. Natalya and Noemi were deep into a side conversation, while Marcel was intrigued and somewhat apprehensive about sled repair.

"Do you think I'm going to have to do that tomorrow?" he asked.

"You'd better," Hannah quipped.

"I hope not."

"Don't worry about it," William said to Marcel. "Tosh makes you work hard at first, but it gets better. Trust me."

"How's your experience been so far?" Erik asked the French boy.

"I think he's had a great time," Natalya chimed in, having finished her conversation with Noemi.

"So I guess you're done with that secret talk," William said lightheartedly.

"Girl stuff," Noemi replied with a smile.

"Uh huh," grunted William.

"I have had a wonderful time so far. This place is so amazing. Never had I dreamed it could be this detailed. The University was a true gem," said Marcel.

"Wait," Hannah said. "You went to the University?"

"Yes, in the Elven Neighborhood. It was a campus, and what they are doing there is fascinating."

Hannah looked at Erik as if he had stolen something from her. "Don't I get to go?"

"Of course," Erik said quickly. "That's on your schedule for tomorrow."

Hannah was relieved. The University was a place she definitely wanted to see.

"If you'll excuse me," Noemi said, looking at her watch, "I've got to go."

Natalya looked at her friend strangely. "Why? Where do you need to be?"

Noemi seemed to struggle for the words. "I'm meeting . . . I have a meeting with . . ."

"With?" Natalya prodded.

"I have to go," Noemi finished and rushed out of the Hall.

"What was that all about?" William asked.

"I don't know. She's been acting strange all day. I have no idea where she's going. I don't have any memory of a meeting we're supposed to be at."

"Maybe she's just supposed to go," offered Marcel.

"Not likely," Natalya responded.

William took a drink of Liquid Breeze but almost spit it out when Erik blurted, "So, are you going to pop the question to the parents?"

William wiped his lips. "Keep it down."

"Come on, buddy. Tell me . . . I've been dying all day

to know."

"Know what?" asked Marcel, clearly not understanding the conversation. Neither was Hannah.

"These guys haven't told you?" Natalya faked a shocked look. "William has a girlfriend, an Elven girlfriend he's been in love with for two years."

Hannah stared wide-eyed at William.

"It's true. Her name's Holly," he admitted.

"So you're going to marry her?" Marcel asked.

William flushed. Suddenly, he was on the spot. "Keep your voice down."

"It's obvious you love her. It's your last year here in the NP, unless you marry and live here permanently."

"What?" said a shocked Hannah.

"Keep it down!" rebuked William with a wave of his hand.

"Well?" Natalya said, raising an eyebrow. "She can't live on Earth, so the only choice is for you to live here."

"I know," William said quietly. "Yeah, we've talked about it."

A different butler elf walked to the table with a pitcher of Liquid Breeze but Erik brushed him away.

"So are you asking Holly's parents tonight?" Natalya was now whispering.

"I am."

There was a massive pause. Everyone at the table seemed frozen, none more than Erik, William's closest friend. It was he who finally spoke. "This is . . . awesome, man."

William grinned broadly. "Thanks."

"Congratulations," said Natalya. "I think you make a great couple."

William nodded. "The only problem is *my* parents.

They won't understand, let alone believe."

"Ah," Erik said, flipping his hands nonchalantly. "You'd be surprised. They'll come around."

"I don't know . . ."

Suddenly, William stopped speaking. The lights flickered and the five friends found themselves in sudden darkness.

"What the . . ." Natalya blurted.

Everything was pitch black.

"Power outage," Erik said. "This is what the elves were talking about earlier — these power fluctuations. Looks like it hit the Hall."

"Have you ever had one before?" Marcel asked.

"No," Natalya answered.

The lights reappeared quickly, illuminating the room as before.

"That was weird," said William, glancing at Erik.

"I don't know what's going on with the power but something isn't right," Erik said, looking around the room with concern.

CHAPTER NINE
Training Run

"I don't have much time to talk," the woman's voice said over the phone receiver. "I've routed most of the power that's needed. It's going to be massive when it's completed."

"No one has suspected?" the deep voice asked from the other end.

"They're concerned, all right. They have their best people working on it, but they won't figure it out in time. Trust me," the woman reassured the voice.

"I don't like to trust anyone."

"I know, but in this case, you'll have to. What about on your end? Is everything ready in Metaline Falls?"

"All is in place."

"Good. We only have tonight to do this."

The auditorium was unlike anything Hannah had been in before. She'd gone to arenas and stadiums for various sporting events, but never had she been in such a grand place. The auditorium seated thousands and every chair was filled with elves.

The walls were a deep red and decorated with elaborate tinsel. There were small Christmas trees spread throughout the various aisles and high ceiling lights spread warmth from above.

Hannah and the other humans had been escorted to the very front of the stage by a very tall and very old elf that was obviously an usher. When Hannah had taken her seat, the old elf smiled and said, "Such a pretty girl."

Hannah flushed.

The place was filled with chatter and ambient noise. Hannah turned to Marcel who was seated to her left. He looked at her and neither one said a word, but both had the same thought: *incredible!*

Surprisingly, it didn't take the ushers long to seat people and at six o'clock straight up, the lights dimmed and onto the massive stage walked an elf Hannah figured had to be about as old as the usher who had seated her.

The auditorium went ballistic with applause and whistles. The elf bowed and raised his arms to indicate he wanted to begin, but the crowd was not letting him. They continued cheering. Hannah didn't know who this elf was, but when she looked over to her right and saw Erik pounding his hands together, she figured she should do the same.

The elf nodded appreciatively to the ovation, raised his arms again, and the crowd finally subsided into quiet.

"Good evening," the elf spoke smoothly, his voice amplified. "We are here to officially christen our two newest members. For thousands of years we have been here to continue to help children all around the world because of something called Christmas Spirit. And tonight we honor two humans that will continue to carry that torch."

The crowd applauded enthusiastically.

"To do the honors," the elf paused purposefully as the applause died down, "I give you, Santa Claus."

If the crowd had erupted earlier with the sight of the old elf, they exploded when Santa Claus stepped onto stage from the right. Everyone stood and cheered, shouting and hooting.

Hannah was awestruck.

Santa Claus. *The* Santa Claus.

As she analyzed him from his glistening black boots up, he was just as Hannah pictured he would be. Around the tops of his boots was a fluffy white material. His brick-red pants where loose and free-flowing. The black belt around his waist was thick and the glistening gold buckle had been intricately designed. Hannah could distinctly make out the letters "SC".

From there, Hannah traced up his thick, long-sleeved coat that was the same, exact color of his pants with round, black buttons up the center. The cuffs and collar of the coat were the same fluffy white as the material around the tops of his boots. His beard was full and white, yet not very long. It looked somewhat like out-of-control white groundcover traipsing across his face. Santa's eyes were a deep blue and complemented his pale face and mop of white hair. On his head was a stocking cap, red like the rest of his outfit, along with the white fluff at the end of it, all of which covered his potato-like frame.

He walked forward and shook the old elf's hand and bowed before the audience. Hannah felt goose bumps running down her spine. She was filled with an indescribable joy. She was as happy as she had ever been in her life. She had no problems, no fears. There was nothing negative or bad in her life at that moment. She was looking at the real Santa Claus, a person she believed existed, but figured she would never see.

The crowd wouldn't let Santa speak for another five minutes as they paid tribute to him with more applause, whistles, and shouts of acclamation. Eventually, they tired enough for Santa to speak.

"It is wonderful to see all of you."

When Claus spoke, Hannah felt as though extra life was being pumped into her. His voice was rich and deep and perfect.

"Again, for another year, we come together to honor what we are about. All of you, especially this month, are working hard and making preparations for the Eve. As I watch you and listen to you, I am as proud as any elf has ever been. You do things for others, not for yourselves. You put the needs and wants of millions in before your own. It amazes me.

"When I look at Earth, and when you look at Earth through your Windows, it is discouraging. There seems to be so much evil, so much tragedy that you think it is impossible to overcome. Children are starving. Children are being hurt by others, both physically and mentally. Children don't have a place to call home. Children worry that they'll be shot or beat up as they leave school. Parents are afraid to let their children play outside for fear that someone may take or harm them. It is a world ruled by fear, and yet, children continue to believe.

"And what do they believe in? Do they believe there are elves in the North Pole? Yes. Do children believe that there is a Santa? Yes. Do children believe there is a place where evil does not exist, where there is only joy? Yes. It is here. It's because of all of you that the North Pole has endured all these thousands of years and that it will continue to do so.

"Tonight, we honor two young people, the finest on Earth."

Hannah's heart raced. It was like she was running a sprint around a track. Her breath came in spurts and her chest rose up and down quickly.

"When Marcel and Hannah were recommended, and I looked at their lives. I was most pleased. You would be hard-pressed to find any children more deserving that these two. I will begin with you, Hannah."

Claus pointed directly at her. She turned an instant tomato red. He smiled and raised his finger slightly. Hannah was magically lifted out of her seat, up over the lip of the stage, and gently placed in front of the icon himself.

The crowd ignited with applause. Hannah felt more joy. Tears burst from her and she hugged Santa with everything she had. She was not sad in any way, but knew what the tears of joy were for the first time.

Claus put his arms around her and squeezed. If love were visible, you would've seen it covering Hannah.

Santa's warm, velvety coat felt good on her face, and the smell of fresh peppermint tickled her nostrils.

When she finally pulled away, the crowd quieted once again and Claus looked into her teary eyes. "Belief is something we elves have always had, but for humans, belief does not come easy. Humans are constantly bombarded with the powers of unbelief. They are taught *not* to believe in things because it isn't logical. Children are taught *not* to believe in the unseen things. . . .

"But here stands Hannah, who has always believed. She will be an intricate part of the workings here at the NP. I have high hopes for her, and I know that while she's here, she will be treated with dignity and respect.

"Ladies, gentlemen, children . . . Hannah Green."

The assemblage stood and cheered. Claus smiled gently and motioned for Hannah to look out at the crowd of thousands. They were cheering her because she had belief, and it was because of her belief that the NP would continue.

Hannah Green had never felt better in her life!

William Wood had been in the house many times over the two years since joining the NPSP, but he could not think of a time when he was more nervous entering Holly's house than tonight.

As Holly led him through the front door and toward the kitchen, neither of them said anything to each other, for Holly was almost as nervous as William. What did she have to be nervous about, really? Her parents adored William and treated him like family, yet did they know what he was about to ask? Did they have a clue that he was about to propose marriage . . . and at such a young age?

William remembered the first time he'd been in the house and how he'd been so impressed by the hand-crafted furniture and antique interior look. He'd been to a few elves' homes but none was better decorated than Esther's, Holly's mother. She was a marvel at making a house feel warm and inviting.

When he and Holly entered the kitchen, Holly's sister and father were seated around the long, oval table, while her mother was busy working at the old-fashioned wood stove. Holly's father, Chuck, smiled genially. "Take a seat and have a cup of eggnog," he said, motioning for them to take a seat.

Holly's sister, Erica, smiled at William. She understood why Holly liked him. He was handsome, and though Erica was a couple of years younger than Holly, she was old enough to appreciate William's rugged good looks.

Holly grabbed the glass pitcher which was full of thick eggnog and poured a glass for William, then for herself.

"Thanks," William said with a warm but nervous smile.

Holly smiled back.

William had rehearsed the scene in his mind a hundred times: what he would say, how he would start the conversation, what he would do if Holly's father frowned. His heart palpitated. He figured he would just ease into the conversation, eat dinner, and then during dessert, pop the question.

He took a drink of eggnog, his hand shaking slightly.

"How are the new NPSP Members working out?" Chuck asked.

"They're excellent," William said, setting his glass down. "I'm really happy with both of them."

"Someone told me that Marcel's from France?"

"Yep," said William, trying to control his breathing which all of the sudden seemed to have gotten to be more difficult than usual.

"That's good. It's been many years since we've had someone from Europe as an NPSP Member."

William nodded pleasantly. 'This is going to be a long evening,' he thought.

"Dinner will be ready in a few minutes. We're having turkey and the works," Esther said, turning from the stove to smile at William.

"Smells great," said Holly, watching her mother take a dish out of the oven.

"I've got a couple of nice surprise appetizers tonight," Esther said.

Erica, who had been staring at William the entire time, as if he were some sort of scientific anomaly, asked suddenly, "Are you going to marry my sister?"

It was as if time had completely stopped. Had Holly's sister just asked the question? Every eye in the room was now on William. He looked at Holly's father and swallowed hard.

Junior Claus was almost fifty years old. His head was like his father's, a mass of tangled white hair. He was overweight, with a large, what he called "eggnog" belly. His face was covered with a thick, pepper-colored beard — the black portions being the only thing left of its younger color. He was standing in the rear paddock where the Juvenile reindeer were kept. Though he'd like to use the Nifty Nine tonight, that was out of the question.

NP Juvenile reindeer are usually around ten years old. Most of the Nifty Nine were in their thirties. Junior was about to take an extra harness off the top hook against the wall, when a movement to his right caught his eye. He turned, and there was his sister, Alisha.

"Hey, what are you doing here?" he asked, returning his attention to retrieving the harness. "You're not in the auditorium listening to Dad?"

"No," Alisha said, her hands in her pockets. "Just wanted to walk a little."

"Yeah," Junior mumbled, inspecting the harness.

"Tonight a training night?"

"Yes. Tonight I fly over Metaline Falls in Washington state."

"Oh," Alisha said with a nod. "Are you excited?"

"Always a rush to ride in the sleigh, even if it's not the official one."

"Yeah," Alisha concurred.

"Somethin' bothering you?" asked Junior, noticing the strange look on Alisha's face.

"Just these power fluctuations. They have me worried."

"Me too."

"I think I'm going to head home," Alisha said quietly. "Have a good flight."

"Good-night," Junior said, before walking out of the paddock with the harness and onto the cobblestone streets, which glistened from the fresh falling snow. Lampposts illuminated his way easily and he enjoyed the fact that the streets weren't crammed with elves. Mostly everyone was in the auditorium or in their homes.

Hailey, as always, would have the Juveniles ready to go. All Junior had to do was show up and ride. This particular practice session was his twentieth, and by now, he had the process down. Most of his practice rounds were really about sightseeing.

He walked past the massive Christmas Tree which, for once, wasn't being decorated, and stopped to marvel at it. Each year it was decorated differently with an assortment of ornaments and tinsel. This year's effort was one of the best Junior had seen in a while, probably because Kirken, the elf in charge of this year's decorations, begged for a larger decorating team and had gotten it.

"Wonderful Tree this year," came a voice from behind. It was his wife's Gail — a voice he'd heard for almost thirty years.

Junior turned surprised. "What are you doing here? I thought you said you were going to the auditorium."

"I told the kids to go. I had some things I needed to do at the house."

"Forever cleaning," Junior said, shaking his head.

"I decided to take a walk and figured I'd escort you to your sleigh."

"Why, thank you, ma'am," Junior said playfully.

They locked hands and continued along the cobblestone road, walking over the arch bridge that overlooked the Cocoa River.

"When you get back, I'll have fresh oatmeal cookies."

Junior smiled. "Really?"

"I'll make sure they're right out of the oven."

"You're a kind woman."

"I know . . ." his wife said sarcastically.

"Most of the time," Junior quickly added with a smirk.

"Watch it, mister. You never know what I might put

in those cookies."

Junior laughed. "Raisins."

"Laced with ipecac."

"Not funny, Gail" Junior said, still laughing.

"You don't think so? I thought it was quite funny." She gave him a wink.

They enjoyed their remaining walk together in silence, continuing to hold hands until arriving at the Airstrip.

"Hello, you two. The reindeer are ready, sir," Hailey said pleasantly.

"I brought an extra harness," Junior said, holding up the one in his left hand, while still holding his wife's in the other. "Last time I went out, one broke."

"Good idea."

The sleigh looked almost identical to the real thing, only this one was about a fourth smaller, which made it easier for the Juveniles. And as usual, it was shiny and lustrous.

The Juvenile reindeer were anxiously awaiting, all of them staring back at Junior as if to send him the message that it was time to go.

"They've been a bit giddy tonight," Hailey said, looking at them. "Don't look at me like that, Tangles. You've been the one I've had the most trouble with."

Tangles, the lead reindeer, snorted indignantly.

"I swear, having Rudy as his father has not helped. He was born with attitude, and the fact that his father's the head deer doesn't help."

"He's got a great nose . . . better than Rudy's," Junior admitted.

"Yes, but don't tell him that. He'd be blaring it all the time. It's bad enough I have to put the muzzle over it when he's in the stables."

Gail laughed. "It's what keeps you busy, Hailey."

"Indeed," Hailey said, sounding somewhat exasperated.

"I best get going," Junior said, throwing the harness up to the cushioned driver's seat.

His wife hugged him. "Have a pleasant evening."

"Thank you."

"I'll be here waiting when you get back," Hailey said.

"You don't have to wait all that time. Go get a cup of hot cocoa or something."

Hailey smiled.

Junior lifted into the air like a slow motion jump, hovering above the sleigh for a moment, then settling down into the lone seat. Reaching into his cloak pocket, he took out two long white gloves and pulled them over his hands.

"Did you wash that suit before you put it on?" his wife asked.

"Of course."

"Liar," Gail mumbled.

Junior laughed. She was right about the Santa suit, but he wasn't going to admit it. He looked out toward the Juvenile reindeer and called them by name. "On Banges, on Leif, on Jenn, on Teal. On Karis, on Grath, on Elsie, on Linsa, and off Tangles we go!"

The reindeer bounded forward, the bells on their harnesses ringing in perfect harmony, the sleigh moving along the Strip smoothly. Within a few moments, they were airborne.

Hailey turned to Gail. "As many times as I've heard him say that, it just doesn't sound right."

Gail nodded. "I look forward to the day the reindeer

are actually a part of the Nifty Nine and their names are changed."

"No doubt."

Junior was quickly into the Tunnel of Belief and surrounded by white light. Getting to Earth only took a few minutes with nine reindeer and when he looked over the side of the sleigh, he was staring at the distant lights of Metaline Falls — the small town found in the north-easternmost corner of Washington state, along the Pend Oreille River. Surrounded by the Selkirk forest, it's a remote area, which is exactly what Junior needed.

In his previous flights, Junior had been all around the world, but this was his first time in Washington state. The Juveniles were in top form and the sleigh glided smoothly through the cold night air, which had no effect on him or the reindeer.

He was now gliding along the tops of the pines and the wide river. It was a cloudy night — a necessary ingredient when doing practice flights. The town lights reflected off the river's smooth surface. Ahead was the bridge that spanned the Pend Oreille River and enabled people from town to get to the main highway. Junior figured he would stay low, along the surface of the river, and glide underneath the bridge, but he never got the chance.

Tangles was the first to go limp. He was the lead reindeer and dictated the pace of the sleigh. When his body suddenly stopped, the reaction was chaotic. The sleigh banked hard to the right. The other reindeer tried to compensate as Junior held the reigns tight, yanking left as hard as he could. The team started to pull out of it when Jenn suddenly went down, her limp body dangling like a broken puppet in the reigns, similar to

Tangles.

Everything was happening so fast, Junior didn't see his adversaries as they took aim at other reindeer. Banges, then Teal, went limp as the sleigh jerked along, now skimming the top of the river. There was a sudden burst, like the sleigh had been hit with something heavy. Junior held tight to the reins as the sleigh shook violently. Another blast hit the front and Junior got a fresh look at what was causing the shaking. It was a hook of some kind, attached to a thick cable.

Another crash and this one sent him airborne. He soared over the confused and unconscious reindeer, falling to the water. His face was the first part of his body to connect to the cold, and it not only sent shivers down his spine, the water felt like a hard punch to his face.

Junior was now surrounded in darkness, frigid darkness. He was spinning and turning uncontrollably from both the turbulent river and the force of being propelled so forcefully out of the sleigh. He scrambled to get to the surface but his suit was soaked and difficult to swim in. He clawed at the water like a raging dog, trying to get to the top for needed oxygen, but it was impossible. The current was too strong. Everything was going dark. He made one more valiant push upward but it was no use. He was going to drown. The darkness came quickly and overpowered him.

CHAPTER TEN
First Date

William's fears about asking for Chuck's blessing for Holly's hand in marriage was misplaced. Although Erica's surprising question left him speechless at first, it was a perfect opportunity to address the issue and bring it forward for discussion.

After William thoroughly explained how much he loved Holly, how much he felt in his heart that they were meant to be together forever, Holly's mother and father were ecstatic. Holly's mother dried the tears from her eyes and her father was shaking William's hand with joy.

"We were waiting for this day," said Esther.

"Didn't we just talk about this last night?" said Chuck, looking at his wife. "This is a great day, a great day!"

William nodded, smiling and staring at Holly, who simply glowed.

"Wait," said Chuck suddenly. "What about your parents, William? We'll have to have the ceremony here, and . . . they won't be able to come," he finished, although progressively slower at the end.

This was the only part that William didn't like.

142 | North Pole Santa Patrol

"You're right. They won't be able to see it. I figured we'd have to videotape it with an earthly recorder."

"Yes, yes, definitely!" said Holly's father.

"And Dad," said Holly, "we want to have the ceremony this Christmas Eve."

"What?" said Holly's mother, lifting a towel from her shoulder. "You don't have time. You have to pick out your dress, the cake, the decorations . . ."

"All of it is taken care of," Holly said reassuringly, "all except the invitations."

"What? How?" asked her mother.

"Gloria already did everything for us." Gloria was Holly's dearest and most trusted friend.

"You mean . . . wow," said Chuck. "You just figured that we'd say yes?"

"We were hoping," said William.

"Well, I'm saying yes. I'm saying yes, yes, yes!" Chuck looked like he was going to burst with joy. "So, tell us the details. What do you have planned?"

"I brought some mugs for us," Gallest said, pulling them out of his coat pockets as they walked along the street with the hoards of other elves exiting the auditorium.

Hannah was congratulated over and over again. Pats on the back. Smiles. Head nods. Everyone was kind and pleased with her. "What are the cups for?" she asked.

"To drink from," said Gallest, lifting them up as if Hannah couldn't see them very well under the lampposts.

"Does the ice cream shop in the Neighborhood sell beverages?"

"I changed the plan a bit. I have something special in store for you tonight," said Gallest mysteriously.

"What is it?" asked Hannah.

"You'll see in a second."

"If we're not drinking something at the ice cream shop, then what are we drinking?"

"That," Gallest said, pointing to the meandering Cocoa River.

As elves crossed the northernmost arched bridge, Gallest veered right, and took Hannah under it. There was a light attached to the pylons of the bridge that illuminated the little area in wonderfully soft, white light. The dark-haired elf bent over and scooped the cups into the river. He gave one to Hannah with a smile.

"Thanks," she said, looking at the steaming mug in wonder.

"Go on, take a drink."

Hannah had to admit it felt a bit awkward drinking cocoa from a river, but the smell was tantalizing. She put the small mug to her lips and drank. The taste was fantastic, like the richest chocolate she'd ever tasted. It was smooth and made her entire body warm, as though she was sitting in a hot-tub.

"Good?" Gallest asked, raising the cup and taking a drink.

"Excellent," Hannah said.

"I love coming underneath the bridge. The light and the river . . . it's so pretty . . . like you."

Hannah froze. Had he just given her a compliment? Had he just said that she was pretty? Although it sounded a little odd, like he'd rehearsed the line before, it was nonetheless a sweet attempt. Hannah was happy that it was somewhat dark because Gallest couldn't see her face turn crimson.

"Thanks," she said, quickly taking a drink.

Gallest seemed a bit uncomfortable and took a drink as well. There was an odd silence that followed. Hannah wasn't sure where the conversation was supposed to go next but not saying anything wasn't an option.

"What's the best part of living here in the NP?" she attempted.

Gallest looked relieved. "Yeah . . . ah . . . for me . . . it's the Neighborhood."

"The Elven Neighborhood?"

"Yes. It's unlike any other, believe me."

"How so?" Hannah wondered, feeling the extra color drain somewhat away from her face.

"I've seen many humans and how they live today. Everyone seems afraid of other people. Humans have neighbors that they don't even speak with or know. I've watched for years from my Window and I'm convinced that's why it's so bad on Earth."

"Because we're not good neighbors?" Hannah asked, taking a drink.

"In a way. Humans don't care for one another like we do in the NP. I know all of my neighbors really well. We all do things together in groups, but humans are not that way. They'll have a few friends, but there isn't the kind of caring for one another like here."

"I care . . ." Hannah said.

"Oh, I know you do, especially for your immediate family. I get that. But where humans fall short is how they don't care for those they don't know. That's not the case in the NP with elves. Look how many people talked with you tonight, just walking from the auditorium. Did you get the sense from any of them that they really didn't care about you?"

Gallest was right. Every elf Hannah encountered had been genuine and caring. "No, they were all very kind and sincere."

"Exactly. Do you think you'd see that on Earth?"

"We are on Earth," said Hannah before taking another drink.

Gallest took another swig as well. "Yeah, but I mean where humans live. Do you see that on Earth very often?"

"Well . . . no."

"See."

"But . . . do you have crime here?"

"Crime?" Gallest laughed. "We don't know what crime is. Can you imagine malice or deceit being here in the NP? It would never happen."

"It does in my world. So people don't trust people who they don't know."

"But humans take it to an extreme."

Hannah sighed. "Maybe. I've never felt love and kindness like I have here, except from my parents. It's too bad I can't spend like a month here."

Gallest nodded. "You need to take advantage of every minute of the days you do get. In your free time, I'll show you around more, maybe take you to the Neighborhood."

"Seriously? What about the University? Do you think you could take me to the University?"

"Absolutely," Gallest said, finishing his cocoa and dipping into the river for another cup. "But tonight, I want to take you someplace amazing."

William and Holly stood on the small porch of her house. He was as happy as he had ever been in his life. Holly's parents were excited and supportive. In just a few days, Holly would be his wife, his actual wife, and he would be staying in the NP forever. It was a dream come true.

"I can't believe how well it went," Holly said in a quiet whisper.

"I know. It felt so good and now that everything is out on the table, we can move on with our preparations."

"Gloria has been so awesome getting things ready," said Holly, taking William by the hand.

"She's the best," William concurred, looking into eyes that loved him unconditionally.

"You know, there have only been two marriages between elf and human in all the history of the NP."

"I know. It's rare," said William, looking up at a hanging bushel of mistletoe and picking off one of the red berries.

He loved mistletoe!

Hannah stood at the back door of the gargantuan Wrapping Center. Gallest excitedly opened the door and led her into the dimly lit hallway. Hannah was surprised that there wasn't a lock on the door or some sort of security device, but then, after all, she was in the NP, where there was no crime or malice.

"Where are we?" Hannah asked as Gallest led her by the hand to the elevator at the end of the hallway. Doors split off to their left and right, but Gallest ignored them. He pushed the down arrow and the elevator doors opened.

"We're on the backside of the Center. I'm taking you to the night shift."

"The night shift?" Hannah asked, walking into the elevator.

Gallest pushed the G button. "I wanted you to see the night shift and how they work."

The elevator doors closed.

Hannah was excited. She didn't know exactly why she was, but Gallest's enthusiasm was contagious. The elevator made a faint ringing sound, came to a stop, and the doors opened. Gallest led her forward to a sort of catwalk overlooking a massive assembly line, complete with conveyor belts and machines in red and green Hannah had never seen the likes of before.

There were hundreds of elves on the assembly line moving inhumanly fast. Boxes would shoot down the belt and the throng of elves would go to work, grabbing from the massive towers of wrapping paper and ribbon on the wall behind them and wrapping the nearest gift. The speed at which they did this was impossible for a human. They moved so quickly it was like they were a blur of red light.

"The night shift," Gallest said proudly. "These are special elves that are born with the ability to move incredibly fast. They're destined to be gift wrappers and they work during the night."

"All night?" asked Hannah in awe.

"No. They only work in five hour shifts and then they're relieved."

Hannah watched intently as an elf pulled a box from the conveyor belt, set it on the table in front of him, turned and tore off wrapping paper, then wrapped the gift in seconds before tearing off a ribbon and tying it around the package. He placed the gift back on the moving belt and grabbed another unwrapped gift.

The group of elves suddenly shouted, "Hey" in unison, helping Hannah to realize there was music playing. She was so initially awestruck by the scene she'd failed to hear the jazzy Christmas music filling the place. The elves were following along with it.

"I think this is amazing," Hannah said, looking at Gallest.

"You won't see them during the day. They only work at night."

"Why?" asked Hannah.

"Day shift is too busy with so many people working."

"Oh," Hannah nodded with understanding.

Gallest led Hannah along the catwalk slowly, watching as the amazing elves hummed, danced, and occasionally shouted to the music, all while wrapping gift after gift that the conveyor spit out.

"Where do the wrapped gifts go?" Hannah wondered.

"Into the other side of the conveyor there," said Gallest, pointing. "Then they shoot across to the next room over and they're addressed."

"Addressed by elves?"

"All of them by hand."

"No way!" Hannah smiled. "So there's a bunch of

elves in the next room over that are addressing these gifts?"

"Right. You want to follow the catwalk over and I'll show you?"

"Yes!"

"We have him," deep voice said over the receiver.

"There weren't any complications? No one saw you?" the female voice asked skeptically.

"No. It went perfectly, no problems."

The woman laughed sinisterly. "I've waited for this moment for too long."

"As have I," deep voice said. "Step one is completed. Now we'll see if they play into step two."

"Oh, Claus will. If he's anything, he's predictable. He'll call in the NPSP, no doubt."

"I'm counting on it."

There were few elves on the cobblestone streets when Gallest led Hannah out of the Wrapping Center, back to the Guest Quarters. She didn't know how long they'd been watching the lighting-fast elves wrap and address, but the time went by much too quickly. Gallest was a pleasant guide and Hannah felt good being with him.

"Tomorrow night," Gallest said as they rounded the corner toward the Guest Quarters, "I'll show you another great spot."

"Really?" Hannah was excited. "Where?"

"It's a surprise."

Hannah wished they could stay out longer but sensed that Gallest felt it was time to say good-night. They approached the glass doors of the Guest Quarters and Gallest stopped, looking into Hannah's eyes.

Her heart raced.

This was a date, and on first dates, wasn't there a kiss involved?

The kiss came quickly, but not like Hannah had anticipated. Gallest took her hand in his, bent over and gently kissed it. This wasn't exactly what Hannah had in mind, but it was a sweet gesture nonetheless.

"I had a great time tonight," the elf said.

Hannah gulped and flushed red. "I did, too."

"See you tomorrow?"

"Yes, for sure," Hannah said, her spirit leaping.

The glass doors swung open and Willis stood regally, waiting for Hannah. Gallest nodded to Willis and looked at Hannah a final time before turning and leaving.

Hannah practically ran to the doors and spouted a quick "hi" to the butler elf. She was into the foyer and ready to head to her room when Natalya stopped her.

"Hannah . . . have you seen Noemi?"

"Noemi?" Hannah asked. "No. I've been with Gallest."

Natalya smiled. "Gallest, huh?"

"Yes."

"But you didn't see Noemi anywhere?"

"No."

"That's weird," Natalya said, almost to herself. "She was supposed to meet me here an hour ago."

Hannah shrugged. "I'm heading to my room."

"Yeah, you should. It's late, and you've got a busy day tomorrow."

Hannah nodded. "Good-night."

"You're in a good mood . . ."

"Yeah . . . tell you about it tomorrow." Hannah smiled.

"Good-night," Natalya replied before sitting down in one of the cushioned chairs.

Hannah skipped down the hall and into her room. The entire day had been unbelievably awesome. She had learned more about the NP than she ever dreamed possible. It was an astounding place of joy, beauty, and love. There was no other place in the world like it, and Hannah wanted to stay her whole life. She plopped down on the bed and looked at the ceiling with contentment. Her thoughts went to Gallest. He was fun and sweet and handsome, and the thought of him made her smile. She couldn't wait to see him again. She always believed the North Pole existed, and that Santa delivered gifts every year, but to see it all in real life . . . .

She had no idea what time it was but sensed it was late. She slid off her bed and went to the closet. Hanging with the other clothes were pajamas that looked similar to the outfit she was wearing. She quickly changed, and went into the bathroom to brush her teeth. She was not surprised to see the new red and green toothbrush lying on the folded hand towel, but laughed when she picked up the white tube of toothpaste labeled *Elven Squeeze*, with the subtext, *for a snowy smile*.

As she brushed and stared at herself, something about her looked different. There was a glow to her that she'd never seen in herself before. She couldn't explain it, but she looked as happy as she had ever looked — a perfect happy.

When her head hit the pillow, she felt the bed shift to accommodate her body with extra cushion and it was only a few minutes before she was sound asleep.

CHAPTER ELEVEN
Snowball Fight

Hannah awoke to see heavy snow falling past the bay window. It took a moment to realize that she wasn't dreaming. She lay in bed, watching the snow fall and elves pass by below on the cobblestone streets, busily going in every direction. She was forced out of bed when she heard loud knocking at her door.

Hannah climbed out from under the warm covers and stretched up to the ceiling before walking over to open the door. Noemi and Natalya greeted her, dressed in heavy coats, stocking caps, and gloves.

"Come on!" Natalya said, slapping her gloved hands together. "It's time to go."

Hannah stared.

"It's time for the snowball fight."

"Snowball fight?" Hannah asked, her eyes widening.

"Hurry up. Just about everyone's already down at the field, waiting," Noemi added, gesturing for Hannah to get a move on.

"What do you mean?"

Natalya smiled. "Every year we have the annual snowfall fight. It's time. Now we expect you out in the hall in two minutes, dressed and ready. The snowfield is

154 | North Pole Santa Patrol

barely regulated so you'll need to dress warm."

Noemi playfully pushed Hannah backward and shut the door. "Shouldn't have let her sleep in."

"She had a busy day yesterday. Much busier than Marcel," Natalya said, a mischievous smile rising on her cheeks.

"What do you mean?"

"She spent the evening with Gallest."

"Gallest?" Noemi looked stunned. "The elf that works at the Window?"

"Yeah. I didn't get a chance to talk with her about it, but she was bouncin' off the walls last night."

Noemi smiled. "Romance is in the air."

"Little early for that. This is only her second full day in the NP."

"Yeah . . . poor Marcel. He seems a little bit overwhelmed."

Natalya agreed. "But he seems to be enjoying it."

"Oh, he's loving it, but still . . ."

"What about you? You seem to be happier this year. Are you still not going to tell me why you stood me up last night? I waited in the foyer for like three hours."

Noemi grinned. "I told you," she said sheepishly. "I can't. It's a surprise."

"For some reason, I don't believe you," Natalya retorted.

The door swung open and Hannah was dressed in snowball fight essentials. "I still don't know what we're doing," she said.

She followed Noemi and Natalya down the hallway and into the foyer where Willis opened the glass door for them. "I see it's time for the snowball fight."

"Aren't you coming?" Natalya asked as she walked

through.

"Of course. Wouldn't miss it. I'll be there shortly."

"See you there," Noemi said as the three shuffled onto the streets packed with elves, all seemingly going the same direction and to the same destination.

"It's crowded today," Hannah observed.

"It's the snowball fight. Mass elves come to this. The NP shuts down for an hour and we go at it."

Hannah looked at Natalya slightly apprehensively. "We go *at* . . . what?"

"Good luck today, Hannah," said an older elf, walking next to her.

"Thanks," Hannah replied, somewhat bewildered.

"Here are the teams," Natalya launched in. "It's you, me, Noemi, and Abom versus . . ."

Hannah cut her off. "Who? Who's Abom?"

Natalya looked at Noemi then back at Hannah. "Erik and William didn't tell you?"

"No."

"Abom . . . Abom Nibble."

Hannah stared, lost.

Noemi laughed. "She doesn't get it yet."

"Say the name real fast," Natalya suggested.

"Abomnibble . . ." said Hannah.

"Say it again."

"Abomnibble . . .oh . . . *Abominable* . . ."

"Abominable Snowman," said Natalya.

"The Abominable Snowman?" asked Hannah in wonder.

"That's technically not his name but it's been that way for ages. His real name is Abom Nibble. Back in the Dark Ages, his name was leaked by one of the Members and the legend was born of the now infamous,

Abominable Snowman — that he was supposably this terrible creature that did horrific things. All nonsense. He's the most lovable guy," Natalya said as they walked slowly through the jammed streets while snow fell heavily around them, illuminated golden from the lighted fog hovering above the tall mountaintops. "Abom lives in the forest that surrounds the NP."

Hannah shook her head in confusion. "Does he have claws and . . ."

"No, no. But he is huge. He's like eight feet tall. He looks like a giant polar bear pretty much except that he can talk," Noemi answered.

"And he's on our team?"

"Yeah."

"Who's on the other team?" Hannah wondered.

"The guys . . . Marcel, William, and Erik," said Noemi.

"Don't forget to tell her about Frosty," Natalya added.

"Frosty? The snowman?" Hannah asked incredulously.

"Right. He plays each year just like Abom. He's tough," Noemi said, like all of this was common knowledge.

"Only in the NP," Hannah whispered. She could tell today was going to be a host of surprises, just like yesterday. She was about to go into a snowball fight with the Abominable Snowman and Frosty.

What was next?

———————————————

Junior Claus awoke slowly. Everything around him was a fog of white and blur. His head, especially the right side of his cheek, beat with the tempo of his heart. He was face-up on a double bed. A lamp adjacent to him glowed softly white. When things finally cleared, Junior sat up and surveyed the room. It was elegantly decorated. The furniture and cabinetry was exquisitely crafted.

"Like the room?" came the deep voice from the corner.

Sitting in a leather recliner was a man dressed in black pants and a turtleneck in the same color. His black hair was slicked back and he had unusually blue eyes. Junior had never seen this man before.

"Let me be the first to make the introduction. My name is Unbelief."

Junior blinked, trying to process what had happened. He was on the training run and then he was attacked, and this must be the attacker! Judging by the sunlight beaming through the window, it was morning. But how long had he been unconscious? He tried to move his arm but felt the cold pressure of handcuffs. His right arm to the base of the bed.

"Sorry about that," Unbelief said with a wry smile. "Can't have you leaving, though."

"Your name really isn't Unbelief. It's just what you're calling yourself."

"There's no reason for me to give you my real name. I find that Unbelief suits me better."

"If you think I'm going to cooperate with you . . ." Junior started.

"Oh, you will. If you don't, the people you care about most are going to disappear. You're going to sit tight until we get what we want."

"And that is?"

"The NPSP."

Junior frowned.

"Then your father."

Junior gritted his teeth angrily.

"And then Christmas."

"You'll never get them," said Junior with conviction.

"You have reason to say that," the man said, shifting in his chair slightly. "For centuries, people have tried — come close a couple of times — but this time, it's different. I've spent considerable time and resources making this plan come to life. And it *will* come to life, I assure you. Christmas, as the billions of people know it, will end this year."

"Impossible!"

"Not really," Unbelief said, pushing himself up and out of the chair. "Not everyone is as loyal as you believe. That's your downfall. You and your father's. I don't believe in anything. I simply know or don't know, and I know that there is nothing you can do to stop us."

Hannah stood in amazement. She was in a field of freshly packed snow up to her ankles. The wind gently blew and she was glad she'd brought her stocking cap, gloves, and coat because it was cold. Not bitterly cold, but chilly enough for her to appreciate extra clothing.

Surrounding her were three-story-high bleachers carved out of huge snowbanks and every spot was filled with elves, bundled in extra winter attire. She had been led into the arena-like area through a tunnel of snow that looked as though it had been chiseled away by a giant drill.

Natalya stood at her side, along with Noemi. The arena was flat and open, about the length of a football field and about twice as wide. Ahead of her at the other end were her opponents in the snowball fight: William, Erik, and Marcel.

Next to them floated a huge X, hovering magically. It was silver and shimmered like fine polished metal. There were two other Xes, both of which were further away, but looked the same — silver and hovering above the ground. She had no idea what the Xes were for, and before she could ask Noemi or Natalya, the crowd of elves erupted in applause.

Swooping down with elegance was none other than Rudolph. Hannah stood agape. The magnificent animal was forty yards away and yet his red nose was beaming, even in the daytime. Sliding off him with surprising agility was Santa Claus. He raised his arms and bowed as the elves cheered.

"Good morning," he said, and like yesterday evening, his voice was amplified, though Hannah didn't know how he was doing this.

"Good morning," shouted the crowd.

"Time for the annual snowball fight. Here are the rules, as usual. The objective is to capture and hold as many of the Xes as possible. The team whose total time reaches ten minutes first, wins.

"There are three territories to control. You control them by touching an X."

Santa moved to the floating X nearest him and touched it. It instantly went a brilliant, glowing red.

"If you're on the Red Team," Santa pointed to Erik, William, and Marcel, "the X will turn red. If you're on the Green Team, Noemi, Natalya, and Hannah, it will turn green."

The X changed to a magnificent forest green.

"You can control the territory only if it is uncontested. This means that you only gain time if your opponent is not within ten feet. Once an opponent gets within ten feet of any X, the X is contested and time won't accrue until one of you is the victor.

"In order to get people, you must make snowballs and throw them at each other. When you have been hit ten times, you're frozen and cannot move for twenty seconds."

Hannah looked at Natalya with concern.

"Don't worry . . . you're not really frozen," Natalya whispered. "You just won't be able to move for a while until it releases you."

"It?" Hannah asked, but Natalya didn't answer.

"The time will be displayed over there."

Santa pointed opposite him toward the snow wall that had two large squares adjacent to each other. Inside each square were large, black numbers that read: 0:00.

"As you capture and lose and recapture the territories, the time will add automatically. Please note that in order for your snowball to count as a hit on someone, it must be at least the size of a tennis ball.

"Now, as you know, it is customary that our guest stars play as well. First, playing on the Green Team with Hannah, Noemi, and Natalya . . ."

All of Hannah's clothing suddenly went solid green, as did Noemi's and Natalya's.

A loud cheer from the crowd followed.

". . . is our own, ABOM!"

Running into the arena was a creature of legend, a creature that haunted some kids' nightmares, yet here he was bounding on two legs. His massive frame, which was well over eight-feet tall, was covered in thick, white fur. His face was a cross between a gorilla and a polar bear. His arms were the size of most men's legs, at the end of which were fingers the length of rulers. They did not, as Hannah duly noted, have claws.

Abom waved to the crowd and moved toward Hannah.

"Hannah," he grunted. "Hello."

Hannah tried to say something but all that came out was a squeak. This seemed to strike Abom as funny because he laughed, a deep belly laugh. "You look like Noemi and Natalya did when they first saw me."

All Hannah could think to do was nod her head.

Santa continued. "And playing on the Red Team . . ."

All of the boys' outfits went a deep, brick red.

" . . . the Frosty!"

Rolling out from the tunnel was a snowman, just like Hannah had made many times over, just like the traditional snowmen you see every year in books. For eyes, he had small rocks. His nose was a long carrot and for a mouth, he had small interwoven pinecones. On his head was a black top hat that sparkled with small bursts of red and green.

Marcel was amazed as the creation rolled toward him. Frosty had three perfectly circular parts: his head, midsection, and the largest section, his lower body. His lower body intrigued Marcel the most because it spun as he rolled forward, spitting out snow left and right like a wheel turning in mud. When he stopped and stood in front of Marcel, he towered over seven feet.

This Frosty didn't have sticks for arms. Rather, they were made of snow and attached to his mid-section, complete with an elbow, forearms, wrists, and very human-looking hands.

"Hello there, Marcel," he said, his voice kind and warm.

Marcel, like Hannah, seemed to have lost his ability to talk.

"Go on, say somethin', man," William said, shoving Marcel in the shoulder.

"Hi," Marcel managed.

"Are we ready?" came Santa's voice.

The crowd of elves cheered madly.

"Play!"

Marcel looked confused. He understood the game. Control the Xes but . . .

"Come on. Start making 'em!" Erik shouted, running toward the nearest X.

This whole thing was a complete surprise to Marcel. Erik and William had told him nothing at breakfast about this snowball fight, or about the Abominable Snowman or Frosty!

Marcel decided to focus and get in the game. He reached down, scooped up the snow and was about to pack it with both hands, but found there was no need. The snow seemed to pack itself into a perfect sphere and within moments, Marcel was armed. Charging toward the nearest X, following Erik, he threw it as hard as he could and the snowball connected with Abom's massive back, but it didn't faze the creature. Abom was in an intense frenzy with Erik. Marcel rolled up another ball of snow and threw it. Another hit. He rolled another and fired, but this time when it hit Abom, the creature froze, like he had been petrified. Ten hits. Twenty seconds of frozenness, and maybe twenty seconds of a controlled territory.

Marcel shot a glance at the scoreboard and watched the seconds tick away under the Red Team's score. Suddenly, a wet ball of snow hit him across the face. He'd been tagged by Noemi.

Another hit him in the back. It was Hannah.

Marcel ducked and avoided another of Noemi's blasts. He bounced back up, snowball in hand, and fired back at Noemi. The ball missed her face by inches. He took another blast in the head from Hannah. Then another from somewhere else. Had that been a snowball Erik misfired? How many times had he been hit?

The whole scene was a massive melee of snowballs being thrown in every which direction. The elves cheered as seconds accumulated for both teams. Clearly the advantage went to Frosty, who was able to move a bit faster than everyone else, due to his ability to roll in the snow and Abom, who was a snowball-making machine, with his massive hands and fingers.

Marcel was moving to a different X to help William, who was trying to fend off an attack, when he felt shots hit the back of his coat. He tried to wheel around to see who had thrown them but found himself frozen, statue-like. He couldn't move. He could breathe, but he couldn't move. It was the strangest feeling to only being able to use his eyes. Twenty seconds of this turned out to be surprisingly long.

Once freed, he immediately scooped and fired, hitting Abom once again, then connecting with Noemi in the nose, though he wasn't aiming for her face. She ducked into it.

"Get to the other X," he heard William yell from behind.

Marcel obeyed but he wasn't able to guard very long as he was pummeled by Abom and Hannah until he went rigid once again. This time, Marcel was actually glad to have a break. Running through the snow with his extra clothing was making him somewhat fatigued.

Ten minutes of total accumulated minutes was not easy to obtain. By the time the match was almost at an end, the only ones throwing with any vigor were Frosty and Abom. Everyone else was defending their territories by avoiding snowballs, hoping to acquire whatever seconds they could.

Marcel looked over at the scoreboard, his heart pounding.

RED TEAM: Nine minutes, forty seconds.

GREEN TEAM: Nine minutes, thirty seconds.

Giving it everything he had, he reached down, formed a snowball, and charged at an X again.

"Hungry, Junior?" asked Unbelief, staring out the window that overlooked six-foot palm trees in the glowing sunshine.

"I don't want anything from you," Junior answered stoutly.

"That'll change," Unbelief said smugly, not bothering to turn around to talk with Junior.

"Where am I?"

"Someplace tropical . . . actually, my island."

"Your island?"

"Yes — been in my family a long time. Nice accommodations, wouldn't you say?"

"I wouldn't know. I seem to be handcuffed."

"We can't have you sneaking around the place, Junior. I already told you that."

Junior sighed, staring at the back of Unbelief with increased disdain.

"You know, you and I are about the same age. You're almost fifty . . . I'm fifty, though I must say I look much better than you," Unbelief said egotistically.

"So what's the plan?" Junior asked in an irritated voice. "Ransom?"

Unbelief turned and faced him. "Something like that," he whispered.

"Why don't you just tell me? It's not like you plan on letting me live."

Unbelief smirked mischievously. "Now, now. I'm a man of my word."

"You're a man who is against everything I stand for. It's people like you that have made the Earth the cesspool it is."

Unbelief's nostrils flared. "No, it's you, Claus, with your conceited ways, as if you're better than everyone, you and the elves."

"What?" Now Junior's nostrils were flaring. "Where do you get that nonsense?"

"Take your Naughty List — how some kids get Gifts and others don't. Wouldn't you call that a bit judgmental, a bit egotistical to think you're the judges of millions of kids and whether or not they are deserving of gifts?

"Or what about your precious North Pole Santa

Patrol and how only a few select, elite kids from all the Earth get to experience the wonder of the NP. All kids deserve to see it and live it!"

"I agree!" Junior countered, matching Unbelief's harsh tone, "but that's not the way it works."

"Well, this is the way it's going to work in the future. There isn't going to be a North Pole to go to. There won't be a Santa Claus to believe in because everything he is, and everything he stands for is about to be destroyed forever."

"Don't underestimate elves!"

"I don't. That's why I have one on my side. If it wasn't for her, our plan couldn't have been carried forth."

"Her? Who is it?"

"If I tell you now, I'll miss the wonderful expression on your face when you see her."

Junior's head swam with ideas of escape. By the looks of it, the house or mansion he was in didn't seem to have high security. If he could just break free of his handcuffs, he could get away, but what good would that do him? He didn't know exactly where he was and had no clue where the reindeer and sleigh were being kept, let alone know if the Juveniles were still alive.

"Do you know how long I've waited for this moment?" Unbelief said boastfully. "Ever since my parents told me that I was part of a society of people dedicated to preserving the real truth . . ."

"Please!" Junior grunted. "The real truth? I am the real truth."

"No! You're an illusion, a figment of a wild imagination."

"How can you say that when I'm right in front of

you!"

"You're not a figment of my imagination. I don't believe in you. I simply know of you and how the NP works. There is the difference between me and the millions of others on Earth. I know you exist, I don't have to believe you exist."

"But it is precisely believing that . . ."

"That what?" Unbelief cut Junior off. "That makes us stronger? Makes us better? Is that what you were going to say? Rubbish! It is the truth, not believing in some mysterious Claus that will make us stronger and better!"

CHAPTER TWELVE
The Suits

Marcel, William, Frosty, and Erik stood together in the middle of the icy field victoriously, having narrowly defeated the girls by nine seconds. It had been the closest match in three years and the crowd of elves cheered the players with great enthusiasm.

The girls, along with Abom, were hardly disappointed, having spent every ounce of energy in the game. Not that the boys were any better.

"Bravo. Good game, everyone!" Santa bellowed, standing between the two teams from the middle of the field. "Of course, it is tradition that after the snowball fight . . ."

"CHAOS!" shouted the elves.

"Chaos!" echoed Santa, reaching down and pulling up a handful of snow, packing it, and jettisoning it into William's face. "Every elf and human for themselves!"

What ensued next was truly chaos as elves clambered down from the ice bleachers and took part in the action, making snowballs and launching them at anything that moved. Though tired, all the players were partaking in the fun too. Thousands of snowballs filled the air like a massive storm, some finding their targets, others not even close, yet all of it done in a good-spirited, fun way.

169 | North Pole Santa Patrol

How long the battle lasted, Erik did not know, but by the time the last snowball had been thrown, he couldn't raise his arm for anything and neither could anyone else. Santa looked like a drenched target, his cheeks red from taking blasts in the face. William's face looked just as red and Hannah had taken a shot from Marcel directly in the forehead that looked like a red golf ball was lodged above her eyes.

"Okay . . . okay . . ." said Santa, his voice still magically amplified.

Any remaining elves that had snowballs in their hands dropped them.

"It's going to take me a week to get out of these wet clothes," Santa quipped. "Is there anyone who didn't hit me?"

The crowd of elves laughed.

Santa Claus was exactly how Hannah had pictured he would be. Besides his traditional appearance and attire, he was a most kind and fun-loving man. There was not an ounce of malice or bad temperament about him.

"We've got a busy day," Santa continued, "so I'll let you get back to your responsibilities."

The crowd of elves dispersed slowly, talking with each other and the humans. Hannah noticed that Hailey had hastened to Santa and looked very upset. Santa's expression of happiness turned suddenly serious as the two talked.

William, standing next to Hannah, saw it as well. "I've never seen Hailey like that. I wonder what she's saying to Claus."

Hannah nodded. "Santa doesn't look pleased."

"What's going on?" Erik asked, walking up to

Hannah and William, followed by Marcel, Natalya, and Noemi.

"Over there. Look at Santa and Hailey. There's something wrong," said William.

"I've never seen Hailey upset like that," Erik commented. "What's that she just gave him? Looks like an old piece of paper."

"I wonder what that's about."

Hannah barely finished her sentence before a blast of red and green light encircled Santa and he disappeared.

When the king of Christmas materialized, he was standing in the middle of his living room, staring down at the note Hailey had given him moments before. Normally, the open living room, decorated in pine, was Claus's favorite, but at the moment, the warm décor meant nothing to him. He was in shock. Never before had he felt so empty and lost. He had to think. This situation was not a hoax and he couldn't think of another time when he was more frightened.

"Merry," he called quietly.

There was no response.

"Merry," he said, this time louder and with more urgency.

Merry came into the room from the kitchen, wearing an apron over her red suit that was nearly identical to Santa's. She was a portly woman with silvery long hair and round spectacles that would often slip down her nose. "What is it? I'm making a pie."

Santa looked at her in anguish. Merry's stomach

lurched immediately. She had only seen this look in her husband one other time.

"What is it?" she gasped.

Santa held up the thick piece of paper in his right hand. He did not give it to her, only held it up as if it were evidence being admitted in court. "Sit down."

"No, what is it?" Merry cried.

Claus paused and took a deep breath, trying to catch both his thoughts and some air. "Junior has been captured."

"Captured? What do you mean? By whom?" Merry took a step forward.

"Last night he went on a training run . . ."

"So?"

"He did not come back. Hailey went to check on the Juvenile reindeer and found only Tangles with this paper wrapped around his neck."

Merry was now shaking.

Claus held the paper in front of him and read it.

CLAUS: I have your son. If you wish to see him alive, you will cancel Christmas this year. The day after Christmas, you will be contacted and your son will be returned to you. Failure to do this will result in his death.

There was a terrible silence that fell, broken quickly by Mrs. Claus as she said, "Who took him?"

"It is signed, Unbelief."

"Unbelief? What is that?" Merry asked, choking up.

Claus shook his head. "I don't know. This is the first time I've heard it."

Merry was in tears. Claus went to her and held her tightly. As she sobbed, alternatives and solutions bubbled in his mind. Whoever or whatever Unbelief was, it knew about the NP. But why stop Christmas?

"What . . . will . . . you . . . do?" Merry asked between gasps.

Claus stared into the dying fire in the brick fireplace in the back of the room and did not know what he would do. He had little choice it seemed. "I'm not sure," he finally whispered.

Merry pulled back, wiping away tears. "You have to get him back. He's your successor . . . he's our son!"

Claus nodded but did not say anything more. Merry turned slowly and walked back into the kitchen. A deep, penetrating sickness hit Claus. He'd never before felt such hurt. As he turned his attention back to the paper in his hand, he was struck with an idea. He closed his eyes and concentrated. In a matter of seconds, there were four flashes of green light illuminating the room briefly. When the light died away, there were four elves standing together in the room, each with a look of genuine surprise.

The elves standing in front of Claus were ancient. Each had very little hair and what was left was gray. Each stood hunchbacked, age taking its toll on their bones. They were dressed in loose-fitting red uniforms.

"What in the name of Saint Helens are you doing?" asked Ogle, the most portly of the bunch.

"Oh my goodness," echoed Browl, the tallest of them. "I've never been summoned like this. Claus? What is going on? I was about to go for my walk."

"Yes, Claus, what are you doing?" asked Noven, touching his face just to make sure he hadn't actually died.

Clive stared incredulously, holding his cane in his right hand.

"I'm sorry," whispered Claus. "Please, sit down."

The four elderly elves looked at Claus in total bewilderment as they chose their seats. Clive and Ogle took the pine sofa. Noven and Browl took the identical-looking pine chairs. Claus sat in the rocking chair and moved it so that he was facing them. In his right hand he held the letter tightly, so tightly it prompted Ogle to ask, "What are you holding?"

"Last night, Junior went on a training run. Apparently, he has been captured by humans or a human, called Unbelief."

Claus paused, allowing what he said to be absorbed. All four elves were in complete shock.

"I know this because Hailey went to check on the reindeer this morning and found only Tangles in the Juvenile pens. Rolled up and tied around her neck was this note. It says that there can be no Christmas this year or Unbelief will kill Junior. If I obey, this Unbelief will contact me after Christmas and arrange for Junior to be brought home alive," Santa said somberly. "I summoned you here like this . . . I didn't know what to do but I need wisdom and you are the Wisdom Council."

"This is outrageous!" Noven bellowed. "We must have Christmas!"

"If we do," Santa said, now almost in tears, "they will kill my son."

"Who are these people?" asked Noven.

"Or person," said Ogle quietly, rubbing his chin. "This is the most terrible news I have ever heard in my two hundred years of life."

"Yes," agreed Browl in his low voice.

"I must think aloud . . ." continued Ogle. "If Junior was going on a training run last night, this Unbelief person must have known about it. How could he know about it unless he was told by someone . . . someone in the NP."

"What? That's preposterous!" Noven said dismissively.

"No, it's not," countered Clive. "It stands to reason that someone in the NP told Unbelief of the time."

"But who would do that? That would mean that we have deceit amongst us!" said Noven.

"I do not know," Clive said, "but I think we should assume, starting now, that there is a traitor or traitors in the NP, human or Elven. And if there is, it means that he or she has told this Unbelief everything about the NP. Why else would he ransom Junior like this? Because he knows that one year without Christmas, without you, Claus, will destroy so much belief that it would more than likely kill Christmas itself. Can you imagine if children no longer believed in you, Santa, if you didn't show up at all? The world would become an even more terrible place."

"And who's to say that they won't kill Junior anyway? We have no guarantee that they will bring him back safely," said Ogle honestly.

Santa wiped away a tear and nodded in agreement.

"What options have we?" asked Noven.

Ogle took his hand away from his chin, almost having rubbed it raw. "First, we must find out who is giving this information to Unbelief. Second, we must find out who Unbelief is. Third, I think we should assume that they will destroy Junior no matter what and therefore, we should not trust their word. We are going to have to get him back ourselves."

"How?" asked Clive. "Where would we start?"

"I am the oldest here," Ogle said quietly. "I best

you by almost a hundred years, Browl, and you are the second oldest."

Browl nodded.

"My great, great grandfather would sometimes tell stories to me when I was small. Just before he died, he told me one about our ancestors and the North Pole Santa Patrol. He told me that many years ago the elves created the North Pole Santa Patrol in case of a catastrophe. Now, the NPSP, as we know it today, is about the humans being here to propagate belief. But in its inception, the NPSP were humans granted empowerment, along with the duty of propagating belief."

"Empowerment? What do you mean?" Clive asked.

"The humans were given special suits to be used in a time of crisis. The elves did not bestow the powers on the individual humans themselves. They bestowed them on the suits."

"Suits? What are you talking about? I've never heard of these suits," grunted Browl.

"They have been stored away in the bottom chamber of the Gift Manufacturing Plant." Ogle paused, his eyes dancing side to side in thought. "If these suits indeed grant the humans powers, then we need to find them. I propose we send the humans to find this Unbelief and to bring back Junior," said Browl.

"That's your plan?" asked Noven. "It assumes that we can find the suits in the first place."

"My grandfather said the suits are located in the bottom chamber of the Gift Manufacturing Plant. We must start there," said Ogle.

"And you think that if we find these suits, the humans will be able to stop Unbelief?" Clive said, running his hand over his almost-bald head.

"But we need humans to propagate belief here in the NP. Without them, Christmas is doomed," reminded Noven.

"So we leave one of them here to propagate the belief, and we send the other five," said Ogle.

"But does one human have enough belief for all the children on the planet? I would doubt that," Noven said.

"Tell me, do we have a choice?" asked Ogle.

Browl grunted. "We should at least keep two of the humans here for propagation."

"Very well. Two will stay," said Ogle.

"What concerns me here is the fact that Unbelief knew Junior was going on that training run, which means someone in the NP had to give Unbelief the information," said Clive, looking at Claus. "Who knew?"

"Many of the elves knew. It'd be impossible for me to pinpoint exactly how many of them knew and who they are," said Claus.

"As hard as this is to say, I don't believe we can trust anyone from this moment on," said Clive seriously, shaking his cane in the air.

"This assumes that one of us isn't the person who told," said Ogle.

There was an odd pause in the room as each of the elves looked at one another.

"However, in order for us to go forward with some sort of a plan, we must tell key people," added Ogle.

"Then we need to have a meeting with key personnel . . ." said Claus.

"We need to proceed with caution. If not, this could cause great panic and right before Christmas would be chaos," Ogle said.

"So what's first?" asked Noven.

"I think we find the suits first. If they do exist, then we can move forward."

"We have to do this post-haste," said Noven. "Claus, take us to the bottom of the Gift Manufacturing Plant. No one works down below the first floor anymore. There won't be anyone there."

"Yes, Claus, take us there," concurred Ogle.

Santa looked toward the kitchen and saw his wife, standing in the archway. How long she had been listening, he didn't know, but judging by the tears, it had been awhile. He desperately wanted to console her, but knew that he didn't have the time. He had to act now.

Taking a deep breath, he opened his palms and in an explosion of light, the five disappeared into nothingness, only to materialize seconds later in the bottom level of the Gift Manufacturing Plant.

All of them stood in darkness. Claus quickly remedied this with the word: "Illusias."

Immediately, the white ceiling lights came on, illuminating the area. They were standing in an empty oval room. The floor was a polished white marble. In the center of the room was a bookstand.

"I've never been down here," marveled Noven, staring at the bookstand.

"There's no reason for us to. We're standing in one of the oldest rooms in the NP," said Ogle. "It hasn't been used for centuries. I believe my great, great grandfather said that only Claus can initiate the suits."

"How?" Claus asked. "There's nothing there."

Ogle motioned them forward to the stand that suddenly glowed softly white. The stand was hand-carved wood with intricate symbols of reindeer, candy canes, and trees. Claus stared, intrigued, reminded that he'd never been in this room. His father had told him of it occasionally growing up, but he'd never ventured here.

"Put your hands on each side of the stand," said Ogle.

Claus did so. Immediately, a green mist, coming from nowhere, emerged over the front of the stand and a word materialized in fancy, green calligraphy: *DESIRE?*

Claus paused, and then said, "The suits of the North Pole Santa Patrol."

As if the floor were somehow alive, it opened, a hiss of steam rising up to their right. Within seconds, eight seven-foot tubes of glass rose upward. Inside each were identical looking suits — dark red with silver pinstripes. In the left hand pocket were the embroidered letters: NPSP. Dangling behind each suit was a silver cape. Each tube was illuminated and the light bouncing off the suits made them glisten like gold.

"Amazing," whispered Ogle, almost to himself.

Claus turned to the old elf. "Thank goodness you remembered this, Ogle."

"Don't thank me yet. There is still much work to be done."

They all moved to the tubes and admired them. Though they'd been locked away for so long, they looked clean and new.

"Can we open the tubes?" asked Browl.

"No," replied Ogle. "If I remember right, only the chosen human NPSP Members can get the suits."

"How? I don't see any doors on the tubes," observed

Noven.

"To be honest, I'm not sure."

"We need to get all the NPSP Members down here," said Santa.

"Agreed," replied Ogle.

Claus raised his arms and there was a small flash of green light. Almost immediately, green and red explosions popped up around them. The first to appear was William. Next came Marcel, followed by Erik. Hannah, Noemi, and Natalya all appeared almost simultaneously. Facing them was a somber Claus, behind him the four elder elves. Each of the NPSP Members looked confused.

Claus opened his palms and padded chairs appeared behind each of the Members, as well as himself and the elves. "Let's arrange our chairs in a circle. There is much to discuss."

The Members didn't have a clue about what was going on but they obeyed and a few moments later, everyone was seated in a circle, all eyes on the jelly-bellied Claus. His demeanor was much different than earlier during the snowball fight. He was very serious and grave now. "It is a most distressing day," he began grimly. "I was informed just a few minutes ago that my son, Junior, was abducted last night during a training run with the Juvenile reindeer."

The more experienced NPSP Members looked thunderstruck, while Hannah and Marcel looked even more bewildered. Claus paused, and it gave time for William to ask his question. "By abducted, you mean kidnapped?"

"Yes," replied Claus. "By someone or some organization calling themselves Unbelief."

"Oh my . . ." said Natalya with shock.

"This Unbelief is demanding that we shut down Christmas this year and in return, he will release Junior to us unharmed the day after Christmas."

"What?" William blurted. "You can't shut down Christmas! That would be catastrophic. People depend on the Gifts they are given, even though most of them don't know they are given them."

"I know that," Claus said. "That's why I called the Council. I'd like to introduce them."

Claus made the introductions brief. When he finished, Marcel asked, "Were these the same elves that chose me?"

Claus nodded.

Marcel looked at each of the old Elven men and nodded in gratitude.

Santa continued his briefing. "Thanks to Ogle, we have a possible solution. The North Pole Santa Patrol now propagates belief for the millions of kids on Earth. However, centuries ago, during a Christmas catastrophe, the elves created magical suits endowed with special powers. Those suits are what are inside the tubes you see.

"It is our proposal that four of you go to Earth and try and find Unbelief and rescue Junior. Two of you will stay behind to continue propagation."

"Just two?" asked William.

"I believe two will be sufficient, though it will tax your mental strength and your own belief. I know that each of you believe strongly in Christmas and the NP, but whichever two stay behind must understand that it will be difficult," Claus said.

"How could this have happened?" asked William.

"Training runs are usually done in rural areas where there aren't very many people."

"We believe that someone from the NP provided Unbelief with information about the run."

"Who could that be?"

"We haven't narrowed down all the possibilities yet," said Santa.

"So that means there's a spy," said Erik, rubbing his cheek.

"It would appear there is, and I don't think we should assume it's just one person. It could be more," Santa added. "I do not believe it is any of the NPSP. We've watched you and we would've seen malice. It has to be an elf."

"But you don't have unhappy elves in the NP," said Natalya matter-of-factly. "This is the happiest place in the universe. And how could an elf capture Junior? Elves can't go to Earth."

"Apparently, someone isn't happy," Claus said. "We do not want you to tell anyone about this. I will tell Hailey not to tell anyone as well."

"What if we don't find Junior?" asked Noemi worriedly.

"We can't dwell on that. We must believe we will find him and that Christmas will continue," said Santa strongly.

"Where do we begin? Where do we start looking?" wondered Natalya. "And who is going to stay here in the NP?"

"I will," said Marcel quickly. "I believe! I know I can propagate belief!"

Claus nodded.

"I will, too," said Noemi. "I know Marcel and I can

do it."

Noemi looked at Marcel and smiled warmly. Marcel returned it with a grin.

"William, Erik, Natalya, and Hannah . . . you will have to find Unbelief and bring back my son," commanded Claus. "More than likely, he's on Earth but there is a chance he's in the NP, which means you'll need to do this quietly. I have a feeling, though, that by doing so, you will be in great danger."

"I'm ready," said William.

"Me too," echoed Erik.

Hannah and Natalya chimed in. "Ready!"

Hope was filling Claus and fueling ideas. Not only was he going to use the Members, he was going to call in favors from a few friends. "I believe that if Unbelief was able to capture my son, he has considerable resources. I think we should assume that there are many people involved and if that's the case, we're going to need all the help we can get. We'll start with the suits."

Browl turned to Ogle and whispered, "What's he up to? He's thinking about something besides the suits, isn't he?"

"I don't know . . ." whispered Ogle back.

Claus stood up and everyone else did the same, turning their attention to the glass tubes. "Ogle . . . what do they need to do?"

The elder elf shrugged. "I'm not sure. Perhaps stand in front of a tube . . ."

The Members chose a tube and stood before it, inches away. A silence followed as everyone wondered what was to happen. Just about the time the old elf was about to suggest something different, all eight suits vaporized into a red mist and shot out of the tops of the tubes.

The red vapors hovered and then whisked down around the Members like miniature comets, flying past their heads, going back and forth from Member to Member. Hannah wasn't frightened as she watched the blurs of vapor twirl around her. She was intrigued, as was everyone else.

This twirling movement lasted nearly a minute before the first suit went into William. He gasped as the red mist pierced his chest and disappeared. The other vapors were soon to follow, and that's when Erik realized that the suits were choosing their hosts. Natalya was chosen next as the vapor went inside her and disappeared. Erik followed, then Noemi and Marcel, and finally Hannah. The two remaining suits floated back in their respective tubes and materialized as suits again.

Before anyone could say anything, red, pinstriped suits materialized over each NPSP Member, magically displacing their current attire completely. Within seconds, the six Members wore identical suits and capes as well as a thick three-inch belt that had clasped pouches attached on each side of the bronze buckle.

"The suits," said Ogle, "have chosen each of you."

The Members were in awe, staring down at their uniforms that fit snugly and were the most comfortable attire any of them had ever worn. Even the black, shiny boots felt light and soft.

"I don't feel any different," said Natalya, feeling the elastic material that covered every inch of her body besides her head.

"Neither do I," echoed Noemi.

"What happened to my other clothes?" asked Marcel.

"Yeah. It doesn't feel like I have on any clothes

underneath this," said Hannah, looking at Ogle.

"I'm not sure," the old elf said slowly. "I don't remember my grandfather saying much about the suits themselves."

"The suits are supposed to give us special powers?" asked William.

"I believe so," replied Ogle.

"So how are we to find Unbelief?" asked Natalya, still admiring her suit.

"The first thing we need to do is go to the stables and have Hailey talk to Tangles and have her tell us everything she can about where Junior was taken," said Santa.

"But why can't you go with them to find Unbelief?" Marcel asked to Claus. "You could use your special powers."

"I cannot, Marcel. My special abilities only exist here in the NP, and I only have special abilities during Christmas Eve. I would be useless in helping you."

"So, what's the next step?" asked William.

Claus turned to the Council. "Thank you," he said benevolently.

"Don't thank us yet," said Ogle quietly. "This is certainly not going to be easy for any of us, especially you, Claus."

"But you've given us hope," said Claus, his eyes fixed on Ogle's thin and wrinkled face. "Hope is a powerful thing, almost as powerful as belief."

CHAPTER THIRTEEN
Assignments

Everyone on the NPSP was in both a state of confusion and excitement. Confusion, because everything was happening so fast and excitement, because of their newfound suits and the possibility of special powers.

When the Members materialized, along with Santa and the Council, they were standing inside the magnificent reindeer stables. To their left and right were paddocks, large enough to accommodate a member of the Nifty Nine easily, although none of the reindeer were present.

Hannah was about to ask where the reindeer were, but before she could, the head stable elf, Hailey, appeared, trailed by her assistant Mayra.

"Where are the Nifty?" asked Santa.

"They're out in the fields," answered Hailey, as she and Mayra approached the group. "Tangles is with them as well."

"Tell us exactly what happened," said Browl, his eyes focused on Hailey.

"It was actually Mayra who found Tangles and the note first. Go ahead, Mayra. Tell them."

186 | North Pole Santa Patrol

Mayra nervously brushed at her long, blond hair with her right hand. "I was here tending to the Nifty in the morning when Tangles came in looking tired and very frightened. It took me a few moments to calm him down. When he finally did, I noticed something around his neck, like a tube. I opened it and found the letter. I immediately went to get Hailey."

"What did you find out from Tangles?" Ogle asked, his question directed to Hailey.

William leaned in to Hannah and whispered, "Hailey is the only elf that can understand the reindeer. She can understand their language. Mayra's in training to take over when Hailey retires."

Hannah nodded.

"There was a large crashing sound and Tangles was hit with something and lost consciousness. When he awoke, he was in a paddock, but there were no signs of the other reindeer, and he had something tied around his neck. This is where things get weird . . ." Hailey paused. "Tangles said there was a man, an armored man that released the paddock gate."

"What do you mean, an armored man?" asked Erik.

"I don't know. Tangles couldn't tell me more."

"Then what was it?" Erik probed.

"I don't honestly know."

"What about the area where Tangles was held. What did it look like?" asked Ogle seriously, hoping to find a clue of some kind.

"Tangles said someplace warm with coconut trees," answered Hailey.

"Someplace tropical," deduced William.

"Sounds like it," said Hailey. "It's on Earth."

"Did Tangles give you anything more?" asked Claus.

187 | North Pole Santa Patrol

"No, sir. He came right back here."

There was a long silence as everyone pondered what Hailey had said.

"None of you are to say anything to anyone," ordered Claus. "I don't want a panic on our hands. Understood?"

Mayra and Hailey nodded.

"I need some time to sort things out. Ogle, I don't believe I will need the Council any longer, but if I do, I know where to find you."

The old elf nodded. "Whatever is needed from us, you have it."

The other three elves nodded in agreement.

"Everything is going to work out," Clive said, raising his cane and pointing it at Claus. "I know it is because I believe it is."

Claus smiled. "I will transport you all back."

"You might as well transport us all to the University library. We old men need to talk together. There may be some other piece of information we have overlooked," said Ogle.

"Very well," Claus said, and in a flash of green light, the Council disappeared.

Claus faced the Members. "I don't want you to go anywhere else today but your quarters. You can all be together if you like, but I don't want you leaving the building until I've talked with you again."

They all nodded. Claus said nothing more to them before magically transporting them away, leaving only Mayra and Hailey.

Claus sighed. "Thank you both for keeping this quiet and for getting to me immediately."

"You're welcome," said Hailey.

"Yes, sir. You're welcome," Mayra said warmly.

"Continue with your duties just as you normally would."

"Okay," Hailey and Mayra said together just as Claus disappeared behind an explosion of green.

Mayra turned to Hailey. "What were those new uniforms the Members were wearing?"

"I don't know," answered Hailey, intrigued. "They had the NPSP logo but I've never seen them before."

"What's going to happen now?" Mayra asked in a worried voice.

"Believe me, I'm not worried," said Unbelief in his low voice before taking another bite of papaya. "I have everything in place."

Dewey sat across the patio table and said, "But do you think they'll go for your demands?"

Unbelief smiled, looking out from the deck to see the large swimming pool and hot tub. Beyond them was a fifteen-foot brick wall that encased the entire estate, which was set in the heart of the lush vegetation and palm tree forest of the island.

"I know the elves' mentality. I can just hear the Council and their desire for Christmas to carry on. I have no doubt that they will not accept this offer. In fact, I'm counting on it. They'll do everything in their power to come and save Junior."

"But Santa's power . . ." Dewey said.

"Santa's power only works on Christmas Eve. He's

useless any other day. As I've told you before, they
will have no choice but to send the NPSP in their suits,
which is an added bonus. With the defenses we have,
they don't have a chance."

"Yeah, but what about these suits?" Dewey said.

"I don't know," Unbelief said, rubbing his hands
together slowly. "They are only legend, and little is
known about them. It doesn't matter. I have planned
everything perfectly."

Santa Claus walked through the front door of his
cabin alone. The Council had retreated to the University
to discuss the situation further and hoped to come
up with deeper insight. The Members were gathered
together in the Guest Quarters trying to sort out all
that had happened. Before he had time to shut the front
door, there was a flash of red light and his daughter,
Alisha, stood before him, a look of great concern on her
face. Merry walked into the living room and stared at
them nervously.

"Is it true?" Alisha blurted out. "Mom sent me a
note and . . ."

Claus took his time shutting the door and slowly
nodded his head as he walked toward the brightly
burning fireplace in. The warmth felt good to him and
he watched the flames in a sort of trance.

"NO!" said Alisha. "He couldn't have been caught."

"He was," whispered Claus painfully.

"But, Dad, how . . ."

"I'm not sure. I do know for a fact that someone

here in the NP, or some people, tipped off whoever got him because it sounds like they were ready for Junior and knew where he was going to be."

Alisha looked at her mother, who wiped tears from her puffed up, red eyes.

"What are you going to do?" Alisha asked, directing her question back to her father, who continued staring into the fire.

"I'm going to send the Patrol to get your brother."

"The Patrol? Are they ready for that? Isn't it dangerous?" Alisha asked.

Claus turned and looked at her. "Yes, it's dangerous. Do you think I want to send them in there? We have no choice. The people or person who has Junior say that if I continue Christmas, they'll kill him. If I don't go through with Christmas, I'll have Junior back the next day."

Mrs. Claus blew her nose in a wet, white handkerchief.

"It sounds like these people are powerful. If they brought down the sleigh and the reindeer . . ." Alisha said, her voice full of tension.

"They call themselves Unbelief. But to be able to stop the sleigh and the reindeer, they would have to have inside knowledge, which is why I believe one of them was once a Member."

Alisha stood, thunderstruck. Merry did the same.

"It makes sense," Claus continued. "To take Junior's sleigh down, you'd have to have intimate knowledge about it, the kind of knowledge that a Member would have."

"But the Members are the best kids in the world. They wouldn't . . ." said Alisha.

"Over time, a previous Member could lose their belief, which is probably what happened."

"So your plan to save my brother is to send a bunch of human kids?" protested Alisha.

"We have no choice."

"You could send me. I'm able to go to Earth," Alisha suggested.

"But your special abilities would not exist outside the NP. You'd be a normal woman, and what protection would you have? None. No, your place is here continuing to do what you're doing. If the other elves find out about any of this, there will be chaos and panic. That's something we do not need right now. Keep this to yourself, Alisha."

Alisha nodded sheepishly.

"Merry, I'm afraid we have very long days ahead of us. Could you fix me a cup of hot tea? I need to be alone to think about a plan . . ."

Merry looked abashed, yet at the same time understood why her husband needed to be by himself. Alisha, however, looked sullen. She obviously didn't like whatever idea her father had in mind because it involved the NPSP and not her.

"Go on, Alisha," said Claus kindly. "Go back to doing your job. Show no emotion about this."

"Show no emotion?" scathed Alisha. "How am I supposed to do that? My brother has been kidnapped!"

"You do it for the greater good, Alisha," Claus said resolutely. "No matter what, Christmas must go on."

"Even if it means . . ." Alisha said in a whisper.

"Even if it means Junior's life," said Claus with painful finality.

Merry broke into tears.

Alisha looked mortified. "Father, you can't!" she said.

Claus stared down at his boots sorrowfully. "I don't have a choice, Alisha."

William's quarters were larger than any of the other Members'. How he'd gotten the biggest room, he didn't know, but he was thankful because the entire NPSP were there, sitting on his bed or in the comfortable chairs scattered around the room. Only Erik stood, staring out the window that overlooked the cobblestone streets below where elves were busy going about their day.

"I still don't see what's so special about these suits," said Marcel, looking at his chest as though he expected something to come blazing out of it.

"They feel comfortable," said Hannah.

"If Claus told us they have special powers, then they do. I trust we'll learn about those powers when we need to. Right now, I'm more concerned with what the plan is. None of the elves can leave the NP except for Santa and his immediate family, which means we're going to have to be the ones that get Junior," said Erik somberly, still staring out the window as he spoke.

"Is there any other choice?" asked Noemi, sitting in a chair nearest to Erik.

"I don't think so," said William.

There was a knock on the door. Everyone stared intently as William got up from his chair and opened it. He was surprised to find Holly standing there, a look of pure joy etched on her face. She immediately noticed the Members behind William and her smile drained a little. Clearly, she had hoped to find William alone.

"Hi, sweetie. I was hoping . . ." her voice broke off, and she stared at William with sudden concern. He looked grave. "What is it?"

William sighed deeply and motioned her in. He didn't know what to do. Claus had been very specific not to tell anyone, yet here was his fiancé. Holly said "hi" pleasantly to everyone, but the looks from the others were telling her something was definitely wrong.

"What's going on?" she asked.

William shut the door and motioned for her to take an open chair, but she refused. She wanted an answer.

"I can't tell you . . ." William finally said, looking at the others as if they were somehow going to support him.

"What do you mean? It's obvious something's wrong. Just tell me."

He shook his head silently.

"Is it about the wedding? Is it about me?" Holly's voice was now breaking into a higher octave. "What is it?"

"Holly . . . I can't tell you," William whispered.

"It's about the wedding, isn't it?" she shot at him agitatedly.

"No," William replied.

"Then what is it?" Holly demanded, her hands now on her hips.

"Claus told us we couldn't tell anyone," chimed in Erik. "I promise you, Holly, it doesn't have anything to do with you or the wedding."

This seemed to calm Holly a bit. "But there is something wrong, isn't there?"

William nodded slowly. "You can't tell anyone that

something is wrong, okay Holly? We don't want people asking questions."

"That doesn't make sense, William. We don't hide things from each other in the NP."

"But this has to be hidden. Listen, you have to trust me on this," William pleaded.

"Well," Holly said plainly, "you'd all best not go out anywhere because you look depressed."

There was silence as Holly looked around at each of them intently. "When will you be able to come over?"

William gritted his teeth. "I don't know. We're waiting for Claus."

Holly looked worried. As much as she wanted to know what was going on, she respected William's need to keep it secret, though she herself had never kept a secret in her life.

"I hope to see you soon," she said to William before turning and leaving the room.

"She's right, you know," said Erik after Holly had shut the door. "We go out looking like this and elves see us, they'll be asking what's wrong, just like she did."

Claus had stayed up through the night but finally felt that his solution was somewhat plausible, although risky. But there was no way of avoiding risk. Taking most of the NPSP and sending them on a mission outside the NP and putting them in danger was serious. Equally as serious was the fact that only two Members were going to be left to propagate belief, which was unheard of. He wasn't even sure two humans could support the belief of millions of children, but he had no choice and he knew it.

Merry had given him his peace, retreating to the study after fixing his tea. From his rocking chair, Claus stared out the rectangular window of the cabin that overlooked the snow-covered front yard. He watched large flakes waft down and add to the white mass of the early morning.

Snow was the ultimate team player, he thought. A single snowflake was nothing, but with billions of them there was incredible beauty and peace.

He closed his eyes and concentrated on the Members. In a burst of red and green light, the six-person Patrol stood in his living room once again.

"Good morning, everyone." he said. "Give me a second."

There was another flash of light and Hailey was standing in the room with them.

"Hello, Hailey. Sorry to take you away from your day, but you need to be here as well. Please, all of you take a seat."

The Patrol Members found their seats quickly, all of them quiet and anxious to hear what Santa had to say. Claus paused and rubbed his hands on his protruding belly, as though for luck. "I feel very guilty about what I'm about to ask you to do. There is no doubt going to be danger involved and I cannot be there or use my powers to help you."

He sighed deeply.

"In order to get my son back, I believe you're going to need help, and even though you are wearing those suits, I can't guarantee that they will be able to help you in every way needed. I believe that Unbelief has many resources and that they're going to do everything in their power to hold on to Junior.

"I've made my final decision. Both Noemi and Marcel will stay to propagate."

Claus looked at William. "William, you're going to go to the Land of Love and solicit the help of Cupid."

William felt like someone had just punched him in the stomach. Did Claus just say the Land of Love and Cupid?

"Cupid? *The Cupid*?" said William incredulously.

"Yes," Santa answered.

"Excuse me, sir, but how is Cupid going to help us?" asked Erik.

"Cupid, and the other Archers, will help by spreading love, and believe me, you're going to need as much love as you can muster."

"But how am I going to . . . where is Cupid's . . ."

"Cupid and the Land of Love are far from here, but not to worry. The reindeer, Cupid, will take you there."

"Am I going alone?"

"Yes. You'll be the only one allowed in," said Claus.

"Why?" asked William.

"Because of your love for Holly. I would be willing to make a wager that your love earns you access into the Land of Love."

"So Cupid the reindeer knows . . ."

"He's actually the only one that knows where Cupid lives. It's a long story I don't have time to tell you. For now, you'll have to trust me when I say that our own Cupid will be able to get you there."

"But . . ."

"Patience," said Santa. It was obvious William wanted

more details, but Santa was ready to move on.

"Erik, you're going to go to the Tooth Fairy. I have a feeling she's going to be able to help you immensely."

Erik opened his mouth to say something, but Santa continued before he could speak. "The Tooth Fairy is very, shall we say, cautious about having humans see her. In fact, only a few humans have ever seen her. It will no doubt be a challenge getting you in."

"The To . . . Tooth Fairy?" Erik stammered.

"Yes, the Tooth Fairy," answered Claus. "Donder will be able to take you there. He's the only one that the Fairy trusts."

"But . . ."

Again, Santa said, "Patience."

Just like William, Erik wanted to discuss the situation a bit more than Santa was offering.

"Natalya," said Claus, moving his gaze to the long-haired dirty blonde. "You will be going to see the Sandman."

Natalya stared, puzzled. "Sandman? The guy in charge of sleep?"

"Yes. He travels aboard a mighty ship. Finding it should not be a problem for Dancer. He's the old man's favorite."

"How is the Sandman going to help us, Claus?"

"I'm not taking any chances. All of these people owe me one way or another, and I don't think they'll mind if I call on them to repay a few debts."

Claus turned to Hannah. "For you, Hannah, you're off to see the Easter Bunny."

Hannah sat, dumbfounded. Did Santa just say the Easter Bunny?

"Dasher will be taking you."

Hannah's mind was blank. All she could think to do was to nod in agreement.

"But Santa," pleaded Natalya, "if the Easter Bunny and the others are going to help us, don't we need to know where this Unbelief is? And how exactly will the Sandman be able to help?"

"I do not know how Sandman will help you. I'm counting on him to offer you some good suggestions. As far as exactly where to look for Unbelief, well, that's different.

"I could think of only one other solution. And it involves you, Noemi."

Everyone's eyes shot to her. What did Noemi have that Claus wanted?

Noemi swallowed hard. "It comes from me?"

"What is your brother's name?" asked Santa.

Noemi looked confused. Why did Claus want the name of her brother? She answered him quietly. "Jayden."

"And wasn't it almost a year ago that Jayden was miraculously saved . . . cured?"

Noemi nodded, clearly astonished that Claus knew this.

"Tell everyone what happened that day."

Noemi wasn't sure where this conversation was going. She'd never talked about what happened to her little brother after that day in the hospital yet Claus seemed to know all about it. She took in a deep breath.

"About a year ago, my little brother almost died from cancer. He was in the hospital and they had told us that he probably wouldn't live through the night."

Noemi paused. She found that suddenly talking about it made her relive the horrible feelings that

199 | North Pole Santa Patrol

accompanied the situation.

"Go on," Claus encouraged.

"It was the late afternoon and I'd gone down to get something to eat for my parents. They were still up with Jayden in the hospital room. I wasn't actually there when it all happened, but my parents told me."

"Keep going," said Santa.

"My parents told me people came into the room, some of them dressed in strange uniforms, some of them not. One of them, an old man, put his hands on Jay and . . . took away the cancer. When I got back to the room, the whole place was crazy. Jay looked normal. His skin looked healthy, and his body was whole again. The doctors were all trying to calm him down, trying to figure out what was happening. It was amazing, a miracle."

"And the old man and the people that had come into the room . . . what happened to them?" asked Claus.

"That's the strange thing because on that day that old man supposedly healed almost every child in the hospital, but then he disappeared. No one ever saw him again."

Claus nodded, gently rubbing his belly, satisfied with Noemi's account.

"How does that help us?" Noemi asked.

"Because one of those people can help us locate Unbelief."

"The girl," whispered Noemi to herself. "That's right. The girl."

"What girl?" asked William, completely lost.

"One of the people that visited my brother that day was a girl. Her name was . . .was . . ."

"Samantha," Claus finished.

"That's right. It was Samantha. Jayden said that she had this incredible power — that she knew things most people didn't — that she was like the most knowledgeable person on earth."

"What?" said Erik.

"It's crazy, I know, but if I told you everything that happened to my brother before this . . . you'll just have to believe me. Jayden said that this Samantha knew things."

Noemi looked at Claus hopefully. "You think Samantha might know where Unbelief is?"

Claus smiled. "It's worth a shot. I'm sending you with Rudolph. He'll be able to guide you to her."

"But how did you know about her?" asked Noemi, looking dazed. "I never told anyone."

"Noemi, I'm Santa Claus. It's my job to know things."

"You want me to go today?" Noemi asked.

Claus turned and looked at Hailey. "I assume Rudolph can be ready for flight?"

"Not a problem," Hailey said.

"Very good. Noemi, I want you to go with Hailey now."

He withdrew what looked like a doggie biscuit from his right coat pocket. He brought it up to his mouth and whispered something to it, then held it out. Everyone looked perplexed as to why Santa had just done this, all except for Hailey, who took the thing quickly and stuffed it into her front pants pocket.

"When you get back to the NP, we'll be here. You'll find Samantha at her home. She's on winter vacation now, and she is very glad to be with her family. She's had a most interesting and somewhat difficult year. She will help you if she can."

"How do you know this?" asked Noemi.

"I used my Window," Santa said with a smile, and in a flash of light, the two girls disappeared.

CHAPTER FOURTEEN
Samantha

Hailey was moving fast and Noemi was at her heels. When they approached the largest paddock in the stable, Noemi's heart raced. She'd seen Rudolph up close only once and the magic and beauty that emanated from him was breathtaking.

"Come on, Rudy. Claus has an important job," Hailey said, swinging the door of the paddock open.

Rudolph, the red-nosed reindeer, had a very shiny nose, and it glistened with an intense red hue, even when he wasn't using it. He was the largest of the Nifty Nine, almost eight-and-a-half feet tall. His elegance and regality were staggering. His fur was perfectly combed. His eyes were large and brown and looked down at Noemi with love and compassion.

"Noemi's going to need to ride you today."

Rudolph bobbed his head understandingly.

"Claus is sending you on an important mission. I want you to be extra careful. There are people who are out to get you. Yes, you," Hailey emphasized. "Some things have happened and I believe you are in danger when you fly. Be aware."

Rudolph's eyes narrowed, and again, he nodded.

"Claus wanted me to give you this," she said, taking

out the biscuit and giving it to him. The reindeer ate it quickly.

Hailey waited a moment and then said, "Do you understand?"

Rudolph nodded.

"Excellent! Noemi, go ahead and mount up."

Noemi looked at Hailey. "What was that . . . that thing Santa gave you and what you gave Rudolph?"

"Information," Hailey said. "Hurry and mount."

Noemi reached up and grabbed Rudolph's thick horns and pulled up, swinging her leg over his back. Once she was comfortable, Hailey led them out behind the paddock and into the fenced field that was coated with a glistening carpet of snow.

"Good luck," she said, and with that, Rudolph exploded into the air. He was much more powerful than Donder, who had been the one to pick Noemi up this year on her journey to the NP.

Noemi watched as the lights of the NP sped away and within seconds, Rudolph was inside the Tunnel of Belief. The white light encompassed her, and she closed her eyes and held on tight to Rudolph's rack. When she felt the light dissipate, she opened her eyes and saw nothing but clouds. Rudolph was in a steep descent, plowing through the white with great confidence, though Noemi felt apprehensive about not being able to see anything. Visions of colliding with an airplane filled her mind but it was obvious Rudolph had things under control.

The clouds and fog turned out to be a blessing, since it masked Rudolph's approach to Samantha's house. Noemi couldn't even make out the row of houses until they were right on top of them. Rudolph knew exactly where to go and circled once around Samantha's home before landing hard on the roof. The animal immediately bent down, allowing Noemi an easier time of getting off.

"You sure this is it?" Noemi questioned the animal, whose nose twinkled red.

Rudolph nodded, snorting twice as though she should not question him.

"Great. How am I supposed to get down to the house?"

Rudolph's nose glowed a bright red and before she knew exactly what was happening, she was lifted off the roof and gently lowered to the driveway. At this point, Noemi wondered if anyone had seen her and how she was going to explain what had just happened, or the reindeer on the roof.

She gathered herself and then realized the obvious. She hadn't changed her clothes. Still adorned in the new NPSP suit, how was she going to explain it? She looked more like a costumed character belonging in Halloween rather than Christmas.

She made her way up the cement walk and knocked on the door. Her heart was pounding. What exactly was she going to say to Samantha? Would the girl believe her story?

Noemi was about to knock again when the door opened. She was immediately relieved to see it was a girl. She had long, dark-brown hair, almost the same color as her eyes. Noemi was hopeful this was Samantha. It would make things much easier.

"Hi, um . . . Samantha?"

Samantha looked inquisitively at Noemi for a moment. "Yes?"

"I'm Noemi. I've been sent . . . I mean, I really need to talk . . ."

Samantha stepped closer. "You need to talk with me, don't you?" she said in a quick whisper.

Noemi nodded.

"Sam, who's at the door?" called Samantha's mother from the living room.

"It's a friend, Mom."

"Don't be too long. We have to go to the store soon," Samantha's mother said quickly, sounding as though she had her mind on other things rather than Samantha's friend at the door.

"Come in. We'll go up to my room."

Noemi stepped inside. Samantha rushed Noemi past the living room, where her mother was bent over the Christmas Tree, fumbling for something. To their right and up the stairs, the two girls went. Samantha's room was at the end of the hall, and when Noemi was inside, Samantha shut the door behind them.

She turned to Noemi and said in a whisper, "You're from the North Pole."

Noemi's mouth was agape. How could this girl have possibly known that? Maybe it was suit that gave it away.

"That's right," Noemi said.

"And you need my help."

"Yes," Noemi replied.

"With what?" asked Samantha, sitting on her bed cross-legged. Noemi stood next to her.

"What I'm going to tell you, you probably won't believe," started Noemi.

"Trust me, Noemi. You can't shock me."

"Yeah, you didn't seem shocked when you opened the door and saw me in this," Noemi said, looking down at herself and referring to the suit.

"It takes more than that to shock me these days."

"Okay," Noemi said, pressing her hands together and gathering herself up. "I'm from the North Pole and we need you to help us find Santa's son, Junior, who was kidnapped by someone or something called Unbelief. They are holding Junior for ransom and threatening to kill him if Claus goes through with Christmas. Claus wants us to find Junior and rescue him. The problem really is . . ."

"You don't know where Unbelief is," Samantha finished.

"Right," said Noemi hopefully.

Samantha seemed to know a great many things, just as Santa had indicated. She frowned and looked down at the bed, as if in deep thought. Moments passed slowly, and Noemi wondered what Samantha was doing. It was obvious she was in concentration mode . . .

"Unbelief . . . oh, yes . . ."

It seemed as though Samantha was getting information from some source, as if it was being poured into her mind.

"His real name is Fred Noggen. Have you heard of him?"

"No," said Noemi.

"He's one of the richest men on earth. He's the one behind the kidnapping."

"But why?" asked Noemi.

Samantha paused, again like she was listening to answers being put in her head. "I'm not entirely sure, but I do know where he's got Junior."

"Where?" said Noemi optimistically.

"Here, let me get a piece of paper."

Samantha went to the corner desk and pulled out a piece of white paper from the drawer. Noemi noticed a picture that for some reason looked familiar to her. It was Samantha, along with two other boys, smiling pleasantly. At the bottom of the photo, there was a caption that read: BEST FRIENDS.

"Here, take a look at this. I've written you some coordinates."

Noemi moved to the desk and looked over Samantha's shoulder as she began to draw. "Mr. Noggen likes to own things, like this island in the South Pacific. I'm writing the exact GPS coordinates here."

Noemi was mystified. How could this girl possibly know the GPS coordinates for an island owned by a rich man?

"I'm going to draw you a diagram of the island." Samantha paused, her eyes darting back and forth. "You should know that Noggen is anticipating an escape attempt."

"How do you know that?" asked Noemi in awe.

"Trust me. I just know," Samantha said assuredly. Noemi believed her.

There was a sudden knock on the door. "Samantha, are you in there?" asked her mother.

"Yeah. It's just me and Noemi," Samantha answered easily, as if her mother should know Noemi.

There was a long pause. Noemi fully anticipated seeing Samantha's mom open the door but, to her relief, didn't. Instead, she mumbled something that sounded like "okay" and moved away.

"The island is going to be tough to get on. Most of the shore is high cliffs. There is a beach on the southern side. That's probably your best bet to land in," Samantha said while completing the sketch of the island. "You'll find Noggen and Junior most likely in his mansion that's in the center of the island. I would suggest you take the reindeer and drop directly into the mansion from above, but, on second thought, that'd be crazy. Noggen has turrets on top of the roof at each corner. But if you could find a way past, you could drop in through the skylight in his bedroom."

"Skylight and turrets? How can you possibly . . ."

"You're astonished because I'm telling you, even though you're the one riding on an animal that flies," Samantha said smoothly. "No, I think your best bet is the beach. It's safest. But be warned. The whole island is being watched and guarded."

"Guarded?"

"Oh, yeah. Noggen has plenty of help with him."

"You know that for sure?" asked Noemi apprehensively.

"Yes."

"So he has guards?"

"Yes," Samantha answered. "Mostly mechanical. You'll find that Noggen is holding Junior in his Tech Room, which is down a hallway and to the right from his bedroom. Look for a tall man with greasy black hair."

"This is not going to be easy," Noemi said, coming to the sudden realization.

"Listen, I have friends. We could help you," Samantha said, looking up. "We're part of a . . . of an organization called . . ."

"I think you've done enough. Claus needs this right away," said Noemi, feeling rushed. She needed to get the map and the information back to Claus as fast as possible.

Samantha nodded, turning her attention back to the drawing for a moment, then giving it to Noemi, who folded it in quarters and put it in her hip pocket. Samantha stood up and walked over to the bedroom door, pausing before opening it. Again, Noemi's eyes went to the picture of Samantha and the two boys.

"They're my best friends," Samantha said, as if she could now read Noemi's thoughts. "Their names are Juan and George. Juan is the dark-haired one."

"I don't know why they look so familiar," said Noemi.

Samantha turned to her and smiled. "It's too bad we don't have more time. We both have some good stories, I imagine. But now we've got to get you back up to the roof so you can get back on Rudolph and head to the North Pole."

"How did you . . ."

"I have what's called the Gift of Knowledge. I know things…"

Samantha opened her bedroom door and led Noemi down the hallway quickly. "My brothers and Dad are out at the movies. It's just my mom and me," Samantha whispered. "She's in the kitchen now. We'll sneak down and go out the front door."

Noemi was breathing heavily. She didn't know why but she was even nervous now. The two girls made it to the bottom of the stairs and turned to the front door. Samantha opened it and rushed Noemi out first. She followed, shutting the door quietly behind them.

As if Rudolph knew Noemi was ready, there was a great rushing of wind, and the animal landed in the front yard, standing regally in the shimmering snow.

Samantha stared in astonishment.

Noemi didn't waste any time hoisting herself up and looking at Samantha, whose mouth was slightly open in wonder. Before she could say anything, Samantha's mother opened the front door and stopped cold, staring at the red-nosed reindeer in total awe.

Rudolph gave a snort and Samantha's mother let out a small yelp just before the animal ascended into the air with great speed and power. As Noemi ascended, she shouted, "THANK YOU!" and they disappeared into the thick, overhanging fog.

Samantha turned to her mother, who still stared into the sky, her eyes like large marbles. "Come on, Mom," she said, taking her by the elbow. "I'll try to explain this one."

"That . . . was . . . reindeer . . ."

"Rudolph, Mom. It was Rudolph."

"This is Conner, over. I've got Rudolph coming in with a . . . it looks like a Member," the elf said into a miniature walkie-talkie. He was the lone elf in the lookout tower adjacent to the landing Strip. Gliding in graciously was Rudolph with Noemi on his back.

"Copy that," the voice on the other line said. "I'll be right down."

Landing on the Strip was a lot like landing on an airplane runway, Noemi figured, since it was lit up clearly and the way Rudolph approached was a lot like a plane, touching down and slowing quickly. Noemi hadn't even dismounted before she was sucked away by a powerful green and red light. When her vision cleared, she was standing in the center of Santa's living room. The rest of the Members were all there, seated comfortably.

It took Noemi a moment to gather her thoughts. Santa waited patiently, sitting in his rocker, rubbing his protruding stomach in a circular pattern.

"You were right," Noemi sighed. "Samantha did know about Unbelief."

"That didn't take long," said William, pointing at Noemi.

"Yeah, what did you find out?" Erik asked.

"Well," Noemi said, taking out the crude map Samantha had drawn. She moved over to the circular table next to the window, and everyone in the room gathered around. "Unbelief is not a bunch of people or things. It is one person. His real name is Fred Noggen."

Santa's eyes shot up and out the window as though he had just heard something strange. Everyone picked up on it and looked at him.

"What is it?" asked Natalya.

"You said his name is Fred Noggen?" Santa asked, turning his serious gaze on Noemi.

"Yes, Fred Noggen," Noemi said the name slowly.

"Do you know him?" asked Natalya.

Santa nodded. "He was once a Member."

The group was flabbergasted. How could a former NPSP Member think about kidnapping Santa's son?

"It makes sense now, though," Santa said in a whisper. "He would know how things work and how elves think. I don't know how he got help from inside, but somehow he did. This makes things more dangerous."

"Yeah," said Noemi, throwing up her arms. "This Noggen guy has like an army guarding your son on some island in the South Pacific. Samantha said it was surrounded by cliffs and only had one real beach access point."

"Hmm," said Santa, stroking the end of his thick beard. "What are these? GPS points?" he asked, referring to the crude map.

"Yes. That's the location of the island," said Noemi. "His mansion is almost in the exact center. That's where they have Junior."

Santa nodded.

"Did she tell you anything else?" asked William.

Noemi shook her head. "Not really. She's incredible, though. She said she has the Gift of Knowledge and that she knows a whole bunch of stuff."

"Yes, she does," said Santa. "She's one that's benefited from a Chest."

"What's that?" asked Marcel.

"Many years ago the elves created a Chest, like a treasure chest, that would give humans certain Gifts, just like the Gifts created for people in the Gift Manufacturing Plant. It took the elves decades to develop, similar to when they first started on the Candy Canes. The elves kept the Chest in the music room at the University. It was a magnificent room, full of different instruments, and they were unique in the fact that they had a life of their own. The instruments could play by themselves — many a concert was given in the auditorium.

"However, an elf named Jerrod, who is no longer alive, tried to use the Chest on himself to gain Gifts. But the Chest was created for humans and when he opened it up, there was a great explosion, and the Chest, along with the musical instruments, disappeared from the University. We wondered what had happened to them. We assumed everything had been destroyed. A few months later, though, we learned we were wrong."

"What happened?" asked Hannah curiously.

"The Chest and the instruments were somehow transported to earth in the explosion and found by a young man. This young man played the instruments and opened the Chest, bestowing on him great power."

"And then what?" Erik asked, intrigued.

"He gave his brother some of the power that he had gained, and it turned out to be a mistake. The brother tried to destroy everything, and soon the two were battling each other."

"What became of them?" asked Marcel.

Claus waved his hand. "It's not relevant, really, except that Samantha got her Gift of Knowledge from the power of the Chest. It doesn't surprise me that she knew so much about Unbelief. Without her help, we couldn't have proceeded."

"What about a Candy Cane? Can't we take one to the island? That's all we need to do," said Noemi excitedly.

"A nice thought Noemi, but we don't have anymore left. And as you know, it takes almost three years for the Candy Canes to grow to maturity and give off their aura," explained Claus.

"What about magical peppermint?"

"I can't think of a way it would be useful in this case. It's not a very powerful alternative," said Claus.

"Then let's take my Candy Cane from my house," Noemi suggested.

"There are two problems. The first is that once a Candy Cane is activated and brought into the light, its aura is bound to the location in which it was opened. If we moved it, it would do no good. Its power would be gone. And second, if we did that, the aura around your house would go away, and your parents would be in a serious panic."

"You said that the Candy Canes grow . . . like plants?"

"Yes. They're extremely difficult to grow and can only be grown under the right conditions. That's why the lower level of the Blackhole Research Center is dedicated to growing them."

There was silence in the room, most of them staring at the unfolded map on the table. Claus looked at them warmly. "Let's have something to eat and then we'll head to the stables."

"These numbers can't be accurate," Alkin said to himself as he looked at the screen embedded in the wall showing the power readings of all the major buildings in the NP. He had been trying to find the source of the power fluctuations that had everyone working in the Operations Center concerned. Today's readings were even worse than yesterday's. It seemed as though more power was being drained, but why? Elves working in the other buildings were asking questions and raising legitimate concerns. He was getting tired of giving them vague answers.

Gallest walked into the room and greeted Alkin

with more disconcerting news. "Sled Repair is down almost fifty percent than normal capacity. It seems like the energy that is being siphoned off is being taken from there today."

Alkin shook his head. "First, it was the Hole, then the Stables, and now Repair? This doesn't seem natural for some sort of glitch. It's almost as if someone or something is trying to do this without us tracking them. It's hard when we can't isolate the power drains."

"What are you suggesting?" Gallest asked, his eyes narrowing. "That someone is actually trying to steal power? Who would do that?"

"More importantly, Gallest. *Why* would they do it?"

CHAPTER FIFTEEN
Easter and Sand

Merry Claus was an outstanding cook, and by the time the Members left for the stables, they felt warm and refueled. Perhaps it was the hot cocoa or the pasta dish or the scrumptious snowman cookies . . . it was a welcomed lunch and the Members appreciated it.

Hailey had the Nifty Nine ready in the field adjacent to the stables. In a flash of green, the Members and Claus appeared, startling Hailey just a bit as she stroked Dancer's neck with a thick brush.

"Sorry about that," Claus said warmly.

"It's all right," Hailey replied. "I knew you were coming. It just happens so fast that sometimes it takes me by surprise."

"Yes, it does happen rather quickly," remarked Santa with an understanding nod. "So, are we ready?"

Hailey nodded. "They're all set. They know where to go and what their objectives are."

"Go ahead and mount up," Claus said.

The four Members mounted their reindeer quickly. Hannah with Dasher. William aboard Cupid. Natalya riding Dancer, and Erik on Donder. Each of them looked confident and reassured, though Hannah did not feel that way. She was not sure what to expect and had to admit that there was a sense of apprehension within herself. What if she didn't succeed? What if she couldn't get any help from the Easter Bunny? She couldn't think that way. She had to stay positive. Besides, what was there to worry about with the Easter Bunny? It wasn't like she was going to visit the Headless Horseman and ask him for help.

Santa looked at each of them proudly as Noemi and Marcel stood by his side. "I know all of you will do well. I hope to see you back soon, preferably by tonight. Now, if you'll allow me, I will send you off," Claus said with a voice of power and majesty. He stepped forward and pointed toward the cloud-covered sky. "On Donder, on Cupid, on Dasher, on Dancer. Now dash away, dash away, dash away all."

Hannah grabbed hold of Dasher's reins and held on tightly. The animal was ascending quickly, as were the others. In a moment, she was surrounded by a great white light, so blinding that she couldn't see anything. She tightened her grip. It seemed like it was forever as Dasher galloped through the Tunnel, and it wasn't until Hannah felt the light diminishing that she opened her eyes fully.

Dasher descended quickly on a lush, green field of grass, but this land was unlike any Hannah had ever seen before. The colors were magnified a hundred-fold, and the green grass was more than green — it had a luster and emanated color so richly, it was almost too much to look at.

Dasher landed softly, the grass rustling below him. Hannah stayed mounted for a moment and stared around her before finally dismounting. She was in the middle of a field, surrounded by a forest of high-growing trees, a species she'd never seen before. They looked similar to pine trees but the needles were much thicker and wider, and the trunks were the width of a small car. Bright sunshine beamed down at her from a cloudless sky. A moment ago she was in the NP and now she was someplace completely different.

Hannah turned to Dasher as if the animal would provide some sense of help. He seemed to understand and motioned forward with his head. Hannah looked in the direction Dasher had indicated, but all she saw was the dense forest ahead of her. She decided she would try it and see what she could find, although she was still a bit apprehensive. She could not have imagined a few days ago that she would not only see the actual North Pole, but that she would also be seeing the world of the Easter Bunny.

She walked to the edge of the field to where the forest began. She turned back and looked at Dasher, who once again gave a nod of encouragement. Hannah nodded back, and made her way into the dense thicket. She was relieved to see there was an animal trail, no doubt made by rabbits, meandering its way forward, navigating through the multicolored shrubs and trees.

The further Hannah walked, the more the forest changed. The trees looked completely different, with wild hues of yellow and green. Flowers were in bloom everywhere as though it was springtime on a steady growth of Miracle Gro. The land was fantastic, and Hannah knew she'd never seen color and beauty like this before . . . ever.

How long she walked, she didn't know, but it seemed liked hours, following a trail that passed through a vast colorful forest and small streams of water that were the deepest green she'd ever seen, yet were small enough for her to jump over without any problems.

Just as she rounded yet another corner, the trail opened up, and in a massive field of emerald green grass were thousands of bunnies, dashing back and forth, carrying what looked like ribbons in their mouths. All of them seemed to be excited as they did this. There was a strange chatter, like massive mouths banging their teeth together rapidly.

The bunnies looked normal to Hannah. There was nothing special about them except that they were carrying the most colorful ribbons she had ever seen.

She took a deep breath and walked out into the field. She wasn't three steps into the short grass when every rabbit stopped, like they'd been petrified by some unknown source. Every eye locked on Hannah. There was a very uncomfortable pause as Hannah had a sudden vision of thousands of bunnies storming her.

She cleared her throat.

"I'm Hannah . . . from the North Pole. Claus has sent me."

The animals did not react. Their ears perked a little straighter, but none of them moved. Perhaps they didn't hear her.

"I'm Hannah from the North Pole. Claus sent me. It's very important," she shouted loudly.

Another pause.

The bunnies remained frozen.

Then there was a stirring at the very end of the field. Hannah couldn't make out what was happening because it was so far away, but something was definitely moving. It was large, about the size of a German shepherd, and it was bounding toward her quickly.

Hannah's heart raced. She got the distinct feeling she was not supposed to be here.

She could make out the animal now. It was the largest bunny she'd ever seen, rocketing toward her. A moment later, it was within ten feet.

One long look and Hannah knew instantly that this was the true Easter Bunny. The glowing white fur, the deep, piercing blue eyes that radiated with curiosity. Its ears were pointed up, cocking its head to the side as if to survey Hannah from a different angle.

"Hannah from the North Pole," the Easter Bunny spoke with a strange yet soothing voice.

"Yes," Hannah whispered, not entirely surprised the animal could speak.

The rest of the bunnies in the field were curious and surrounded the girl in the red suit.

"Never before has a human been here," the Easter Bunny said.

Hannah quickly deduced that the Easter Bunny was male.

"Oh," is all she could manage.

The bunny took a hop closer and sniffed Hannah. "You are Hannah Green."

"How did you know my last name?" Hannah said, amazed.

"Indeed . . ."

He sniffed more.

Hannah decided to start in. "I've come because Claus needs help."

The Easter Bunny hopped back a little but did not take his eyes off her. "Why?"

"His son has been kidnapped by a man of Earth — a powerful man that's demanding Claus not fly this Christmas — that Christmas not happen this year. Santa sent some of us to certain places for help," Hannah said.

"Indeed," the Easter Bunny replied.

"Is there anything you can do to help us?"

The Easter Bunny slowly nodded. "Claus has been our greatest ally. He has helped us more times than I recall. If he has sent you here, asking this of us, it must mean he is in great need."

"Yes," Hannah said.

"Do you know where you are standing?"

Hannah looked around. She was in a field of vividly green grass, but somehow that answer didn't seem real impressive. The Easter Bunny continued without waiting for her answer.

"This is the field of wishes. It is a vast field where many wishes are asked for. The ribbons you see in the mouths of the bunnies are human wishes that we try our best to capture and to put into eggs for Easter. Alas, there are billions of people on earth, making billions upon billions of wishes, some ridiculous, some very sincere. It is our job to try and get all the legitimate wishes we can and help them come true.

"Take a look at the field. Look closely . . . go on. On the grass, at the ends of the blades of grass. . ."

Hannah looked to her left at an open patch of emerald. She concentrated, staring at the ends of the blades and sure enough, she saw them. They were as small as the head of a pin, yet they glistened in the sunlight, a shimmering speck of light.

"Go over and pull one," the Easter Bunny said.

Hannah looked at the animal for a moment, and then went toward the shimmering light. She bent over and could now see not just one, but hundreds of specks of light all glistening. She reached out and with her thumb and first finger, pulled.

The light instantly turned solid and as she pulled her fingers up, it transformed into a thick ribbon until at last Hannah pulled it free from the grass. The ribbon itself was yellow and shimmering brightly.

"That wish belongs to a boy named Hayden Angus. He is twelve. He wishes that his parents would spend more time with him."

Hannah looked at the ribbon in awe. There were wondrous markings on it, like miniature calligraphy, but Hannah could not decipher it. Her gaze met the Easter Bunny's once more.

"What am I supposed to do with it?" she asked.

One of the nearby bunnies hopped to her feet and craned its head back, opening its mouth. Hannah looked at the animal and then put the ribbon into the bunny's mouth. The bunny closed its teeth around it and bounded away briskly, half the ribbon hanging out.

"What happens to it?" asked Hannah, watching the bunny go.

"It's taken to be blessed, then put into an egg. On Easter, it will be delivered back to Hayden with a bit of Easter magic," the Easter Bunny replied.

"Wow," said Hannah, forgetting for a moment the urgency of the situation.

She was brought back to reality when the Easter Bunny asked, "What is it that you are to do, exactly?"

"A few of us have to go into the man's house that kidnapped Junior and help Junior escape. Problem is,

Unbelief's house . . ."

"Unbelief?" the Easter Bunny stopped Hannah.

"That's what he's calling himself, Unbelief. Claus can't use any of his powers because it's not Christmas Eve, and the elves don't have any more Candy Canes."

"I wish I could help you more, Hannah, but we are bound by the natural laws here, and we cannot go to Earth. Only myself and only on Easter Sunday."

"Oh . . ." Hannah said.

"But I may be able to give you something that might come in handy."

The Easter Bunny closed his eyes for a long time. The rest of the bunnies still watched silently. Finally, the animal opened his eyes and reached to the grass with his mouth, pulling up a ribbon from the blades.

This ribbon was the same size as all the others: around twelve inches. It was nearly an inch thick, the same as the others Hannah had seen. The only difference was that this one did not have any markings or calligraphy. It was a brilliant shade of purple, smooth and deep.

"Take this," the Easter Bunny said in a kind of muffled voice, since he had the ribbon still in his mouth.

Hannah reached out and took it, examining it with great interest.

"Put it in your belt, and when you need it most, use it."

"Use it?" Hannah asked.

"Did you notice it had no writing on it?"

"Yeah," Hannah replied.

"That's because it's a free wish, Hannah. If it is within my power — and keep in mind, Hannah, that my power is limited once outside our haven — you

224 | North Pole Santa Patrol

shall be granted whatever it is you wish for. Simply put it up to your mouth and whisper your wish."

Hannah stared at the ribbon in wonder.

"Can you make more of them? The other Members . . ."

"I cannot. It is all I can give."

Hannah nodded, and put the ribbon in one of the small compartments in her belt.

"I get the sense that you are in a great hurry."

"Yes," Hannah said. "The quicker I get back to NP, the quicker we can try and go get Junior."

"Then Godspeed, young Hannah," the Easter Bunny said with a final nod before turning and bounding back to the other end of the field. The other bunnies went to work as if Hannah hadn't been there at all, scurrying here and there with ribbons hanging out of their mouths.

Hannah felt like she needed to stay, that there was much more to learn but knew that time was everything and she had to get back. She took one more look at the beautiful field and then ran back as hard as she could.

Natalya did not know how long she'd been riding Dancer. Though it seemed like forever, in reality it was only an hour. She did not know in what part of the world she was and she was so high up above the large city, it was impossible to try and guess. If she could make out some of the architecture below, she might've been able to deduce where in the world she might be, but it was impossible. The city was just a twinkling mass of light.

Dancer galloped underneath thick clouds that provided a strange silhouetted ceiling over Natalya's head. Dancer seemed to know where he was supposed to go, at least that was what Natalya was hoping because she had no idea where to find the Sandman or what exactly she was supposed to do when and if she ever did finally meet him. Claus hadn't given her much information to go on, but that didn't matter. She would carry out her duty to the best of her ability.

That was one of Natalya's best attributes: her loyalty and unwavering belief. She was the youngest of her family, having grown up with two older brothers, and had always been the one to be there to help, always willing to lend a hand to a friend or her family. Now she was helping, not only Santa, but the world. The full reality of that fact hadn't set in on her yet.

She was staring into the dark night, not feeling the effects of the wind or cold temperatures, and thinking about her mom and dad, which explains why she didn't see *it* at first. But as Dancer swerved hard to the left, it jolted Natalya into paying more attention to her surroundings, and there, coming into full view, in blazing glory, was a glowing sloop, the likes of which she'd never seen before, let alone the fact that it was flying gracefully through the clouds, pushing them out of its way as it swathed a path.

Natalya had studied the Caribbean as a history project last year, focusing on the pirating days of the seventeen hundreds. She had to write a report on the different types of ships used during that time, and the smallest of them was the sloop.

Dancer put on a burst of speed and circled around

behind the ship, gliding carefully onto the deck and coming to a stop. Natalya was frozen in wonder. She was now aboard a giant flying sailboat belonging to the Sandman, the king of sleep. She dismounted and thought that her boots hitting the wood deck seemed to echo, as did her footsteps.

The deck was empty and quiet, though the ship creaked as it sailed through the night sky. Natalya stared back at Dancer, his face illuminated in the light of the ship that emanated from the deck. She was hoping that somehow the reindeer could communicate and inform her about what she was to do. She figured she'd just start searching, but before she took another step, a man appeared to her left like he'd just popped up from the wooden planking.

Natalya took a step back, not out of fear, but because it was quite unexpected. The man standing in front of her wore a plain brown robe, with thick gray hair that fell to his shoulders. His beard was just as thick and gray, though not near as long as the mop on top of his head. His eyes were a metallic blue that, even in the low light, Natalya could make out easily.

"Ah . . ." she grunted.

"Dancer . . ." the old man's eyes left Natalya and fell to the animal. Dancer immediately sprang forward and looked very content as the Sandman serenely rubbed his back. Natalya got the impression that the Sandman had missed the reindeer. After a time of silence, the stranger looked again at Natalya.

"It has been a very long time since I've had a visitor from the NP," he said, his voice deep, almost rhythmic.

Natalya didn't know what to say. She could only stare.

The Sandman continued. "What brings you to my ship?"

Natalya finally found her voice. "I . . . I've been sent to ask if you can help us."

"Really? And who would be *us*?"

"Santa Claus and the North Pole Santa Patrol."

The Sandman squinted. "What's happened?"

"Santa's son, Junior, was captured and taken by a human, Fred Noggen. He calls himself Unbelief. We believe that we can get Junior back, so some of the Patrol Members are going to try and rescue him."

The Sandman raised a finger and pointed. "They have changed the uniforms for the NPSP Members?"

Natalya looked down at her suit momentarily. She'd forgotten she'd had it on. "These suits are different. They have magical properties."

"Indeed," the Sandman whispered. "Magical properties of what sort?"

Natalya shook her head. "I don't know. I haven't discovered what they are yet."

"I see," the Sandman said, staring at her with a critiquing eye. "Well, there is only one way I might be able to help you."

Natalya raised her eyebrows hopefully.

"Follow me."

He turned and walked toward the aft. Huge sails billowed overhead in the night air and the fog that surrounded the ship was as dense as ever. Natalya couldn't see anywhere past the keel of the ship, but figured that she was safe. After all, how long had the Sandman been in existence? Surely he knew how to sail without hitting anything.

The old man led her to what looked like a trapdoor.

He opened it, pushing it back so that it slapped the deck with a loud thwack. He descended down the small, narrow stairs and into the belly of the ship.

Natalya followed.

The enormous keel was filled with glittering, sparkling sand. It was fantastic to look at. It glowed with an amazing brightness that didn't strain Natalya's eyes, but rather captivated them — a combination of beige and white mixed together.

"The Sands of Sleep," he announced grandly.

Natalya could only stare and for a long time, the old man let her take in the simple beauty of it all.

"This is the only way I can help you. You can have some of the Sands. Perhaps it will in some way come into use for you."

Natalya nodded, her head now filling with questions about this man. "What do you do? How does all this work?"

The Sandman looked at her warmly, as though it was a pleasure to have been asked this question. "I help people on Earth by allowing them to sleep. Do you see the tube in the very back, over there?"

Natalya saw a black tube running up from the enormous mound of sand, up into the deck and then disappearing. "Yes, I see it."

"The Sands of Sleep are being vacuumed through that pipe and out into the sky below. The Sands seek out those people who are in deep need of sleep, people too stressed out or people who haven't gotten a good night's sleep in a long time. The Sands are able to go through any object easily, all in order to find the person in need of sleep. They make their way to the eyes and once they touch the eyelids, spread their deep, soothing properties

229 | North Pole Santa Patrol

to the person, allowing them a deep, restful sleep."

"So Sand is being dumped right now?" Natalya asked.

"Yes, out the aft of the ship. I'll show you before you go."

"But won't the Sands run out if you're constantly dumping it?"

"A good question. The Sands of Sleep never dwindle. They always replace themselves."

"How is that possible? They just make more of themselves?" wondered Natalya.

"Yes. This ship and the Sands have special powers. *This* ship, for instance, cannot be seen by humans."

"Then how can I see it?" asked Natalya.

"Because Dancer wants you to."

"Dancer? How does Dancer have anything to do with it?"

"A very long time ago, Claus helped me when I was in need of some assistance," the Sandman said reflectively, obviously remembering back. "And it was Dancer that accompanied me during the difficult journey. I have a special fondness for the animal, so I made my ship available to him alone, in order to find me in case there ever might be a need, and tonight there seems to be a need.

"I'm going to go up and get a sack so that you can take some of the Sand with you. While I'm up there, jump into the Sand. Walk around in it."

"In the Sand?" asked Natalya curiously, pointing at the massive mound of Sand before her.

"Yes, in the Sand," said the Sandman, a grin emerging from under his beard. "I'll be back in a minute."

He made his way up the stairs and out of sight. Natalya turned to the Sand and stared. It was shimmering and walking into it somehow intrigued her, though she didn't know what to expect. She took a hesitant step forward, then jumped in. As soon as her boots sank into the substance, she was instantly calm. She was at peace, and felt there was absolutely nothing in this world to worry about. She took a step and was surprised at how easy it was to walk in. She figured the Sand would be so thick and dense, she wouldn't be able to walk, but that wasn't the case. The Sand rose to her chest, yet she could walk through it as though it were nothing.

She walked in miniature circles for minutes, thinking of nothing, but completely content with her life. This was a feeling she'd never had, and it was exhilarating. She didn't want to leave, which is why it took the Sandman ten calls to get her attention.

"While you're in there, fill it up," he said, tossing her a burlap sack.

Natalya grabbed it, a look of serenity on her face. She then started scooping Sand into the bag and before long, had it filled. She hoisted it over her shoulder and made her way back to the Sandman.

"In order for the Sands you carry to work, you must see this man, this Unbelief, then open the bag."

"I just thought of something. Can't you send some Sand from the ship?"

"No. While I was on deck, I checked the delivery manifest to see if Fred was on it. He wasn't. Therefore, the only way to force sleep upon him is for you to actually see him and release the Sands."

"Okay," said Natalya with a sigh. "I'm calm and . . ."

". . . at peace," the Sandman finished. "That's the power of the Sand. It is why I continue spreading it throughout the world. In sleep, we find our deepest desires and fears. In sleep, our bodies rejuvenate and reenergize, but so many people on Earth today try to do so much and cram as much as they can into their lives, that they don't sleep nearly long enough or sound enough. I thought that my work would become easier over the years, that people would understand the importance of allowing their bodies to sleep, but alas, I am far busier now, sending out more of the Sands of Sleep than I ever have, and I suppose that will continue."

Natalya stared at the Sand again, captivated.

"Come. I will show you how the Sands are released."

CHAPTER SIXTEEN
Of Teeth and Love

Erik wondered if Donder was lost. Did he really know how to get to the Tooth Fairy? Erik was seriously doubting it. Donder had been galloping through the surrounding white fog for at least an hour and yet nothing had changed. They were completely surrounded by a thick, white cloud. Erik was about to say something when finally, ahead of them, he could see a blurry, circular, white light.

Donder sped up and blasted forward. The light now was so bright Erik had to shut his eyes, but just as he did, Donder banked hard to the left and Erik slipped off. He was free-falling, eyes wide open now, plummeting through light. Donder was nowhere around. Where was he falling to? He could see nothing but white light.

Abruptly, his descent slowed and some force brought him from his prone position to an upright, standing one. He was still descending, but at a very slow and controlled pace. The great light that had enveloped him was dissipating and as Erik stared down past his black boots, he saw it.

In a field of deep purple grass were thousands of crystal-blue mushrooms and swirling around them were trails of golden light. As Erik drew closer to the ground, he realized that the golden trails were fairies, roughly the size of his hands. They were everywhere and countless.

The force that kept him upright released him once his feet touched the ground. The field he stood in was covered with mushrooms, all the same size and shape, all about as high as his knee. The multitude of fairies had discovered him and soon had him so surrounded that he saw nothing but their glowing human-like bodies and faces.

Each had a pair of translucent wings that, when beat together, created small sparkles of light that jetted out from behind, hence the golden trails everywhere. Most of the fairies looked young and had a variety of different features, some with blond hair, others with brown — some with green eyes, others with blue.

The fairies were clothed in simple robes that glowed with a soft, white hue, giving them an almost angelic look. Erik was about to ask if any of them knew where the Tooth Fairy was, but didn't get the opportunity as the fairies suddenly parted. Floating forward slowly was a female fairy, her long hair flowing past her shoulders, her robe a deep gold, unlike the others. In her right hand she held a wand with a star formation at the end that glistened white.

Erik stared in wonder. He figured the fairy couldn't have been more than twenty years old, judging by human years anyway.

The noble fairy approached, now inches from Erik's face. "What is your name?" she asked, her voice small, yet elegant and warm.

Erik stared, his name finally coming to him. "I'm

Erik. I'm from . . . the North Pole. I've been sent here because we need your help."

"You haven't lost any teeth in a while, have you?" she said, a pleasant and inviting grin crossing over her face.

Erik paused. "Ah… no. Not since I was a kid."

"That explains it," the Tooth Fairy said, slapping her forehead with her free hand. "Once you have all your adult teeth, I forget your name. Part of the way things work around here. Can you imagine if I had to remember every single name of every child that had lost a tooth? Goodness, I'd be a basket case."

"You're the Tooth Fairy?"

"Why, yes. I thought the wand would have made that obvious."

Erik liked her sense of humor. "So, I'm like in . . ."

"Fairyland," the Tooth Fairy finished. "Yes, it's where the fairies live. We manufacture and recycle teeth for all the people of the world."

Erik was stunned. He felt like he was back as a first-year Member in the NP. "You manufacture . . ."

". . . teeth," the Fairy said kindly, grinning so wide Erik could've counted her gleaming white teeth, had he wanted to. "This is where you got your teeth. Both your baby and your adult teeth came from one of these mushrooms."

"My teeth?"

"Yes. We're constantly making them. I'm just the only one that's able to go to Earth and live within that plain of existence. Surely you didn't think I was a one-woman show, did you? Look at the all help I have," the Fairy said, lifting her arms to indicate the throng of fairies still surrounding Erik, looking on curiously.

"We haven't ever had a human visit here," the Fairy continued. "When I first saw you falling, I wondered if it wasn't an elf. We've had elves here before, but never a human. It's amazing you can even be here. I imagine it has something to do with that suit you have on."

Erik looked down at himself. His suit glistened in the golden light. "How do you know about the suit?"

"I have my ways. You've come here for help, you said. What is it that you need?"

Erik swallowed. "There is a man that's named Unbelief who lives on earth. He captured Santa's son while he was on a training run with the Juvenile reindeer and he is threatening to kill Junior if Santa doesn't go with his demands."

The fairy frowned. "What are the demands?"

"That there's no Christmas this year."

"What?" the Tooth Fairy was outraged. "Unacceptable! Think of the children. Christmas must go on!"

The crowd of fairies clapped and hollered in a language Erik couldn't understand, though he figured the Tooth Fairy could. "What does Claus want to do?"

"That's why he sent me here. He wanted to know if you could help someway."

"Claus . . . asking me for a favor? I am honored, though I don't quite know what I could give you that would help you on Earth. Here, I'm quite powerful, but on Earth, I have fewer abilities."

"Anything would help," said Erik.

"You know," the Fairy said, tapping her wand into the palm of her other hand, "I could give you something."

"Like what?"

The Fairy made a circle with her wand and instantly, a white orb of light appeared, solidifying into what essentially looked like a golf ball. "Take it," she said. "It will help you."

Erik grabbed the object, surprised that the feel was so spongy and soft. "What is it?"

"Inside are wisdom teeth."

"Wisdom teeth? I had those pulled a couple of years ago," said Erik.

"And you didn't put them under your pillow, did you?" the Fairy asked with raised eyebrows.

"Well . . . no."

"And why not?"

Erik looked for a reason, but couldn't come up with one.

"That's why I couldn't remember your name right off the bat, Erik. Had you put your teeth under your pillow, I would've known who you are."

"But why are you giving my wisdom teeth back?"

"Because," the Fairy said, "we give you wisdom teeth for a reason, and that's to add wisdom to your consciousness. Wisdom helps you decipher, analyze, and make decisions better. But no, what does almost every single person do nowadays? They have their wisdom teeth taken out. Why? Sure, it's a little painful at first, but what kind of wisdom isn't painful?"

Erik looked at the spongy golf ball in his hand. "What am I supposed to do with this?"

"Eat it," the Fairy said plainly.

"You want me to eat this . . . thing."

"Yes, put it in your mouth."

Erik looked at it for a long time then popped it in his mouth. It was too big to swallow, which forced him to

237 | North Pole Santa Patrol

chew it. The flavor was vanilla and sweet tasting.

Even before the last bite hit his stomach, Erik felt a jolt in his mouth and immediately felt large teeth moving in from the back of his jaw. His wisdom teeth were beginning to grow at record-breaking speed.

"Won't be long," the Fairy said.

She was right. It took just a few minutes before all four teeth were in, without pain. Erik remembered the jaw pain and headaches he had when his first wisdom teeth were beginning to come through.

"Wisdom is all I have here that would help you," the Fairy said, looking around. "We don't have the kind of power the NP does."

"I need to get back to what you said earlier," said Erik, now feeling his newly acquired wisdom teeth with his finger. "You said you make teeth for all the kids . . ."

"Yes, yes," the Fairy said. "All of them. Once a child is born, I assign a fairy, and that fairy goes to work making their teeth. First the baby teeth, then, of course, the adults."

"If you make the teeth, how do you get them into our mouths?"

"I put them there," the Tooth Fairy said, like this was supposed to be common knowledge.

"How?" asked Erik, totally intrigued.

"With this," she said, bringing her wand in front of her face. "A simple flick and pop, they're in. It's the same thing whether it's adult or baby teeth. That way I don't have to go down to Earth to insert them manually. I'd never make it. It's tough enough going down to collect the used teeth each day."

"Why do you collect them?"

"We recycle. We use the old baby teeth to construct

the adult teeth. We constantly reuse. It's the only way."

Erik was mystified. "But our teeth come in slowly."

"Of course. There's less pain that way. The teeth are put into the gums and then slowly come in with time. We worked that out long ago with Father Time. It used to be so painful for people when it wasn't slow. Terrible business, really. But now, we are a well-oiled machine."

Erik wanted badly to learn more, but a pressing sense of urgency drew his thoughts to the NP and the need to get back.

"I wish I could give you more," the Tooth Fairy apologized, sensing that Erik needed to go.

"It's okay," he said. "I guess I'm going to have to rely on my wisdom."

William wondered if he was the last of the Members to return to the NP. The lampposts glowed softly, and judging by the empty cobblestone streets, it was late into the night. Santa wanted them to report back to him as soon as they returned to the NP, even if that meant the late hours.

He walked toward Santa's cabin, a changed man. After having spent hours with Cupid, he felt stronger than ever that marrying Holly was the right thing to do. His experience changed him so much . . . he wanted to go and tell her about it, but knew that his duty was to Santa and the NPSP.

He knocked on Santa's door three times. The curtains were drawn over the windows but he could see firelight dancing in between the cracks. He heard

239 | North Pole Santa Patrol

someone coming to the door. Santa opened it and beamed down at William. "You made it," he said.

"Yes, sir," William replied.

"And what are those things that you're holding in your hands?" Claus asked.

William looked down at his right hand. "They're from Cupid," he said, holding out the red, twelve-inch arrows in front of him. "He gave me two of them."

Santa took the arrows and examined them, motioning William into the cabin with a head nod. "Take a seat; let's talk a bit."

William chose the couch while Santa sat in his favorite rocker, still examining the arrows with great interest. The fire flickered tranquilly and the cabin was quiet and sedate.

"What did he say the arrows can do?" asked Santa.

"They're traditional love arrows," William said, remembering exactly what Cupid had told him. "Whoever gets hit with one of them automatically has twenty-four hours of love. Every negative and bad emotion disappears and is replaced by love."

"But it's only temporary?" wondered Santa, looking up at William.

"Yes. Only twenty-four hours."

"He didn't happen to give you a bow to shoot the arrows with?"

William nodded and showed Claus the large ring around his index finger. In the center of it was a round, red sapphire. "When I rub the sapphire, the bow will appear."

"That's what Cupid told you?" asked Claus.

"Yes."

The fire crackled, taking William's eyes off Santa and

into the red flames, his thoughts drifting to Holly.

"What was the experience like?" Santa asked, setting the arrows down across his lap.

"Amazing, terrific . . . all the things I'd say about the NP, except that their focus is love, whereas here, the focus is belief. In the Land of Love, it's all about loving each other, but you knew that, didn't you?"

Claus grinned.

"Cupid told me that I couldn't have made it into the Land of Love if I hadn't been in love myself. It was my love for Holly that allowed me in."

Claus nodded.

"You knew that I was the only Member that was truly in love, which is another thing in itself."

"How so?" asked Claus, now gently rocking back and forth.

"It's one thing to love someone, like I love my parents, but it's totally different to be *in love*. You think different. You feel differently about things."

"I assumed that you loved Holly, and that you had made the decision to stay in the NP, to begin a life here with her."

William nodded.

"I don't know if these arrows will help you, but I know the experience of going to their land gave you insight into your own love, especially for her."

"You've been there?" William asked, somewhat surprised.

Claus smiled. "It's been a long time, and like you, I was amazed at the kind of love they have for each other and how much they do for mankind."

"Yeah," agreed William. "I didn't realize that there were archers everywhere on Earth, shooting people with

241 | North Pole Santa Patrol

different kinds of arrows. I just thought there were only the love arrows, but there are so many more."

"Much more," Santa concurred. "I have to say, though, I was getting worried. The other Members returned hours ago."

"I figured. It took me forever to get Cupid to take me to the river. He was constantly chasing the archers and the angels. It was like he was a different reindeer."

Claus laughed. "I should've warned you. That reindeer spent almost a full year living among the angels and archers. They are like family to him. It does not surprise me that he got a little sidetracked."

"I'm just so tired," William admitted, the warmth of the fire and the soft sofa making for a combination that called him to sleep.

"Go ahead and lay down. You can sleep on the sofa tonight."

"Okay . . . yeah . . ." William's eyes felt heavy. "I'm just going to lay down here and go to . . . sleep."

CHAPTER SEVENTEEN
To the Island

When William awoke, he felt refreshed and it took
a moment for him to realize his surroundings. He was
in Santa's cabin, on the couch. There was a fire blazing
in the fireplace and outside, penny-sized snowflakes
fell. Seated around the kitchen table for breakfast were
the NPSP Members. Merry, in her red apron, busily put
out the pancakes, eggs, and bacon, while Claus poured
everyone thick hot cocoa.

"Well, it's nice to see you up," said Erik, looking over
at his friend.

William sat up slowly, rubbing his head. "What time
is it?"

"Nine," said Noemi, before taking a drink of hot
cocoa.

"I was tired," William admitted.

"Yes, you were," Santa said, sitting down at the table.
"Come and join us for breakfast."

William got up slowly and meandered his way to the
table, taking a seat next to Marcel.

"How does the suit feel today?" Santa asked.

The suit! William had nearly forgotten. It was
strange, but it was somehow a part of him, like an

243 | North Pole Santa Patrol

extension of himself. "Feels great," he said.

"Good," replied Claus, taking a seat himself. "Now, let's eat."

William was famished and the home-cooked appeal of the breakfast only made his appetite grow. It was pleasant sitting around the table with all the Members and Mr. and Mrs. Claus. Everyone didn't say much as they ate and filled themselves with the hot food. It was Erik that finally asked the question that had been bugging him all night. "What was the Land of Love like?"

William was into his second helping of eggs and waited until his mouth was empty. This provided time for Marcel to add, "Everyone told us about what happened to them, except for you. Why did you end up being out so late?"

William wiped his mouth with his napkin. "It took hours to get to the Land of Love. Cupid took me through this pink mist and when it cleared, we were in a city full of archers — angels with bows and arrows — going everywhere."

"What'd they look like?" asked Natalya.

"They looked human, except they were only about three feet tall. They had wings and when they beat them together, they made a beautiful sound. I loved it. Problem was, Cupid — the reindeer Cupid — went crazy, chasing the angels all around. I had no control, and he did it for hours. The angels played right along. It had to be the biggest game of tag that I've been in. Seriously, it was crazy."

"But you did actually meet Cupid, like *the Cupid*?"

"Oh, yeah. Once I got on the boat."

"The boat?"

William took a drink of hot cocoa before answering Natalya's question. "You ever seen cartoons when two people get in the boat and they go through the tunnel of love? You know, it's the ride where people that like each other go. Well, that's what I had to do. There was a river that flowed pink and I had to get in a boat and ride the current into this tunnel of pink mist again."

"Who rode in the boat with you?" asked Noemi.

"No one," answered William, "but the boat ride lasted a long time. Finally, when I came out of it, I was in a palace, in a large room, and that's where I met Cupid. Pudgy little guy. He showed me how things work in the Land, and then I told him of our little problem."

"And what'd he do?" asked Claus after chewing his last bit of pancake.

"He took me to a wide field of red grass, and showed me how the angels practice."

"How the angles practice what?" wondered Noemi.

"Firing the arrows with their bows. It's actually really hard."

"You mean you actually fired them?" asked Natalya, holding her glass of orange juice.

"Yeah. It took me hours to get proficient. That's partly why I was so late getting back."

"And I thought the NP was imaginative," said Erik, shaking his head.

"So, let's take an inventory. William, you got the magic arrows and bow. Natalya has the Sand from the Sandman . . ."

"And I got wisdom from the Tooth Fairy," added Erik.

"The Easter Bunny gave me the ribbon," said Hannah, just before taking a bite of bacon.

William was intrigued. "You're going to have to fill me in on what happened, because I don't understand what you guys are talking about."

"We got back a lot earlier than you did and had a chance to talk," said Erik.

"So, what happened with you and the Tooth Fairy?"

Erik smiled. "I got my wisdom teeth back."

"Your wisdom teeth?"

As they finished breakfast, each Member took turns telling William about their individual experiences.

"Why don't you use your wish now and wish for Junior to return," suggested William hopefully, after Erik had finished telling about his saga with the Easter bunny.

"We tried that as soon as we got back and talked," said Erik. "It didn't work. The Easter Bunny told me that if it was within his power, he could grant the wish. Obviously, it's not within his power or we'd have Junior back."

"So hopefully it will work when we get to Unbelief on the island," said William before taking a drink of cocoa.

"I wish there was another way, a way that meant I didn't have to send you," said Claus, rubbing his beard, "but I can't think of one. I was hopeful that when I sent you to the other realms, you would be able to get something that could aid you when you get to the island. I just hope the things you did get are enough."

"They will be," said Natalya confidently.

"What about you two?" said William, referring to Marcel and Noemi. "How's it been with us being gone?"

"We've been a little tired," said Marcel, looking at Noemi, who nodded in agreement. "There's definitely a difference with you gone."

"But we can handle it," said Noemi. "It's only temporary."

"Yeah, if it was permanent, it would get old," added Marcel.

There was a knock on the door and Mrs. Claus walked over and opened it. Standing on the threshold was Hailey, in her suspenders and red and green body suit. "I've brought the Nifty, sir."

"Come in, Hailey. Would you like some breakfast?" Hailey stepped inside.

"Good morning, Hailey," said Mrs. Claus kindly as she shut the door.

"Good morning, Mrs. Claus."

"Breakfast?" asked Santa again.

"No, thank you, sir."

"There's plenty of food," Santa said, gesturing to the overstocked table.

"I'm fine, sir, thank you."

"Very well," he said, sighing and looking around the table at the Members. "You all are very courageous, for what you are about to do is not easy, and it's dangerous. I don't know how well the suits you have will protect you, let alone the things you've acquired from the other realms, but I do know that this is the most important thing you'll ever do in the NP and for Christmas. I want you to know how proud I am of you, and that I believe in you and your abilities to succeed."

There was another knock on the door. Claus looked curious, wondering who it was. Merry went to the door and opened it. There stood the four old elves from the Wisdom Council.

"Come in, come in," said Merry, inviting the old

men in.

"Thank you," replied Browl. The rest of them followed.

Claus stood up. "I didn't think you were going to come."

"We needed to see the children off," replied Clive, pointing his cane at the table. "Ah, breakfast!"

Juan and George sat on Samantha's bed and stared at her incredulously. "You want us to believe that this girl came down on a reindeer to ask you about some island?"

"That's what I'm telling you," Samantha said, sitting on the floor against her bedroom wall.

"That's insane," mumbled the long-haired, pony-tailed George. "I didn't think that reindeer . . ."

". . . fly," said Samantha quickly. "You guys don't know because you don't have the Gift of Knowledge, but I do, and I really think this girl may need our help."

"To find Santa's son?" asked Juan, rubbing his hand over his short black hair.

"Yes," Samantha replied. "Can you imagine if there's no longer a Christmas?"

"That's not gonna happen," said George.

"How do you know?" Samantha asked.

"Because there'll always be Christmas."

"Not if this Unbelief person controls things."

"If we help them, we'll expose ourselves," said Juan.

"Isn't that what we've been doing for the last year? Look how many articles have been written about the Brilliants and all the sightings. This won't be any different," Samantha said.

"Do we tell the others?" wondered George.

"I think we should," Samantha replied.

"Wait a second. Everybody's on vacation. Carl told everybody that we were to take the next two weeks off. There's probably no one in the Lighthouse to help us anyhow."

"We should call a meeting then."

"Look, Samantha. You offered the girl help, right? What was her name, Noemi?"

Samantha nodded.

"And she didn't take it?" said Juan.

"She doesn't know who we really are. If she did, she would've."

"I disagree. She's Jayden's sister. He knew we were Brilliants even though he didn't have a Vest. Jayden supposably told her about us, so she does know."

"But not to the degree she thinks she does. If she knew more . . ."

"Maybe," countered Juan. "But I don't think we can get involved, at least, not yet. Let's see if they can get Santa's son out themselves. You'll know, won't you, if they don't succeed?"

Samantha nodded.

"Then I think we should wait."

Hannah was the last one to mount up on her reindeer, again riding Dasher. William was aboard Cupid, Erik aboard Donder, and Natalya riding Dancer. Claus, Merry, the Wisdom Council and the other

Members stood next to them on the Strip.

"Did you see the looks we got walking over here?" said Clive, leaning on his cane. "The others are wondering what we're doing."

"I'm not worried about it," said Claus. "Everyone's too busy to be thinking about why the Members are leaving with some of the Nifty."

"I hope so," said Clive with a nod.

Claus turned to the reindeer and their mounted Members. "I've manipulated the Tunnel of Belief so that it will put you somewhat close to the island. That's as good as I can give you."

"That'll be good enough," said Erik confidently. "Don't worry, sir. We'll get him back for you."

Coming out the of the Tunnel of Belief was an easy transition, though it took considerably longer to get through than Hannah had anticipated. As Dasher galloped over the Pacific Ocean, it was hard not to be captured by the sheer beauty of the water and the mountainous island in front of her. Hannah didn't feel the warm wind brushing against her face, a nice caveat of riding one of the Nifty Nine, but that still didn't stop her from sweating. It was a nervous sweat. Though she thought she had an idea of what to expect, there were still unanswered questions that lingered. Who was Unbelief really? And what was he really planning to do?

Ahead of her, Hannah saw the white sandy beach that prefaced the deep forest of palm and coconut trees. She turned her head and behind her, galloping through the air with ease, were the other Members. Erik gave a confident nod and Hannah returned her eyes to the beach. Dasher was slowing and came to a walk as his hooves dug into the sand.

"Get off," Erik ordered quickly. Everyone disembarked with haste.

The reindeer stood steadfast, surveying the forest in front of them. The island was quiet and only a gentle wind brushed in from the ocean. Normally, an island like this would seem like a paradise, but given the situation and what was at stake, none of the Members felt that way. To them, it was a trap, and they all figured they were about to spring it.

Erik took the lead and pointed toward what looked like a narrow trail going directly into the heart of the woods. "Let's go," he whispered, his silver cape flapping gently behind him. They moved quickly, running up the beach, leaving the reindeer behind. Hannah felt somewhat apprehensive leaving them alone, but knew that they would be little help, and with their massive racks, would have trouble traversing the forest, unheard and unnoticed.

Just as they stepped onto the trail, a noise, like a wheezing vacuum, echoed around them. Red blurs of light flew past their faces and they knew right away that they had been spotted.

As if the forest was now alive, the robots emerged from the trees, many of them perched, some of them lying in the thick groundcover. Nonetheless, they were coming from every direction, all of them identical in their appearance.

Each was painted camouflage green and brown, except for the smooth, white face with two small eye

251 | North Pole Santa Patrol

holes that served as the bot's optics. The white faceless face reminded Hannah of a plain mask that had simply been screwed on to cover the wires and other techno junk that was behind it.

The robots advanced slowly, and Erik was surprised by the fluidity of motion. These were not the traditional stop and go, jerky robots you'd see in old sci-fi movies. No, these creations were very human-looking. Even their hands — which held two white pistols that looked like spray bottles — were intricately designed.

"Surrender," the one nearest to Erik said, its pistol pointed directly at him.

What could they possibly do against so many? There had to be nearly thirty robots surrounding them now. William suddenly had an overwhelming urge to jump. Without thinking, he bent and lifted off the ground, soaring so high and so fast that the tallest of the palms were below him in seconds.

His mind raced.

It had to be the suit. It was giving him the power to jump.

Red lasers shot up from below, but none were close. As quickly as he went up, he began to descend. The leaves of the palms were painful on his face as he smashed his way back down. He figured he'd slam the ground hard, but to his amazement, he slowed and landed smoothly, as if controlled by some unknown power.

It was a chaos of red around him. Lasers flew in different directions as the NPSP Members used their new suit powers to fight. It was obvious that Hannah's suit gave her incredible speed because she was three times faster than the robots, able to dodge their shots easily,

252 | North Pole Santa Patrol

while hitting them with the blunt end of one of the robot pistols she had taken.

Erik's suit was giving him the power of strength. William watched as his best friend lifted a heavy robot by its waist and squeezed it with a loud grunt. The robot exploded into pieces from the pressure.

William saw Natalya repel the robots back with the mere push of her hand. As though some great, invisible power was coming from her palms, she shoved the robots back so hard they looked like bowling pins being knocked back and falling to the ground.

The scene was a melee of swift and decisive action.

William wheeled around and charging him was one of the robots, its pistols outstretched in front of it. William didn't have to think. He just reacted, and like before, kicked off the ground, this time not jumping as high.

He leapt over the robot and when he landed, rolled to his left. A red laser singed the ground a second later. He picked up a tennis-ball sized rock lying next to him, took aim, and hurled it at the robot. The rock struck the mechanical creation in the face, cracking the white mask. William bolted forward, jumped into the air, and swung his foot, striking the face exactly where the rock had hit. The robot staggered backwards, muttered something incoherent, and then exploded with a small bang.

For Hannah, the whole scene was surreal. It was like someone had hit a slow motion switch on everyone but herself. To her, everyone was moving super-slow and yet her functions were normal. The red lasers were ridiculously lethargic and she could avoid them easily, giving her plenty of time to swing her thick stick with power as she went for the heads of any of the robots who were close enough. Hannah knew it had to be the suit, there was no other explanation. It was like the suit was alive and telling her what to do, where to go, when to duck, and when to strike. Surprisingly, she wasn't afraid. Instead, a comforting calm blanketed her, a feeling she could not explain.

When Hannah turned around, even with her new speed abilities, she couldn't stop two red beams from hitting Erik in the face. The blast propelled him off the ground and backwards thirty feet, his body landing with a terrible THUD. Before she could move toward him, she felt a sudden pain in her right cheek, just under her eye. She turned and saw another red beam heading directly at her. . . .

It was too late.

The beam hit and a moment later, everything went white.

Only two NPSP Members remained and one of them was in trouble. Though William's new jumping attributes allowed him great height and distance, there were simply too many robots converging on him. He leapt into the air, hoping to clear a large group of them rushing forward in a single-file line down the narrow trail, but he couldn't avoid all the red lasers and one of them struck him just underneath the chin. The shot sent him into unconsciousness immediately and he plummeted to the ground like a rock.

Inexplicably, Natalya was finding that her ability to move and stop objects (telekinesis) was keeping her alive and the enemy's lasers away. She had backed her way onto the beach, her hands outstretched toward the mass of robots that closed in upon her. She had few

254 | North Pole Santa Patrol

options. Though the red lasers didn't seem to penetrate the invisible shield of energy she created using her suit, she was quickly running out of places to escape to. She thought about using the reindeer, but a quick glance showed that all of them lay on the beach, either dead or unconscious.

Soon she would be trapped between the mechanical guards and the ocean, and she had no escape route.

———————————

"Look at this," said Dewey. "The robots have captured all of them but this last one on the beach!"

Unbelief looked at the large, seventy-two-inch view screen on the wall of his office. It was a live feed from one of the many cameras positioned on the island for security.

"She must have some sort of shielding power," Unbelief whispered excitedly. "Look at the red lasers bouncing off the air like there's something there."

"Yes!" said Dewey.

"It won't be long before . . ." but Unbelief didn't finish his sentence. Without warning, he watched Natalya take off into the air like a rocket. The camera turned in every direction, but the girl was gone.

"What happened?" asked Dewey

"I . . . don't . . . know," whispered Unbelief. He directed his next command to the computer console directly beneath the view screen. "Set cameras and sensors to scan for a thermal signature. We are going to find her."

———————————

255 | *North Pole Santa Patrol*

Natalya was hiding within a large bushy plant that she didn't know the name of, but one that had yellow trumpet-like flowers blooming profusely. She hadn't exactly planned on landing there, it just kind of happened. One moment she was on the beach fighting off the robots, the next she was catapulting through the air at breakneck speed, over the tops of the trees, traveling for what seemed like miles, until finally crashing down roughly in the bush she now found herself in. To her surprise, she was not hurt or scratched in any way, thanks to the magical properties of her suit. These same properties were also responsible for her escape. By using her power of telekinesis, she propelled herself away with all the power she could muster.

She listened carefully. There were sounds of birds and other life in the forest, but no trace of the mechanical hum of her robot chasers. She figured she'd escaped them for now, but knew that she didn't have long before they would be upon her again.

She worked her way out of the bush and stared at the canopy of leaves and branches above her. She was deep in the forest now and truly had no idea where she was. She would have to blaze a trail and hope that somehow, someway, she would be able to find Unbelief's complex and Junior Claus.

She looked to the thick belt and tapped the pouch that held the magic Sand from the Sandman. If she could get close enough to Unbelief, she could release the Sand and he would instantly fall asleep.

———————————————

Claus sat in front of the fire and stared at the flames as they burned brightly. Merry came up behind him, putting a hand on his shoulder. "You've been sitting here since they left. It's late, and I'm tired. It's almost midnight."

Claus nodded slowly. "Am I a fool? Sending those kids out after Unbelief?"

Merry sighed. "A part of me thinks that it was a mistake, but another part of me says that if you hadn't, this Unbelief would destroy our son and Christmas, and we both know that Christmas is to be preserved, no matter what. But I can't help but think that our son is being held against his will . . . it's terrible," she cried.

Claus put his hand on top of hers. "I have faith Merry that the Members we sent will succeed and get Junior out."

"I, too, have faith, it's just so hard . . . he's our son."

Natalya had been on the move, even in the darkness. She figured that sitting around, waiting to be discovered, wasn't the best plan, yet how wise was it to wander around in almost utter darkness? She was constantly slamming into trees and falling down, tripping over rocks and uneven terrain.

A light to her right suddenly emerged, like the headlights of a car. Then to her left another set were turned on. Her heart raced. She'd been found, no doubt. Above her, another light beamed, casting her in complete white. She tried to look up but all she could see was the bright light bearing down at her. She was about to use the power from her suit again and propel her way into the night sky, but didn't have time as a volley of red came at her from all directions. The suit protected her from the body shots, but she wasn't fast enough to stop the ones that hit her face, and within seconds she fell to the ground unconscious.

———————————

The next morning, Claus awoke early and made his way to the living room, hoping to find the NPSP Members sleeping on the couches. This was not the case, and when he saw the empty room, he couldn't help but feel let down. Was it really realistic to expect that the Members would successfully get Junior back in a few short hours? No, it probably wasn't, though he had been hopeful.

He, like Noemi and Marcel, had to carry their duties out with happiness and joy, concealing the gravest of situations to the rest of the elves. For how long could he do that? How long could the remaining Members do that? And what would happen if the rescue team Members didn't return?

Claus sighed and decided he would get out of his red and white pajamas, put on his suit, and go for a walk. Perhaps he might get a nice steaming cup of hot cocoa from the river.

———————————

She locked the latch quickly and spread hay over the trapdoor. She stopped and listened carefully for any noises. It was still early in the morning and she knew no one showed up in the stables for another hour. She waited silently for a minute just to be sure, and then reached for the interphone on her belt, which resembled a fold-open cellular phone that humans used.

Once she folded it open, the view screen sprang to life and she used the illuminated number pad to dial the number. She brought the phone to her ear and listened. It was two rings later before a deep voice picked up the other line. She immediately recognized it as Unbelief's.

"Do you have them all?" she asked in an excited whisper. She had monitored the Strip off and on all night and saw no reports or evidence to show that the NPSP Members had returned.

The man on the other line laughed. "All too easy. They were no match for the bots. Completely unprepared, even with their suits. I have them in combined stasis, like Junior. I've got the computers working on extracting the properties of the suits."

"You put Junior in the combined stasis?" the woman hissed.

"Don't worry. He's still coherent. He can talk. He just can't move any part of his body."

"Perfect," the woman said, sounding relieved. "I should be arriving soon. Everything else is in place. It shouldn't be more than a couple of days."

"So far so good. I have to say, your plan is efficient and effective," Unbelief said.

"I've earned your trust?" the woman asked.

"You've earned my interest," shot back Unbelief

quickly. "The rest is in your court."

"Don't worry about me. I have my job well taken care of."

CHAPTER EIGHTEEN
The Plan Unveiled

December 23

The waiting was the hardest. He didn't sleep. Not that he got much sleep the days before Christmas, but with the rescue Members not returning, it made sleeping impossible. He had faith that they would return with his son and that Christmas would go on, but he couldn't stop the nagging feeling that the Members were in trouble, that they had been captured. If that feeling were true, then what?

He could not bring himself to think about it. He lived his whole life with faith and belief for cornerstones and he could not let doubt creep in.

Merry brought him a cup of tea and sat down next to him on the couch. "What are you thinking?" she asked.

Claus leaned back and sighed. "I'm worried. Last night I visited Noemi and Marcel in their quarters and they looked tired. I didn't anticipate the other Members taking so long. They are simply too many kids on Earth for two Members to propagate. It's impossible."

"What are you going to do if the Members don't show up?"

"They will show up, Merry. I have to believe that."

"Did you tell Noemi and Marcel that the others hadn't returned yet?"

"Yes," Claus replied.

"How did they take it?"

"I think it added more stress to them, which was something I wanted to avoid. It's fair to say they are just as worried as we are."

"What are we going to do?" asked his wife, her voice tense with apprehension.

"We have to continue on. We have a full day ahead of us and we can't show other elves how we're feeling."

There was a knock on the door and Merry looked at Claus anxiously. It was too early in the morning for a social visit. Claus moved to it and opened it, surprised to find Holly.

"It's been a long time, Santa," she blurted right out.

"Come in, Holly," said Claus kindly.

Holly entered and took a seat on the couch next to Merry. Claus chose his favorite rocker. "I know you're worried about William . . ."

"There's so much that still has to be done, and he's not here. I can't ask his opinion and all the questions everyone keeps asking me about where he is. It's just so hard. Where did he go?"

Claus sighed deeply. "What I'm about to tell you, you can only tell your parents, and no one else, Holly. You have to promise me."

Holly looked frightened. "What? Why?"

"Please, Holly. Promise me."

"I promise," she whispered.

"After I tell you, you must also promise me that you will continue to carry out your preparations for the wedding."

"Sir, I'm frightened. What's going on? Please, tell me."

"You have to make this second promise."

"Okay, I promise I'll carry out the preparations. Now . . . please tell me what's happening!"

———————————————

"I can't keep doing this," Noemi whispered to Marcel. "I can't keep pretending nothing is wrong. My head hurts all the time. I feel like I can't move sometimes."

Marcel nodded. "So do I. The fatigue has been getting worse each day."

Noemi went to the large bay window in her quarters and looked at the Elven traffic below, illuminated by light from the lampposts. "Look at them. They have no idea what's going on."

Marcel sat in one of the comfortable chairs, looking at Noemi with concern. "You know, maybe the Members are captured. Maybe they can't get back."

"That's what I think," Noemi said, without turning around. "I think that Claus believes they will make it out, but I don't know. It just doesn't feel right."

"There's not much we can do about it," said Marcel. "We're here in the NP and they're on that island. We can't leave. We have to propagate belief, and Claus really can't do anything, either."

"There's Rudolph," Noemi whispered, still looking out the window.

"What?" Marcel asked. "Did you say Rudolph?"

Noemi shook her head quickly. "Nothing ... it's nothing."

Marcel got up from the chair. "I have to get ready for the day. I'll be at the Blackhole Research Center, and then with Hailey at the stables."

Noemi didn't reply. Marcel paused, then went to the door. "You okay?"

"Fine," said Noemi quietly. "I'm fine."

Gallest looked at Alkin curiously, and then returned his eyes to the view screen embedded in the black desk. The readings for energy use were again off the charts, something Gallest had never seen before until this holiday season.

"The stables again," said Alkin.

"We've already been there," said Gallest, now almost whispering to himself. "There was nothing out of the ordinary."

"Something is siphoning off our liquid energy and trying to harness it, and it's somewhere near the stables."

"We've done every check," said Gallest. "We didn't find any evidence that showed a power drain."

Alkin snapped his fingers. "You know what — maybe we're using the wrong tools."

"What do you mean?" asked Gallest. "We have the latest technologies. How could we possibly be using the wrong tools?"

"I am reminded, Gallest, that you are still young, and have much to learn. Come with me."

―――――――――――――

Marcel's time at the Blackhole Research Center would've been more enjoyable if he wasn't so fatigued from carrying the belief of so many kids on his shoulders. He was intrigued with all the new gadgets and technologies that the research teams were working on, especially the new automatic snow sprinkler system that sprayed snow in different multicolored patterns.

When he arrived in the stables, he found an upset Hailey and Mayra. They looked frantic and panicked.

"He's gone," Hailey said before Marcel could even ask what had happened.

"Who's gone?" he asked, a feeling of dread passing over him.

"It's Rudolph. He's not here."

―――――――――――――

Telling Holly about the rescue attempt was more difficult than Claus imagined. Holly cried so hard that he wondered if she might faint, and in the end, she said she would remain faithful to her promises, but he knew that Holly's situation was a most difficult one. When she left the cabin, Claus got the feeling a part of her had died.

The Members had to return, and soon.

Claus stared down at a long list of children's names on the old piece of parchment he had laid out on the table. He was concentrating on Brent McAllister and identifying the best route to take to his house when a thunderous knock came from the front door. He stood up quickly and went to it. As soon as he opened it up, it was obvious by the looks on their faces that there was more trouble.

"What is it?" he asked. "What's wrong?"

"Noemi," said Marcel. "It's Noemi. She's gone."

"What? What do you mean, gone?"

"So is Rudy," came Hailey's nervous voice. "We think Noemi took Rudolph in some sort of rescue attempt."

"What?" said Claus unbelievably.

"I was in her room earlier, and she was just staring out the window. She said something about how the Members were probably captured and Rudolph . . ."

"I've looked everywhere for him. None of the Nifty saw him," said Hailey.

"Come in," Claus ordered, offering the two Members chairs around the kitchen table. "What about Noemi?"

"She was supposed to be with Alisha at the Gift Manufacturing Plant. We've spent the last hour looking for her and Rudy. Nobody's seen them."

Noemi had been aboard Rudolph for nearly an hour, and she was as nervous as she had been when she had first stolen the animal. When she had approached the red-nosed reindeer and told him of her plan, and what had probably happened to Junior and the others, she hoped he would understand and that he would help her because without him, her rescue attempt would be impossible.

To her relief, Rudolph nodded vigorously, stamping his feet and lowering his head in anger, not directed at Noemi, but at the person responsible for Junior's capture. She had opened the paddock, mounted up, and they had swept into the sky quickly and quietly.

She knew she was taking the gravest of chances, but what choice did she have? Everything pointed to the fact that the NPSP Members were captured and there were only two days until Christmas. The time for action was now. She couldn't wait for a different plan, and yet she couldn't tell anyone because they would try and stop her.

It was going to be up to Marcel to propagate belief while she was gone, and hopefully it wasn't going to be long. Noemi knew that two people were not enough to carry the belief of the world, no matter how much faith one had.

The ocean was calm and the setting sun glistened brightly off the small waves below her. Samantha had said the best way into Unbelief's headquarters was to enter through the skylight in Unbelief's bedroom, but that the turrets surrounding the complex would surely shoot down the reindeer. But could Rudolph make it?

She was about to find out.

In the distance, she could make out the castle-like structure towering over the palm trees in the center of the island. No doubt if she could see it, they could see her on whatever sophisticated radar equipment they had, and Noemi figured it wouldn't be long before the turrets started their volleys. She bent forward and gave Rudolph a pat on the side of his neck.

"Okay," she said. "Now!"

Rudolph nodded and Noemi leaned back, her hands firmly gripping Rudolph's massive rack. She stared at his nose, which instantly turned a burning red, like a hot ember in a fire. Everything was depending on this move because if it didn't work, she would more than likely die.

Her heart raced.

Rudolph charged forward, soaring higher. Then, like a lightning bolt, an intense beam of red exploded from his nose, cutting through the air with amazing speed, directly at Unbelief's mansion, specifically the turrets mounted on the four tall pillars that towered over the structure.

The beam found its target and it wasn't a moment later before the first turret exploded into pieces of burning red. A red laser shot out of one of the other turrets and Rudolph banked a hard left, Noemi holding on for her life. The laser missed, and Rudolph didn't wait. He directed his next shot at another turret, and just like the first, it exploded almost instantly. Rudolph's beams were truly more powerful than Noemi had ever imagined.

Two more beams streaked at them. Rudolph ascended so fast that Noemi's stomach felt like it had been left behind. Rudolph approached ever closer, his red nose striking a third turret, sending it in hot red pieces into the air. Noemi figured another shot was headed their way, but Rudolph's beam found the last turret before it could fire and the explosion was so loud, it hurt Noemi's ears.

They were now almost directly above the main complex. Just like Samantha had said, there was a huge skylight — Unbelief's bedroom.

It had to be. Not waiting, not thinking, Noemi jumped off Rudolph soaring through the air, directly toward the thick glass, her silver cape whipping loudly behind her.

A hundred feet. Then seventy. Fifty. Twenty.

There was an explosion of glass as Rudolph's beam pierced the window seconds before Noemi would have. The glass fell to the floor and Noemi was right behind it. When she landed, it felt as though she'd just jumped off a small step, rather than a one-hundred-foot plunge.

Just as she'd hoped, the suit had protected her.

So far, so good.

She was surprised to find Unbelief's bedroom empty. There was a dim light in the corner coming from a tall lamp, but the rest of the room was somewhat dark.

A door to her left opened and in stepped a faceless robot. Noemi lunged forward and kicked with all she had. Her boot found the bot's abdomen and sent the thing flying into the hallway, slamming into the wall and falling to the ground in three pieces.

Again, the suit. First, it absorbed the drop into the bedroom, and now it was giving her strength.

Noemi remembered what Samantha told her — that she would find Unbelief in the Tech Room. Noemi sprinted forward and rounded the corner, only to be met by two more robots. They raised what looked like guns and fired. Without hesitation, Noemi slid to her left and her body instantly went transparent. The red lasers passed through her as if she were a ghost.

She charged forward, her transparent shell

returning to normal, and kicked the first robot nearly in half. The other robot fired at her again, but not fast enough as Noemi was able to command her suit to become ghost-like yet again. She jumped into the air, materialized to normal, and planted a kick into the robot's thick neck, sending it backwards in a heap.

Noemi panted hard, trying to steady her breath. To her right was a silver door — the door to the Tech Room. She lowered her shoulder and slammed it with everything she had. The door buckled and she fell into the well-lit room in a tumble. She bounced up and stared. In front of her were two robots and two men, one of them, the taller one, matching the description Samantha had given for Unbelief. And behind them, in clear tubes, looking like they were asleep, were the four NPSP Members and Junior, individually encased in glass.

"Bravo!" chided Unbelief, staring at Noemi with delight. "Never thought anyone could get to the turrets. How did you do it?"

Noemi wasn't interested in conversation. She wanted her friends and Junior, but didn't move because the robots had raised their weapons and Unbelief was holding what looked like a remote control in his hand, making it clearly visible for Noemi to see.

"Smart girl," Unbelief said, noticing Noemi's interest in the remote. "You make one move and I push the red button. Your dear friends in the tubes get the gas . . . the kind that ensures they'll never wake up."

The man next to Unbelief gave a snicker.

"Now, we've got some questions for you. First . . ."

Noemi wasn't about to answer questions. She concentrated on the remote and before Unbelief could move, it shot out of his hand and into Noemi's. She instantly squeezed, exploding it like it was a raw egg.

"Shoot!" Unbelief shouted, ordering his two robots.

Before either could fire, they were lit up by an intense red beam and exploded seconds later. Behind Noemi, charging into the room huffing and snorting, was an incensed Rudolph. Fear crept across Unbelief's face. The reindeer barely fit through the doorframe. The man next to Unbelief reached for something in his front pants pocket, but a red beam from Rudy's nose struck him in his shoulder and he went backwards like he'd been hit by a small car. He bounced off one of the glass tubes and fell face forward on the tiled floor.

"I have come here," breathed Noemi with anger, "for my friends. Tell me what you've done to them!"

Unbelief backed up clearly frightened. Next to him was a long silver table, on top of which were different scientific instruments and equipment. Unbelief seemed to be going for a large metal suitcase that was closed near the other end of the table.

"Stop!" ordered Noemi, stepping forward. Rudolph did the same.

The man stopped, staring at her in trepidation.

"It's time you and I had a talk."

It would be the final time she would have to go into the stables. Everything was set. She had enough energy to do what was needed. Now, all there was left to do was to get on Rudolph and go.

She walked quickly to the other end of the stables under the overhead lights that shown bright white, to where Rudolph would be. Coming to the paddock, she stared in shock. Rudolph was gone. Standing in his place were her father, Hailey, Marcel, along with Gallest and Alkin.

"Alisha," said Claus, somewhat surprised. "What are you doing here? Aren't you supposed to be in Gifts?"

Alisha hadn't anticipated any of this. What had happened? Where was Rudolph? Why were they here?

"I . . . I . . ." she stammered.

Claus frowned, but seemed indifferent to the fact she couldn't answer. "Noemi took Rudolph to go and try to save Junior without my knowledge or consent. And Gallest says he's found the source of the power fluctuations, which he believes are at the other end of the stables."

Alisha swallowed hard.

"It's good that you're here. We're about to go find out what's been the source of all this power drain. We can always use another pair of eyes."

Unbelief stared at the thick ropes around his wrists and wondered how this was possible. He had planned everything perfectly. It was a foolproof plan.

Hardly.

Both he and his companion Dewey sat tied up together in the middle of the Tech Room. Facing them were five kids, dressed in suits emblazoned with the initials NPSP, and Rudolph the red-nosed reindeer along with Junior.

"You're a sick person," said Erik, pointing at

Unbelief. "Trying to destroy Christmas ... *Christmas* man! How could you not believe in Christmas and want to destroy it?"

"Yeah, you don't make sense," chimed in William.

"Save me the speech," said Unbelief smugly.

"Right," said Noemi, going to the silver suitcase that sat on the long table with the science apparatus.

"My teeth are telling me ... that sounds weird, doesn't it? My teeth are telling me," Erik laughed at himself. "Okay, they're telling me that first, we shoot them both with your arrows, William."

William nodded, moving to the suitcase and picking up Cupid's arrows. He looked to his hand and rubbed the red sapphire on the ring Cupid had given him. Instantly, a magnificent red bow materialized in his hand. He took the first arrow and loaded it, pulling the string on the bow back tightly.

He aimed for Dewey first.

Dewey was pleading. "Don't, don't do it! It'll kill me."

"No, it won't," said William, "but it will fill you with love."

"Shoot him," Erik said.

William let the pressure off the string and the arrow went into Dewey's chest. Though the man saw the arrow coming at him, he felt nothing as the arrow buried itself in his chest, working its way into him like a worm.

"What'd you do? What'd you just do?" Dewey shouted.

"Those things work?" asked Erik, looking with curiosity, as were the rest of the Members. Suddenly, Dewey's face went slack and he grinned widely. "I love

273 | North Pole Santa Patrol

Christmas."

"What?" Unbelief said, trying to turn so that he could see Dewey. "You hate Christmas."

"No, no," said Dewey breezily. "It is a season of love."

"A season of love!"

William took aim with the next arrow and stared at Unbelief.

"Give him some love, William," said Junior.

William grinned and fired his arrow. It penetrated Unbelief's chest, and just like Dewey, snaked its way into the man.

"No, please . . . no . . ."

"So full of hate and jealousy . . ." said Junior as he watched Unbelief writhe.

"Yeah, full of lots of stuff," Natalya added.

Unbelief's face suddenly turned serene. He looked pleasant and happy. There wasn't a brow-furrowing frown anymore. He looked at William with kindness. "Are these ropes really necessary? It's the Christmas season."

"He doesn't remember?" asked Erik, as William pushed the stone in his ring and the bow disappeared.

"No, he won't remember anything for twenty-four hours."

"Then, in my infinite wisdom . . ."

"Please, infinite wisdom," teased William.

"Hey, I have wisdom teeth. Do you still have yours?"

"No," William replied.

"You see," laughed Erik. "Hannah, you need to use your ribbon and wish that Unbelief and his friend there never remember any of this. They should never remember hating Christmas or Claus."

Hannah nodded, going to the suitcase and taking

the purple ribbon. She brought it up to her mouth and whispered, "I wish that Unbelief and his friend never remember what has happened here today, and that they never remember hating Christmas or Claus."

As soon as she said this, the ribbon faded apart like an exploding snowball, whisking away as if the wind had taken it, until it completely dissolved.

"I'd say the wish was granted," Hannah said, looking at Junior.

"I hope so," Junior sighed. "I was in that stasis for so long . . ."

"How are we going to get back to the NP? We can't all ride Rudolph, and the other reindeer . . ."

"I can help you with that," said Unbelief kindly. "I can show you where they are. We don't want you to be late for Christmas."

"Yes, that's right," concurred Dewey.

"It looks like you'll get out of the ropes faster than I thought," said Noemi.

"The energy signature is coming from below us," said Alkin, looking at the small device in his hand that was beeping rapidly and flashing red. "It's hard to believe this old piece of technology is all we needed to find the signature."

"All of our new tech doesn't scan for snow rays anymore, which was why we could never pinpoint the actual location."

"But there's nothing underneath here," said Hailey.

"I don't know," said Claus, bending down and

brushing the hay away from the floor. Within a few strokes, a trapdoor was clearly visible, its wooden latch snapped shut.

"A trapdoor," said Alkin.

"A trapdoor . . ." said Claus slowly. "I didn't know that this existed."

"Well, whatever is zapping energy from the NP, it's under us," said Alkin, his eyes on the scanner.

"Let's open it," said Claus, moving his gloved hand to the latch.

"Let's not!" said Alisha, her voice defiant and rough. She stood behind the group and in her hand was a square object with a large red button in the center of it.

Claus turned. "Alisha, what are you doing? We need to find out what's down there."

"I'll tell you," she said venomously. "It's a bomb big enough to blow the NP completely away . . . nothing left . . . all I have to do is push this red button and it's over!"

Claus and the rest of them stared in absolute unbelief. This was Alisha, Santa's own daughter, his only daughter, holding in her hand the controls to a bomb. It was unfathomable.

"Alisha . . . what . . ." Claus was almost speechless.

"How many times was it that Junior got everything simply because he was the firstborn, simply because he was the boy! Why should he get all the glory? Why should he become your replacement? What's wrong with me?"

Alisha's harsh voice seemed to knock Claus out of his state of shock. He frowned (something he hardly ever does). "You have a bomb under us right now so you can blow up the NP because you're jealous? Because you're mad at Junior that he succeeds me? You are the princess of Christmas. You will . . ."

"I won't do nearly what he will get to do! I wanted it! I wanted the power!"

Claus shook his head. "I don't believe what's happening. It was you that was giving information to Unbelief, wasn't it?"

"That's right! And now he's captured everyone you've sent. I'm going to meet with him soon and finally see my brother destroyed, along with this place and all of Christmas!"

"What would your mother say?" Claus said, enraged. "We have given you such great responsibility, and this is what you do? You let jealousy rule you? Jealousy doesn't exist in the NP!"

"It does in here," Alisha said, pointing to her own chest. "It's here."

"So, you're going to press the button, are you? Going to destroy the NP right now, along with yourself, eh?"

"Don't test me!" shouted Alisha.

There was a long pause.

Not a person breathed.

Not a person moved.

"Well . . ." said Claus finally. "Press the button . . . but I think you want to live more than you're willing to die to destroy this place."

"You don't know me and what I'm capable of."

"I don't think you're capable of blowing the North Pole up!" said Claus, almost tauntingly.

Alisha breathed hard, venom shooting from her eyes. "You don't know me!" she screamed, and then pushed the red button.

CHAPTER 19
Return

Alisha stared at the small square object in her hand. She had pushed the red button. There should have been an explosion. She pushed it again, quickly, yet nothing. The button pressed down but that's all it did. This was impossible. She had set everything up.

Claus stepped forward stoically. "When Mayra first told me, I didn't want to believe her."

Alisha looked up in disbelief.

"She saw you climbing through the trapdoor and told Hailey. I didn't know what you were up to at first, until I talked with Gallest and Alkin. The power fluctuations were coming from the stables . . . it had to be you, or you'd better have a darn good reason for what you were doing. I had Gallest and Alkin open up the trapdoor and I couldn't believe it. A bomb! I had Gallest get into your room and search. He eventually found the detonator in your diary."

Alisha stared in hatred as Claus continued. "So, Alkin made another one, one that looked exactly like the original. The one you're holding right now."

"I hate you!" she screamed.

"I don't know," said Claus calmly, "if it's me you hate, or the NP . . . but it really doesn't matter. Somehow, someway, I failed you as a father. You are the first one to ever do something like this. I am ashamed of myself and of you."

"Unbelief still has Junior and the others, and if he doesn't hear from me . . ."

Suddenly and serendipitously, a call buzzed on Santa's walkie-talkie. He reached down and pulled it off his thick, black belt, pushing the yellow button on the side.

"Yes," he said.

"Santa, sir!" Mayra was on the other end. "We've got reindeer and NPSP Members coming in, along with the Juvenile reindeer! Junior's back . . . everyone's coming in. It's everyone! I'm gonna call Holly!"

Something inside Claus exploded. It was such joy, such immense joy that he could barely contain himself. Noemi shouted, Gallest whooped, Hailey screamed, and Alkin jumped up and down, pumping his fists.

Claus stared at Alisha with pity. "Your plan is defeated. Whatever you had in store for Christmas will not come to pass. Christmas will go on because of belief, Alisha. I believed from the moment Junior was captured that he would return to us unharmed and that Christmas would continue. It is this belief in people, in the unseen, that makes the NP what it is. Why you never understood that, I don't know. But never again can you live here."

William Wood had never been happier to see the NP. As he dismounted Cupid, a tearful Holly greeted him. She grabbed him and held him tight, crying softly, "I love you. I love you."

William felt nothing but pure joy. He was back in the NP where he belonged, next to his future wife, and away from the horrible stasis Unbelief had locked him in.

"Every minute I've prayed! I knew you'd make it back in time!"

Erik slapped William on the shoulder as he walked by. "Good to be back, huh, buddy?"

William nodded.

"So the ceremony is still on?" Erik said, winking at Holly, who pulled away from William.

"Tomorrow at eight o'clock in the Main Square next to the Tree," she said enthusiastically.

"But all the preparations . . . the cake, the decorations . . ." William started.

"It's all set. I didn't cancel a thing. Claus made me continue and follow through with everything."

"Eight o'clock," Erik said.

"Hi, Holly," said Natalya kindly, walking with Noemi. "Mayra just told us Claus wants us to go to the Guest Quarters. He's supposed to meet us there."

William looked at Holly. "It shouldn't take long."

Holly smiled. "You're safe now. You're in the NP. When you get done, go to the Christmas Tree. You'll find my dad there."

At first, Marcel wasn't sure what was going on. He'd been in a deep sleep and suddenly, he was being shaken by the shoulders. He awoke abruptly, taking a moment to realize where he was and who was standing before him. It was Mayra.

"Marcel!" she said. "Get up. You have to get up!"

"What?" he mumbled. What the heck was Mayra doing in his room at midnight.

"They're back! They've made it!"

Marcel rubbed his eyes. Things were still a bit foggy. "Who's back?"

"The Members ...they've all made it back, including Junior and all the reindeer. Everyone's here!"

The reality suddenly hit Marcel like a wet towel being snapped against his skin. He shot up in his bed. "Are you sure? They're back?"

"Yes, yes!" Mayra said. "Come on. I've been sent to get you!"

"Everything's going to be okay?" Marcel asked, taking Mayra's hand.

She smiled, and in a blinding flash of red and green, they were transported to the foyer of the Guest Quarters. There, seated in the comfortable chairs near the fireplace, were the NPSP Members, Claus, Gallest, Alkin, and Hailey. Marcel was now standing in the center of the room, Mayra at his side.

"Hello, Marcel," said Claus blissfully. "I am sorry that I wasn't able to wait and let you get a good night's sleep, but this news cannot wait. Please, take a seat."

Marcel looked around at everyone, so happy he felt like bursting into song. He quickly took a comfortable chair, as did Mayra. Before Claus continued, he looked at Willis, who stood at attention near the glass doors.

281 | North Pole Santa Patrol

"Willis, why don't you go home."

Willis looked flabbergasted. "Sir?"

"Go!"

Willis was ecstatic. "You're sure?" he asked.

"Quite," said Claus.

Willis smiled with dignity, nodded, and exited through the glass doors. Claus was happy that they were now alone and he could talk freely.

"I cannot tell you how much it pleases me to see all of you, to see your smiling faces, and to feel the joy once again. While you were gone, I felt very little happiness. I thought it would be important for us to talk and debrief a bit.

"First, let us start with the most disturbing news," Claus said, having chosen to start by telling them about Alisha.

"As some of you might have known, the NP was experiencing power fluctuations and drains, which we could not explain. It was worrisome because never before had this happened and we wondered exactly what the cause was. Well, we found out. The fluctuations were a direct cause of a bomb that had been made and placed in the stables."

Everyone stared in disbelief, including Junior.

"It turns out that the bomb was indeed meant to destroy us and the NP. It was manufactured by the same person who had been giving information to Unbelief."

Claus paused. It was painful to continue, but what he had to say had to be said, and what was already done, he could not undo.

"Who was it?" asked Hannah.

"Alisha."

There was stunned silence.

Junior was speechless.

"I did not want to believe it at first, but we caught her just a little while ago trying to escape, and ready to blow up all that is here. If it hadn't been for Mayra and Gallest, we would not be here right now."

"But your daughter . . ." whispered Natalya.

"Yes, my own daughter . . . acting on jealousy, she wanted to destroy everything."

"On jealousy?" said Junior. "She was jealous? Of what?"

Claus turned to his son. "Of you, son, and what you are. You are the prince of Christmas, and one day, the king. You will be *the* Santa Claus. It is the greatest of responsibilities. It is also what made her so jealous. She wanted to be you. She wanted to have the powers you will eventually inherit. But she wanted it for the wrong reasons, and it drove her to do something desperate."

"But she never showed any signs . . ." said Junior.

Claus sighed, nodding his head.

"So, what did you do?" asked Noemi.

"I sent her to Earth to live among the humans."

"For the rest of her life?" asked Marcel, now on the edge of this chair.

"Yes," said Claus sadly. "She will blend in, no doubt, as long as she keeps her hair long enough to cover her ears."

"Never to return?" asked Junior in sorrow.

"Never," replied Claus painfully.

The room was again silent, except for the crackling of the fire.

Claus finally continued. "But I wish to hear about what happened to you all now, and then I'll tell you what's in store for today.

"Junior, why don't you begin on the night you were captured."

It was obvious Junior was in deep thought and concerned about his sister. Claus leaned over and placed his hand on his son's shoulder. "There's nothing you could have done, son. She had her mind made up."

"But it's our Alisha . . . my sister."

Claus nodded. "Sending her to Earth was the hardest thing I've ever had to do."

"I can't believe she was going to blow up the NP."

Claus nodded again. "You need to tell me about what happened to you. I need to know."

Junior shut his eyes for a long time and slowly recounted his experience in detail, including the icy feeling that surrounded him when he was in Unbelief's stasis tube. The other Members described the same feeling when they were put into their tubes, and by the time they were done explaining what had happened, and how they had been captured, Marcel stopped feeling sorry for himself and the fatigue of propagating belief.

Claus asked Noemi to share her experience and how she bravely rescued them. When she finished recounting her story, Claus was amazed at her courageous effort. She alone saved Christmas and everyone in the room knew it.

Claus finished up the summary by telling them how he'd felt and what he'd done to try and stay positive, not telling any of the elves. He was very proud of all of them and it showed in his smile and the warmth that radiated from him.

Everyone's emotions were spent, and sleepiness overtook them. Claus figured as much, but knew that there was much to do, being that it was Christmas Eve.

"I know you're all very tired, but you can't sleep today. We have too much that needs to be done. You Members that have been gone need to make the rounds at the buildings so the elves know everything is fine. Not seeing you has created some apprehension, and I want them to be able to talk with you. All of you should go to the Gift Manufacturing Plant at some point and make whatever last minute Gifts need to be made before we have a wedding and the evening's festivities."

All eyes turned to William. Erik slapped him on the shoulder with vigor. "Lucky guy."

William grinned.

"Now, I need you awake," continued Claus, reaching into his overcoat pocket and pulling out red and green speckled pills, about the size of a vitamin. "Take one and pass them around," he said, handing them to Junior first.

"What are they?" asked Marcel, as Junior took one and passed on to Natalya.

"They will keep you awake," Claus said, standing up with a long sigh. "I have to go and tell Mrs. Claus all the news which, unfortunately, includes Alisha. I will see you all at the marriage ceremony this afternoon."

William was not exactly sure what the pill was that Claus had given him, but it didn't matter because he felt more awake and alert than he had his whole life. It also helped that this was going to be the most exciting day of his life. He was going to marry the girl of his dreams.

Although William wanted to go with the others to mingle with the elves and make last minute Gifts, he knew his priority was in helping Holly and her family. When he arrived at the massive Christmas Tree, now adorned with so many stars and other ornaments that it was nearly impossible to see a needle, Holly's father and three other elves were busy putting together the raised wooden deck that was to become the dance floor after the ceremony.

Holly's father greeted William with a massive hug, telling him how good it was to see him. Holly had told her father and mother what William's mission had been, and they both knew he'd been missing, but were just as relieved as Holly when she told them that William was back and the wedding was on.

"You were cutting it a little close, weren't you?" Chuck joked, stepping back from their embrace.

William smiled. "A little *too* close."

"You all right?"

"Never better," said William. "It's busy," he added, indicating all of the activity going on around them.

"It's Christmas Eve. Look at the elves still on the tree hangin' ornaments, and the streets are more packed than ever. I think everyone takes a Spirit Pill to stay awake."

The Spirit Pill — the red and green speckled pill Claus had just given him.

William nodded. "It took me almost an hour to walk down here. Everybody stopped me and told me how glad they were to see me, how excited they were about the wedding."

"There's going to be a lot of people," Chuck said.

"Where's Holly?" asked William, picking up a hammer and a handful of nails.

"Who knows? There's so many women in the house right now," said Chuck lightly. "Besides, you're not allowed to see her now until the big moment."

"Right," said William, suddenly saddened. His own parents had no idea that their only child was about to get married, or the fact that he would not be returning to Earth.

Erik met Hailey on the Airstrip. Elves were everywhere, polishing the landing lights, sweeping the Strip in anticipation of Santa's take off. Though Erik wanted to make a quiet exit, doing so would be impossible. There were simply too many elves. Hailey stood next to the control tower and held Tangles' reigns.

"You couldn't get one of the Nifty?" asked Erik, out of breath.

"Are you kidding?" Hailey said, shocked. "Each of them are being groomed and manicured. It takes hours. I was lucky to get Tangles, let alone try and explain to people why you need to take him."

"You didn't tell anyone, right?" asked Erik.

"Of course not. I think what you're doing is noble."

"And probably stupid," added Erik.

"Well, you're really pushing it. It's two o'clock, and I still don't know how you plan on . . ."

"Don't worry about that," Erik cut her off in a whisper as an elf came shooting by on a snowmobile-like machine.

"Here, take him."

Erik grabbed Tangles' reins in his hands. "Thanks."

"Good luck, Erik," she said, giving him a warm hug.

He nodded and mounted the Juvenile reindeer. The working elves on the Strip barely took notice as Tangles and Erik flew into the lighted mist.

Hailey watched them disappear and whispered, "I hope your plan works."

"But I don't know the words to all those songs," protested Hannah as Natalya and Noemi dragged her ahead through the crowded streets, toward the Center Plaza, where the Tree stood magnificently. Next to it was the massive wood dance floor, along with hundreds of red and green chairs neatly aligned, facing a makeshift podium and gazebo, where William and Holly were to be married. Mistletoe hung from the top as small flakes of white fell, covering everything in a thin blanket of snow.

"That's where the ceremony's taking place," said Noemi to Hannah as they raced by the last row of chairs. "We're heading for the other side of the Tree."

What Hannah couldn't see, but soon would, was the massive risers set up for the choir, who were about to practice.

"It's a bit past three o'clock. We're late," said Natalya as the three rounded the Tree.

"Oh my . . ." said Hannah, awe-struck.

The risers were full of hundreds and hundreds of Elven women, all dressed in traditional red and white suits. A small Elven man stood on a stool, a baton in his hand.

"Well, just in time," he said with a smirk. "Take your places."

Hannah didn't know what to say. There had to be nearly a thousand women, all standing elegantly together, ready to sing. Noemi and Natalya dragged Hannah up to the third riser in the middle of the sea of red, and they readied themselves.

"I told you . . . I don't know if I know all the songs."

"Don't worry. You know them."

"How?" she asked.

"Because it's the NP," answered Natalya. "It's Christmas Eve, and this is one of the most spectacular things you'll do here."

"Ladies, ladies. Good to see you all here," the conductor addressed the mass of women. "Let's get started with *Jingle Bells*."

He raised his baton. Hannah drew in a breath, as did every other woman on the risers. As soon as his hand went down, the sound that came from the voices was incredible. From the first word, Hannah suddenly felt as though she'd swallowed liquid joy. The feeling was beyond words. It was perfection!

As she belted out the words, she hoped this perfect feeling would never go away. She turned her head and looked at Natalya, who winked.

CHAPTER TWENTY
Marriage and Departure

"What do you mean, you don't know where he is?" said William, now slightly panicked. "It's almost time and he's not here? Where is he?"

Willis fastened William's red bow tie around his neck, which complimented the red and white tuxedo. "I'm sure he's out waiting for you."

"No, he's not," said Mayra. "I was just out there, and he's not there."

"How could he not be out there? He was supposed to be my best man!" said William, looking himself over in the large mirror. "Look at my hands . . . they're shaking."

"It's quite all right, sir," said Willis.

"Not to be nervous like this," said William.

"I'll go check again," said Mayra, shutting the door, leaving Willis and William alone.

"I'm very happy for you," said Willis sincerely.

William smiled. "Thanks. This feels so right, you know?"

"Indeed," said Willis. "It should feel right."

Bells sounded in the distance — wonderful, deep-toned bells. William sucked in a breath. "Here we go."

Erik didn't have a moment to lose. By the time he

stood inside the gazebo, William and Willis were walking up the aisle between the massive number of chairs, all filled with elves.

William saw Erik standing handsomely, dressed in his red and white tuxedo. His best friend *was* here, but where had he been? As William drew closer, a man dressed in a navy-blue suit moved out from the front row and stood in the aisle.

William's heart nearly stopped. Standing before him was his own father and scooting out, already in tears, was his mother.

"Dad?" William barely managed, fighting back tears of joy.

His father walked forward and hugged him tightly, his mother standing next to them both.

"How did you get here?" William asked, pulling away and hugging his mother.

His father smiled and pointed to Erik. "Your best friend," he said.

Erik smiled and winked.

William was bursting. He wanted to jump, shout, do a dance . . . because the scene was complete. He was about to be married to Holly and his parents were here to see it, though he wasn't sure how that was possible. Humans, unless they were chosen NPSP Members, could not see the NP nor be here. What had Erik done?

"This is your day," his father said, holding his son's shoulders. "I'm so happy for you, son. I'll admit, a little surprised, but happy! You go up there and honor your bride to be."

William nodded.

Holly's mother joined them in the aisle. "Come, sit down. It's about to begin."

"Right, right," said William's mother, giving him a kiss on the cheek. "I love you."

"Thanks, Mom," he said.

When they had taken their seats, he moved forward to the gazebo, looking at Erik with admiration. "How'd you do it?" he asked.

"I'll tell you later," said Erik, motioning for William. William turned and watched as the Elven priest walked up the aisle toward them. "I barely had time to change into my tux."

"I can't tell you how much it means to me to have them here," whispered William.

"You would've done the same for me," said Erik kindly.

The orchestra, complete with woodwinds and brass, started the processional. William hadn't even noticed the musicians off to the right of the gazebo. The entire audience stood when coming into view down the aisle was the most beautiful girl William had ever seen. Clothed in a white dress was his bride to be, walking elegantly toward him with her father.

"A beauty she is," the priest said, smiling at William.

"I am the luckiest man alive."

The streets of Seattle were lit up and decorated elegantly. For the first time in ten years, snow fell and besides the people walking the streets, there were few cars. This was because nobody in Seattle drove in the snow much, and it was Christmas Eve.

Alisha couldn't believe she was walking the streets with *humans*. Her plan was to live on a tropical island with Unbelief and be served cold drinks the rest of her life, but now she found herself in the Emerald City, a place she did not want to be.

It seemed that there were Christmas carolers on every block. Holiday lights adorned the windows of the stores and coffee shops. It was as though she had been transported into some derivative of the North Pole. There were even children sliding down the sidewalks, using their tennis shoes as skis.

For Alisha Claus, it was the worst night of her life.

———————————

The marriage ceremony was over, but the partying was still going strong, even at the eleven o'clock hour. People were dancing to the lively beat of the orchestra and band, and there was enough spiked eggnog consumed to fill the Cocoa River. William had the first dance with his new bride, but as soon as it was over, he was pulled in every direction, thanked, congratulated, kissed, and overly-loved by elves he barely knew.

There were times throughout the evening where he looked for his best friend, the friend that had enabled his parents (who were having the grandest time of their lives) to see their son's momentous occasion, but Erik seemed to have disappeared.

Thinking he knew where Erik was, William finally got a chance to sneak away. Slipping out behind the orchestra, he ran along the lighted cobblestone streets toward the first bridge that crossed the Cocoa River. He walked down below it and sure enough, there was his best friend, sitting cross-legged, peacefully watching the river flow by. In his hand was a steaming mug of cocoa.

"Thought I'd find you here," William said, sitting down.

Erik smiled. "I'm not one for crowds."

"I know."

"Want a drink?" Erik said, offering William his mug.

"No. If I have any more liquid, I'll explode. I've drank way too much eggnog."

Erik nodded, returning his gaze to the river.

"You all right?" asked William.

"Yeah," said Erik softly. "It's just hard to let go. This is it for me, man. No more NP. I love this place and the thought of never comin' back, of never being able to see all this . . . it's a lot tougher than last year."

"That's because this is the final year," said William.

"Not for you, though. You get to enjoy it the rest of your life."

"Well, all you got to do is marry some chick in the next few minutes and you could stay, too," William said playfully.

Erik laughed. "Nice. No, I don't think so. But you got yourself a beauty."

"Yeah, Holly's a keeper."

"I'm going to miss you," Erik said. "We won't be able to really talk anymore."

"I'll work on that and see what I can do."

"Don't worry about it. You've got a new life to start. All the things you're going to learn, everything you're going to do here. It's going to be an awesome life for you."

"It wouldn't have been complete unless my parents were here, and you made that happen. How?"

Erik grinned broadly. "Let's just say I wished upon a star and it came true."

"What are you talking about?" asked William.

"I can't give away that secret. Plus, I told Him I'd never tell, not even you."

"Who, Santa?"

"No," said Erik. "*Him.*"

"Who?" asked William again.

"You know who."

William thought a long time, and then nodded. "Upstairs."

Hannah, Natalya, and Noemi still had their NPSP suits on as they sang the words, *"It's a magic carpet on a rail, never takes a rest . . ."* with the rest of the massive choir. Though they sang with the throng of singers, their silver capes made them stand out, as they should. Only a choice few knew of the danger and peril the NP had been in and that the Members had served bravely.

From their vantage point, the three girls could see the Airstrip easily and the massive sleigh that was parked there. Elves were securing the Nifty Nine as well as stuffing last minute physical Gifts into the back end, which was so full, Hannah doubted that another present would fit.

Thousands upon thousands of elves stood on the

sides of the runway, cheering wildly as the Father of Christmas strode to the sleigh. Marcel, William, and Erik greeted him with hugs before he mounted up.

"Where's Mrs. Claus?" asked Erik.

Mr. Claus sighed. "Though it's Christmas Eve, and her joy overflows, I'm afraid her sorrow does, too. She's with Junior at the cabin."

"Is she all right?" asked Marcel.

Claus looked at the young boy warmly. "She's fine, Marcel. Thank you for asking. She's had a rough time, as we all have . . . but Christmas goes on!"

When Claus hoisted himself into the sleigh, the loud crowd got louder, screaming with enthusiasm. Claus waved his hands and eventually the crowd quieted. "It is a magnificent night," said Santa, his voice amplified. "The snow is gently falling and the Gifts of Christmas are about to be delivered, but before I take off, I have the privilege of honoring one of our most distinguished Members ever. His name is Erik Sweet!"

The crowd erupted. Erik was lifted magically off the ground, hovering twenty feet above the sleigh. The cheering was steady for minutes until finally dying down, allowing Claus to continue, Erik still suspended in midair.

"I cannot tell you the amount of bravery and effort this young man has. I am truly in his debt for all his efforts. And now, I give you, Erik, a Gift. . . ."

Santa raised his left hand and immediately, a golden star from the Tree sped toward Erik, disappearing into his tuxedo as though it had been absorbed. Though Erik didn't feel anything, he knew he'd just been given a special Gift that Claus himself had made. There were millions of stars in the Christmas Tree for the millions of children on Earth, but only the golden ones were made by Santa himself.

Erik was lowered to the ground. To the thunderous applause of the crowd, William was lifted into the air next, without warning. "And as you probably already know, we have a new permanent member of the NP, William Wood!"

The crowd cheered madly. Claus once again waited patiently for silence. "To you, William, a Gift."

Raising his arm, another golden star shot away from the Tree and disappeared into William's tuxedo as well. Like Erik, he didn't feel different, but knew he'd been given something precious. Tumultuous applause followed as Claus lowered William to the ground.

"What do you think you got?" asked Erik playfully.

"That's the great thing," answered William. "Sometimes it takes a while to discover what Claus has given you."

"Yeah," said Erik with a nod.

"Don't I get one?" asked Marcel.

"You mean one made by Santa?" asked William.

"Yeah."

"Not until you leave the NP for the last time," said Erik. "That's when you get the special Gift made by the Man himself!"

"To all of you," Santa addressed the crowd, "I thank you! I thank you for your wonderful efforts this year in making this another great Christmas!"

The elves cheered.

"Come on," William said to Marcel, grabbing him by the arm and moving to the side, out of the runway. Erik followed behind.

"Where are we going?" asked Marcel.

"Claus is about to take off," said William, joining the crowd.

The scene was majestic. Large snowflakes trickled down slowly from the sky. The whole Airstrip was lit up in red, green, and white light. The millions of lights from the Christmas Tree adding to the illumination like an artificial sun. The choir burst into song, *"Jolly Old Saint Nicolas, lean your ear this way . . ."*

"Amazing," whispered Marcel.

Taking out a long, black whip, Claus swung it over his head and proclaimed in a most powerful, regal voice: "Now Dasher, now Dancer, now Prancer and Vixen. On Comet, on Cupid, Donder, and Blitzen! And do you recall, the most famous reindeer of all?"

Everyone shouted in unison: "Rudolph!"

The red nose glowed brightly and the grand reindeer made his way forward, the other reindeer following. The crowd cheered as the sleigh picked up speed along the Strip. It wasn't but a few moments and it was airborne, Claus cracking his whip in the air. The sleigh circled once and then hovered over the Tree.

Though they had seen it for the last three years, Erik and William still felt the goose bumps run up their spines, a warmth spreading through their bodies that was inexplicable. The millions upon millions of mostly silver and a few golden stars lifted off the Tree and shot to the sleigh, covering the physical presents with a glowing sea of silver, all invisible Gifts destined for those who believed.

The sleigh stayed hovering for minutes as the stars poured in. The crowd never wavered, cheering and clapping for all the hard work of so many elves. When the last star finally settled, Claus cracked his whip one more time and the crowd became so silent you could hear yourself breathe.

In his last proclamation of the night, Claus said: "Now dash away, dash away, dash away all!"

The sleigh pulled forward quickly and disappeared into the night sky in a flash of white light.

The choir stopped singing as the Elven jazz band started up with a rockin' version of *Silver Bells*. The Airstrip was suddenly transformed into a giant dance stage and every elf was taking part in the action.

"Get in there and dance!" said Erik, shoving Marcel forward.

"But, but . . ."

"Just go find some girl elf and start shakin' that body!" Erik commanded.

Marcel turned a bit red, but then was grabbed by a young girl elf and pulled away. Erik turned to his best friend.

William smiled. "Thanks again! I'm going to find my parents and Holly."

"No problem," said Erik. "I'll see you in the morning!"

"Okay," William shouted over the noise of the band.

Meanwhile, Noemi, Natalya, and Hannah had left the risers to join the dancing crowd. Before they made it very far, a boy elf that looked about seventeen came up from behind Noemi and hugged her.

Noemi immediately went red. She knew exactly who it was. Natalya turned, looking in shock. Hannah simply stared, wondering who the guy was.

"Natalya, Hannah . . . this is Jonathan."

Noemi broke away from Jonathan's hug and kissed him on the cheek.

Natalya laughed. "So this is what's been up with you this year. You've got a boyfriend. That's why you were out late and stuff."

Noemi flushed. "I didn't want to tell you until . . ."

"Don't worry about it, it's cool," said Natalya, looking Jonathan over.

"Let's go dance," he said to Noemi and the two ran off into the crowd.

Natalya looked at Hannah. "Like to dance?"

"Absolutely!" Hannah replied happily.

"I was hoping I might get the first dance," came Gallest's voice from behind them.

———————

The dancing and Christmas Eve celebrations lasted until the early morning, and by the time the elves retreated back to the Neighborhood, everyone was exhausted — joyful, but exhausted, including the Members.

Hannah had spent the majority of her night with Gallest and never knew that she had the stamina to dance for hours. Neither did Gallest. Both agreed that time had passed too quickly. It was six in the morning when they parted on the southernmost bridge overlooking the River.

"I will miss you," were Gallest's departing words right before kissing Hannah gently on the lips. The kiss didn't last long, and when Gallest pulled away, Hannah felt like she was going to explode with joy. He didn't say anything, only smiled and walked away toward the Elven Neighborhood. Hannah stood on the bridge for minutes afterward, watching him disappear in the distance. It was like she was petrified. Noemi was the one that brought her out of the stupor.

"You all right?" she asked.

"I . . . I . . . I will miss Gallest."

Noemi smiled. "Just like I'll miss Jonathan."

"Why do we have to go?"

"I know, it sucks, doesn't it? But we have to, and we don't have a lot of time. Hailey will have the Juveniles ready to leave at seven, so we need to get our things out of the Quarters."

Hannah turned, looking at Noemi in the shimmering glow of the street lights. "Back to reality."

"Right, Hannah. Back to reality."

The streets were empty. Snow fell silently. The two girls walked in silence almost the entire time. When they arrived back at the Guest Quarters, Willis had just finished checking the harnesses of the six white horses that were pulling the large, lavishly decorated carriage.

"Good morning, ladies," the butler elf nodded with regality.

"Hello, Willis."

"I do suggest you get your suitcases packed and change out of your current attire."

The girls looked at each other, realizing they were still clothed in the magic suits. They smiled.

"I'm gonna need a shower," said Noemi.

"Make it a quick one," said Willis, moving to the glass doors of the Quarters and beckoning the girls in. Hannah went through first, but just as Noemi was about to enter, a woman's voice stopped her and she turned.

301 | North Pole Santa Patrol

Standing next to the carriage was Mrs. Claus, her portly figure and spectacles the perfect compliment to her red and white fluffy suit.

"May I speak with you, Noemi?" she asked.

Noemi nodded and turned around, walking back to the carriage. Willis closed the door behind her.

"Mrs. Claus," said Noemi with a short bow.

The old woman looked at Noemi with love. "What you did to save Christmas . . . I can't thank you enough. I have my son back. It is bittersweet that I should gain a son only to lose a daughter."

Noemi nodded slowly but said nothing.

"If it wasn't for you, Noemi, this entire world, and all we stand for, would be gone. There would be no Santa Claus for the children of the world to believe in, no hope for those that are near hopeless, no joy in a world that is full of grief. I will never forget what you did here, and how your bravery saved us."

Noemi felt truly honored but she knew she couldn't take the credit. "It was really Rudolph that made it possible. Without him, I could've never made it."

Mrs. Claus smiled. "It isn't the first time that animal has saved Christmas. I just fear his head may get a bit big. I've made him a special potpie. He loves them.

"I also made you something."

Mrs. Claus took out a watch of her pocket. Glistening like gold, it was a ladies watch, thin and elegant. She handed it to Noemi.

"I can't take this," Noemi said.

"Yes, you can," said Mrs. Claus. "Put it around your wrist and may it always be a reminder for you about this world and how we anxiously await your return next year."

Noemi nodded, clasping the watch securely around her wrist. She looked at Mrs. Claus and they embraced. Noemi felt the gratitude and love emanating from the Queen of Christmas and knew that this moment was very special.

Mrs. Claus pulled away, smiled, and turned to walk down the cobblestone street.

Noemi stood for a time, admiring the watch that looked like any regular watch, except that behind the two hands was a moving scene, an aerial shot of the North Pole, and it looked to be a live shot. There was the massive Tree and the Strip. Noemi knew it was the most precious, physical gift she had ever received.

Erik was the last one in the carriage. Noemi, Natalya, and Hannah sat together on one side, while he and Marcel sat on the other. He knew this moment would come, but it seemed to come too fast. He was hoping that William would at least see him off, but knew his friend had new responsibilities in starting a new life in the NP.

As the carriage, driven by Willies, moved into motion, Erik took a deep breath, staring out the circular windows at the passing buildings and lampposts. The other Members did the same. Erik tried to take in every detail so that he could remember long after today what the NP was all about.

The trip to the Strip went quickly. Willis hopped

off and opened the door for his passengers, who disembarked slowly. Erik had been the last one in, and first one out. He hadn't taken but a few steps when his eyes caught sight of William and Holly standing next to the Juvenile reindeer. His heart leapt.

The two boys hugged, both knowing that this was the last time they would see each other.

Holly was next, embracing Erik tightly. "Thank you for all you've done."

"I'll miss this place," Erik sighed, slowly breaking his embrace with Holly. He turned and smiled at the two people walking toward him. "I didn't know you guys were still here!" he said, extending a hand to both Mr. and Mrs. Wood.

"What a night! Holly's parents were kind enough to have us stay at their house, and I must say, this was the absolute best!" said Mrs. Wood enthusiastically.

"Yes! A large part of me doesn't want to leave," added Mr. Wood.

"So you're both riding a reindeer, I take it?" asked Erik.

"Yes. Hailey has us on . . ."

". . . on Jenn," said Hailey, giving a respectful nod to Erik.

"Yes, right. We're quite excited."

Erik laughed.

Mr. Wood stepped forward, his face now more serious. "Holly's parents told us that this is the last year for you."

"Yes," Erik whispered.

"I know it sounds strange coming from me, Erik, but I'm proud of you. I know your own parents won't know about any of this, but it's because of you that me and the wife got to see our son married. For that, I can't thank you enough."

"You're welcome," Erik said.

The Strip was as silent as the falling snow. The sun illuminated the overhead cloud thicket, casting the whole area in rich yellow. Hailey helped everyone mount their reindeer, saying her good-byes, an especially teary one to Erik.

"Take care of yourself," she said.

"I will."

"And don't forget to look in your suitcase when you get back."

"I won't."

"I'm going to miss you all," said Noemi.

"Me too," added Natalya.

Just as Hailey was about to send off the Juveniles, Junior came running onto the Strip, out of breath, his big belly bouncing like a deflated basketball. "Good lord," he said, panting. "I do not exercise and that run just about killed me."

The Members all looked curiously, laughing at the future Santa.

"I came to tell you," he breathed deeply, "I've never been prouder of the human race than I am today. Because of your bravery and belief, we're still here, and I have a chance at my destiny.

"If you'd let me do the honors of sending you off . . ."

THE END

EPILOGUE

Erik Sweet stood in his bedroom. This was the part he hated. He hated having to come home and face the reality of life on Earth. Life in the NP was so much better. The Candy Cane that had been in his room casting its aura was gone. Though it was close to midnight, it still was Christmas Eve and Erik knew that upon arrival home, the Candy Cane would be gone. There would be no trace of it, just like there was no trace of Father Time's manipulation.

Erik knew that Father Time was responsible for all of the amazing things that happen on Christmas Eve. It was the only way Claus could get to all the houses. Though Erik had never seen the Father, he felt his presence.

In the corner of his room was his suitcase, magically sent by reindeer. He went over to it, picked it up, and placed it on his bed. He unzipped and pulled the front flap back. There, on top of his bundled clothes, was the postcard.

The front of it was an accurate aerial drawing of the NP, the real North Pole. This was the postcard Gustavo from the printing factory had made for all the elves and the NPSP Members. Though the front of the postcards were all the same, it was the back that interested Erik most.

He turned it over slowly. The white background slowly turned red, and green calligraphy magically appeared.

Dear Erik,

As you know, this is the final time you will receive a postcard from me. This card, unlike your previous ones, will hold its magic for your lifetime as long as you believe. In your hardest times in life, in the valleys of trouble, this card will sustain you with its wisdom. Look to it when needed. I am proud of you, Erik!

Erik took a deep breath and went to his dresser. Tucked away in the bottom drawer, under the folded pants he never wore, were his two other postcards. He took them out and looked at them with benevolence. He felt a part of his life was gone, yet a part of it seemed somehow more complete.

He had been a part of the most wonderful group ever. He had been a Member of the North Pole Santa Patrol.

Continue the story at:
santasblog.typepad.com